Sapper is the pen name of Herman C
at the Naval Prison in Bodmin, Corr
Governor. He served in the Royal Engi
as 'sappers') from 1907–19, being awarded the Milita
during World War I.

He started writing in France, adopting a pen name because serving officers were not allowed to write under their own names. When his first stories, about life in the trenches, were published in 1915, they were an enormous success. But it was his first thriller, *Bulldog Drummond* (1920), that launched him as one of the most popular novelists of his generation. It had several amazingly successful sequels, including *The Black Gang*, *The Third Round* and *The Final Count*. Another great success was *Jim Maitland* (1923), featuring a footloose English sahib in foreign lands.

Sapper published nearly thirty books in total, and a vast public mourned his death when he died in 1937, at the early age of forty-eight. So popular was his 'Bulldog Drummond' series that his friend, the late Gerard Fairlie, wrote several Bulldog Drummond stories after his death under the same pen name.

SAPPER

Bulldog Drummond

BULLDOG DRUMMOND
AT BAY

HOUSE OF
STRATUS

This edition published in 2001 by House of Stratus, an imprint of Stratus Books Ltd, 21 Beeching Park, Kelly Bray, Cornwall, PL17 8QS, UK.

www.houseofstratus.com

Typeset, printed and bound by House of Stratus.

A catalogue record for this book is available from the British Library and the Library of Congress.

ISBN 1-84232-544-2

CHAPTER 1

The mist was low-lying. Above it the tops of the telegraph poles stuck out into the starlit night, marking the line of the road which wound over the desolate fen country. A few isolated houses stood like scattered islands in a sea of white cloud – houses in which the lights had long been extinguished, for it was nearing midnight, and the marsh folk do not sit up late.

One house only proved the exception. In size and shape it was just as the others – a typical fenman's cottage. But from one side of it a diffused white glow shone faintly towards the line of telegraph posts. Above the mist the top room showed black and clear-cut. No light came from that window: the illumination came from the sitting-room below.

In it was seated a very large young man. Between his knees he held a gun, whilst on the table in front of him lay the usual cleaning materials, flanked on the left by a large hunk of bread and cheese, and on the right by a tankard of ale. Behind him, on the hearth-rug, a spaniel lay curled up asleep. In front of him, and close to the door which communicated with the kitchen, a bulldog in a basket snored majestically: also in front of him, and close to the door which led into the diminutive hall, a wire-haired terrier hunted ecstatically in his dreams.

The blind was up: the window, regardless of the mist which drifted sluggishly in, was open top and bottom. On the table a lamp was burning, and by its light the contents of the room stood revealed. And when those contents were compared with the living occupant the result was somewhat incongruous.

Over the mantelpiece hung several illuminated texts. They were of a depressing character, which a tasteful colour scheme of yellow beads round red letters was powerless to mitigate. Even a wedding group of the early 'sixties, which filled the place of honour in the centre, seemed unable to give that snap to the wall which the proud owner had doubtless intended. And the rest of the room was in keeping. A horsehair sofa covered with a red counterpane in which were sewn large, round pieces of coloured glass, adorned one wall: a table, complete with cloth to match the counterpane, and a stuffed weasel under a glass dome, adorned another. And in the window, on a small three-legged stool, reposed a Bible of colossal dimensions.

To the expert the solution was obvious on the spot. This was the parlour; that mysterious, unused room which is found in every similar house; that room which, when the door is suddenly opened on the unwary visitor, exudes a strange and musty smell strongly reminiscent of a not too recent death behind the wainscot: that room which is utterly wasted on the altar of lower-class respectability.

On the night when the mist was drifting just ceiling high the room was proving false to its traditions. Gone was the stale smell of ancient bones: even "Prepare to meet thy God" hung at a more rakish angle. The first was due to the open window: the second to the fact that a disreputable cap was slung on one end of the text. But the effect was all to the good. And since the large young man who at the moment was engaged in filling his pipe was presumably responsible for both acts of vandalism, it might be well to turn from the room to its occupant.

His clothes were quite incredibly ancient. Grey flannel trousers: a sweater that had once been white, and an old shooting-coat padded with leather over the shoulders comprised the outer layer. Underneath, grey socks and brown brogues, with a shirt that was open at the neck completed the picture, whilst a collar, made of the same material as the shirt, had been flung carelessly into the coal scuttle with a tie inside it.

After a while he rose and stretched himself, and it was not until he stood up that it was possible to realise how very large he was. He stood at least six feet in height, and being broad in proportion he seemed almost to fill the room. Only the spaniel noticed his movement and opened one liquid brown eye – an eye which followed him as he sauntered over to the window and peered out. Then he returned to the table and, picking up his empty tankard, he made his way past the snorer to the kitchen. A final pint was indicated before turning in.

It was while he was drawing it that the terrier gave a sudden, sharp, staccato bark, and the large young man returned to the parlour to find that the kennels were awake. The spaniel was sitting up contemplating the window; the bulldog, though still breathing hard, had emerged from his basket, whilst the terrier was following up his one bark with a steady stream of bad language under his breath.

"What is it, fellers?" said the large young man genially. "Does some varlet approach our domain?"

Holding his beer in his hand he again went to the window.

"Shut up, Jock, you ass!" he cried. "How can I hear anything if you're making that damn fool noise?"

The terrier made a valiant effort which was partially success-ful; and then the strain proved too great. And this time his master heard it too. From somewhere, not very far away, there came a muffled shout, and Jock proclaimed the fact in no uncertain voice – no just reason, he reflected, for being temporarily winded with a shooting-boot.

The large young man stood motionless, listening intently. The sound was not repeated, but it seemed to him that it had not been so much a cry for help as a call from one man to another indicating that he had found something. But who could be looking for anything at midnight in the fens, with a ground mist lying thick?

The shout had come, so far as he could judge, from the road which passed his own front gate ten yards away. And he was on the point of strolling down the little garden path to investigate further, when a development occurred which was so completely unexpected that for a few moments he could only stare foolishly round the room; whilst even Jock, by this time recovered, forgot to bark. There came a crash of breaking glass, followed by a further crash of still more breaking glass, and the stuffed weasel subsided with a thud on to the carpet.

The large young man had been getting his cap when it happened, otherwise the stone which he now perceived was the cause of the outrage would have spared the weasel and taken him in the pit of the stomach. For the first crash of breaking glass had been the window, which, having been open top and bottom, now had both upper and lower panes smashed. Thence the missile, missing the lamp by a few inches, had smitten the glass dome of the weasel hip and thigh, and ricocheting off the wall had finished up by the bulldog's basket.

"Hi!" shouted the large young man, when he had recovered himself, "what the devil do you think you're doing?"

His momentary amazement had given way to anger: someone had deliberately thrown a stone through the window from the road, and it did not strike him as being in the slightest degree funny. Some tramp presumably, or a belated drunk: in any case, whoever it turned out to be, he was going to be thanked in suitable terms in the near future. Indubitably the large young man was not amused.

"Heel! The lot of you."

He strode down the garden path, and flinging open the little gate stepped into the road.

"Where's the lousy swine who bunged that brick through my window?" he called out.

There was no answer, and for a moment or two he stood undecided, with the two dogs at his heels. He could hear no sound save the cry of a distant night bird, and gradually the difficulty of the position came home to him. The mist, if anything, was thicker; he could see the light from the room he had just left like a dull yellow square in the surrounding whiteness. But the trouble was he had no means of telling which way the stone-thrower had gone after he had done the deed. The fog had swallowed him up completely.

Again he listened intently, and, as he stood there motionless, subconsciously he became aware of the strange silence of the three dogs. He glanced down at them: in the dim light he could see their heads close together over something in the road. He spoke to them and they looked up at him. Between them, in the dust, was a dark patch.

The large young man lit a match and bent down to examine it. And after a while he gave a low whistle. For the patch was still wet, and it was red – that unmistakable red which can only be one thing. It was blood, and why should a tramp or a belated drunk be bleeding?

He straightened up and lit a cigarette: the mystery was becoming stranger and stranger. That the blood was recent was obvious, otherwise it would have dried in the dust. And it therefore seemed fairly conclusive to him that it had come from the man who had thrown the stone. But why should an injured man, who was so badly hurt that he was bleeding, do what he had done? Why hadn't he come up to the cottage and asked for help?

Suddenly Jock began to growl under his breath, though his master could hear nothing suspicious. Until, a few moments later, he heard very faintly in the distance the unmistakable hum of an engine. A motorcar was coming along the road, and the driver had evidently got into a low gear.

5

The large young man hesitated; then, with a quick order to his dogs, he stepped back on to the garden path, and, closing the gate, he stood leaning over it. He felt instinctively that this car, nosing its way through the fog, was connected in some way with the unknown stone-thrower who had come out of the night and disappeared into it again, leaving only the ominous red patch to mark his passing.

Gradually the noise of the car grew louder, until with unexpected suddenness two headlights loomed up out of the mist. They came abreast the gate, and then they halted; the driver had stopped the car. Voices sounded over the noise of the engine: then one of the doors opened and shut, and footsteps approached the gate.

The man who had got out had his hand actually on the latch, when the glow of a cigarette within a few inches of his face caused him to start violently.

"Good evening," said the large young man pleasantly. "Can I be of any assistance?"

He drew hard at his cigarette, and in the glow he got a quick glimpse of the newcomer. The man wore no hat, and his hair was cropped short, whilst his features had that square-cut, Teutonic look which branded him at once as a German, even without the muttered "Gott in Himmel" that he ejaculated under his breath at the shock of finding the gate occupied.

"Have you seen a man?" he began, when once again a door in the car opened and shut, and further footsteps approached the gate. But this time the visitor carried an electric torch which he flashed on to the large young man's face. From there it travelled downwards, pausing for a moment on oil-stained hands, and finishing up with the incredibly dirty trousers.

"Have you been here long, my man?" said the new arrival curtly, and in the darkness the large young man smiled. Evidently by his clothes he had been judged.

"Nigh on thirty year coom next cherry-picking," he answered, hoping fervently that his attempt at dialect would pass muster. What dialect it was supposed to be he had no idea, but to his profound relief it seemed to go down.

"I don't mean that," snapped the other. "Have you been standing by this gate for long?"

"Maybe five minutes – maybe more," said the large young man. "Why do 'ee ask?"

"Have you seen a man come along the road?"

"Old Gaffer Sheepshank, he coom along round about seven. He wor drunk."

The other swore under his breath.

"Just recently, I mean. Within the last few minutes."

"Noa. I ain't seen no one. What sort of a man do 'ee mean?"

But a sudden exclamation from the road interrupted their conversation.

"Emil," called out a harsh voice, "come here at once! Bring your torch."

The large young man thoughtfully ground out with his heel the cigarette he was smoking, and wondered what was going to happen next. For the gentleman who had called for Emil was now examining with keen interest the patch of blood that had happened to show up clearly in the headlights of the car. And then, after a few moments' earnest conversation, Emil returned to the gate.

"Now, look here, my man," he said quietly, "I take it this is your cottage."

" 'Tis my fayther's."

"Is your father here?"

"Not tonight. He be in Norwich."

"So you're all alone in the house?"

"That's right, mister."

"Are you quite sure?" A sinister note had crept into the speaker's voice.

"Course I'm sure. Do 'ee think I'm daft?"

The torch flashed on again, and by its light the large young man saw that he was covered by a revolver.

"Get indoors," snapped the other. "And get a move on, I'm in a hurry. Now," he continued, when they were both standing in the parlour, "what have you done with the man who came along this road a few minutes ago?"

"I tell 'ee I ain't seen no man," was the stubborn answer. "And I reckons you'd better put that there toy away or it might go off. A pretty thing this – in a man's own house."

The large young man sat down in an armchair by the hearth-rug ostensibly to pat the spaniel, but in reality to smuggle his Free Forester tie from the coal scuttle into his trousers pocket. This man Emil defeated him. His English was perfect, without the suspicion of an accent: to look at he might have been an Englishman. And yet there was something intangible about him that placed him as a foreigner. His clothes were faultless – perhaps a shade too faultless for the country. And on one finger of his left hand he wore a ring with a peculiar blue stone in it.

The tie smuggled successfully into his pocket the young man rose, the picture of aggrieved, bucolic indignation.

"Look 'ee 'ere, mister," he said angrily, "I'm tired of thy fooling. Search the house if it gives thee any satisfaction, and then get thee gone. I'm fair sick of the sight of thy ugly fiz, and if I knew who it was I'd have the law on 'ee tomorrow."

But the man called Emil took no notice. His revolver had dropped to his side: his gaze was riveted on the broken window.

"When did that happen?" he said slowly.

"What the 'ell's that to do with thee?"

"Silence, you fool!"

His glance wandered to the broken cover of the stuffed weasel, and finally rested on the stone itself, which he bent down and picked up. Then, balancing it in his hand, he fixed the large young man with a pair of dark, penetrating eyes.

"When did this happen?" he repeated softly.

"What's that to do with thee?"

"Who threw this stone through the window?"

"Danged if I knows, mister."

"How long ago did it happen?"

For the fraction of a second the young man hesitated: then he made up his mind he would tell the truth. It seemed to him that by doing so he stood a better chance of getting some light thrown on a mystery that was growing more incomprehensible every minute.

"Nigh about ten minutes," he said. "T'wor that that took me down to gate."

"So." The other's eyes bored into him. "So. And you did not see the man who threw the stone?"

"Noa."

"Did he call out to you? Speak to you?"

"Noa."

"What did you do after it happened?"

"Got cap and went to gate with pups."

"And you saw no sign of him?"

"Noa."

The man called Emil crossed to the window and shouted, and his companion who had discovered the blood in the road joined him at once. They stood conversing in low voices in a tongue which the large young man recognised as German. One or two stray phrases came to his ear: "*dummer bauer*" (imbecile peasant)... "*zeit verwendung*" (waste of time); remarks which he had no difficulty in interpreting. Up to date, at any rate, it was clear that he had bluffed them into thinking he was a local product. But what infuriated him was that he was still as far off as ever from discovering what all the excitement was about. And then suddenly he caught another sentence: "*sich versicheren*" (better make sure).

Better make sure. Sure of what? He was not left long in doubt, The second man vaulted through the open window and vanished upstairs. His steps could be heard going into each room above: then he came down again and went into the kitchen.

"*Nichts*" (nothing), he said, reappearing.

"Search him," ordered his leader, and the large young man recoiled a pace.

" 'Ere – wot do 'ee think 'ee be a'doing of?" he cried, only to find the revolver pointing unwaveringly at his head.

"Put your hands above your head!"

The order was curt, and, after a pause, the large young man obeyed. Not that there was anything incriminating in his pockets, except that confounded Free Forester tie, and his pulse beat a trifle faster when he saw it extracted and thrown on the table. Worse still, it fell in such a position that the name of the shop where it had been bought lay uppermost for all to see, and Norfolk yokels rarely buy their neckwear from Mr Black, of Jermyn Street. But his luck held; neither man paid any attention to it whatever. Evidently they were looking for something else, and the question which began to hammer at his brain, even before he was allowed to put his hands down, was – what? Assuming that he was a labourer, as they undoubtedly did, what under the sun could they expect to find in his pockets which could possibly prove of the slightest interest to them?

At last the searcher was satisfied, and once again the two men held an earnest conversation. But this time their voices were so low that the listener could hear nothing. Evidently the man who had searched him was urging Emil to do something, and Emil was doubtful. At length, however, he seemed convinced, and having nodded his head two or three times, his companion returned to the car and restarted the engine, leaving Emil and the large young man alone.

"Can you keep your mouth shut, my man?"

The rustle of notes came pleasantly to the ear.

"If so be, mister, that folks make it worth my while."

"A lunatic has escaped from a private asylum," said Emil, "and he is the poor fellow who threw the stone through your window. We are trying to find him, but we do not wish it talked about. Here are two pounds which will pay for mending the glass."

He placed the notes on the table, and the large young man eyed them greedily.

"In a day or two," continued the other, "I shall be returning this way, and I shall make a point of calling in at the pub. And *if* I find that no one knows anything about this there will be three more to mend the cover of the stuffed animal. But if I find that people do know, why then – God help you!"

He said the last three words very softly, and the large young man stared at him thoughtfully. For the moment he had forgotten his role of bucolic yokel; he was only conscious that opposite him was standing a very dangerous customer. And as his eyes fell on that tell-tale tie lying on the table he became conscious also of a profound feeling of relief that his *vis-à-vis'* cricketing education had been neglected.

"You understand what I say?"

"Aye, mister. I'll say nowt."

With a nod the man called Emil left the room and strode down the garden path. And it was not until the sound of the engine was getting faint in the distance that the large young man stretched himself and lit another cigarette.

"What the devil does it all mean, Jerry?" he said, apostrophising the bulldog. "Why does Mr Emil tell me such a fatuous lie, even if he does think I'm a half-wit? Why do people throw bricks through the window, and leave pools of blood in the road? Presumably there is some reason, but for the life of me I can't see what it is at the moment."

He glanced at his watch: it was nearly one o'clock, and he gave a prodigious yawn.

"Tomorrow we will battle with the enigma," he announced. "Tomorrow father will bring the grey matter to bear on what is at present shrouded in impenetrable gloom. Tonight – bed."

And even as he spoke, sharp and clear through the stillness there came the sound of one solitary shot.

The dogs stirred; the large young man stiffened abruptly. The noise had come from the direction in which the car had gone, and he waited tensely. Silence: the sound was not repeated. But there had been no mistaking what it was. Someone had fired a revolver.

"Stay where you are, boys!"

The front door banged behind him, and the dogs, after one wistful look, relapsed once more into slumber, as their master, running with the easy stride of a born athlete, followed the car. The mist was still heavy, but as he got farther from the cottage, clear pockets began to appear from time to time. And it was as he was passing through one of these, that he heard in front of him the thrumming of an engine. He had caught up with the car.

He halted abruptly; then, getting on to the grass verge, he crept forward cautiously. The noise of the engine grew louder; he could hear voices ahead. And then suddenly, looming out of the fog which had again closed down on the road, he saw the red tail light of the car.

Inch by inch he moved towards it, fearful that at any moment a sudden eddy of breeze might clear the mist away and show him up. But he need not have worried: he had arrived at the end of the entertainment. He was still two or three yards from the back of the car when the driver let in his gear, the red light disappeared into the fog, and half a minute later all was silent again.

The large young man stepped out into the road and moved a few paces forward. What had they found in that particular spot to fire at? Was it the man they were looking for – the man who had presumably thrown the stone through the window? And even as he asked himself the question there came the ominous answer. No small patch this time, but a great dark pool stained the road at his feet. Blood again, and he grunted savagely.

"The poor devil must have damned near bled to death," he muttered under his breath.

With the help of a box of matches he searched the surrounding ground, but he could find nothing. At one point the grass seemed a little beaten down, but whether that had been done by the man in the car or by somebody else earlier in the day it was impossible to tell. And at last he gave it up and started back to the cottage.

He walked slowly, his hands in his pockets. Try as he would, he could get no possible solution that fitted. There always seemed to be something that refused to come into line. If, as appeared obvious, a wounded man was being pursued by the occupants of the car – a wounded man, moreover, who was capable of throwing a stone with considerable force, and after doing so of walking or crawling over a quarter of a mile – why had he not come to the cottage? Answer – because he guessed the cottage would be searched. Then why thrown the stone? What good could it possibly do?

He opened the gate and turned up the path, vainly racking his brains for a solution. The dogs stirred lazily, and for a while he stood in the door staring round the room. And then his eyes narrowed. The things on the table had been moved. The oil bottle and rag were not in the same position; the gun itself was not where he had left it.

Quietly he walked across, and sitting down in the chair he opened the drawer of the table. And there he found proof positive; some papers which had been in front were now pushed to one side. Someone had been in the room in the last quarter of an hour. The two notes still remained on the cloth: it was clearly not the work of a tramp or a passing thief. So there was no doubt left in his mind as to whom it was the work of. Somebody had been left behind when the car drove away with instructions to watch the cottage, and he had seized the opportunity of the owner's absence to search it. The point was whether he was still there.

The large young man's eyes strayed towards the kitchen door: it was as he had left it. Unlikely, he reflected, that the man would be in the house, but he decided to make sure. He sauntered across and flung the door open; the room beyond was empty. Presumably therefore, if his visitor was there at all he was outside, hiding somewhere in the little garden.

There the dogs would come in. Only too well did their master know the unfailing courtesy with which they all three welcomed strangers inside the house: in all probability they had sat round the man as he searched hoping for biscuits. Outside it would be a very different matter.

"Jock! Jerry!"

He opened the front door, the terrier and the bulldog beside him.

"See him off! Good dogs! See him off!"

And then things happened quickly. Like a streak of lightning the terrier shot across a flower bed, barking furiously; his grunting companion at his heels. Came a commotion in some shrubs, and a yell of terror followed by ominous tearing sounds. Then footsteps going at speed up the road, urged on evidently by Jock.

Not so Jerry. Not for him such violent exercise at these ungodly hours: besides, his part of the performance was over. Snorting dispassionately, he waddled into sight, and deposited at his master's feet the spoils of war. Then he returned to his basket, whilst the large young man examined the catch.

"First blood to us, Jerry," he remarked approvingly. "The seat of his pants, or I'm a Dutchman. That'll larn the blighter. For all that, I wish to Heaven I could think why we are thus honoured."

He gave another vast yawn, and went over to the window; whatever the solution of the mystery might prove to be, there was nothing more to be done that night. The cottage did not boast of a telephone, and the nearest police station was five miles away. And since his car was being repaired in Sheringham, and would not be back till the following morning, there was no possible method of getting there except by walking, the mere thought of which caused him to break into a cold sweat.

Jock had returned, and his master pulled down the lower sash of the window. Broken glass fell on the floor, though most of it still remained between the two panes – large, jagged pieces, wickedly dangerous for dog's paws. So he raised the top sash carefully, and even as he put out one hand to catch the rest, he saw it. In between the fragments lay a piece of crumpled paper.

For a moment or two its significance did not strike him, and he carried the handful of glass over to the table. Then he extracted the paper and looked at it. In the centre was a frayed hole, and there were two or three crimson smears near it. But it was the scrawled words that riveted his attention.

Mary Jane. Urgent. G G Pont. A5.

He had the greatest difficulty in making out the words, which had been written with a blunt pencil. And when he had deciphered them, they did not seem to convey much. But, as he began to reason things out, the piece of paper conveyed a great deal. Things, at last, were becoming clearer, and with increased lucidity came increased caution. The mist had lifted; the road was deserted, but the large young man went to the window and pulled down the blind. So this piece of paper was what his visitors had been looking for. The writer must have wrapped it round the stone, and thrown it through the window. And the glass cutting it, had left the stone free to go on, whilst the wrapping had remained between the two panes – the one place where no one had thought of searching.

Thoughtfully he folded the paper up and put it in his pocket. And had the man called Emil seen Hugh Drummond's expression as he blew out the lamp, it might have caused him food for thought.

CHAPTER 2

It has been stated somewhere that men can be divided into two classes – those who can and those who cannot stop a dog fight. With equal justification the classification might be, those who look for trouble and those who do not. So that it was a trifle unfortunate for the nocturnal motorists that by no possible stretch of imagination could the recipient of the brick be placed in the second category.

Hugh Drummond had come to his old nurse's cottage, during her temporary absence, for a few days duck shooting, but with the arrival of that cryptic message out of the fog all ideas of that innocent pastime had at once left his head. And when he awoke the next morning to find the sun pouring through the window of his bedroom he was still of the same way of thinking.

That he ought, as a right-minded citizen, to take the message and story to the police was obvious. The trouble was that he did not feel in the least degree like doing so. A hard-worked body of men: it struck him that it would be a crime to overburden them still more. Besides, he felt that the reception of his story by the local constable would probably leave much to be desired. But for the broken windows of the parlour he himself could almost have believed the whole thing to have been a nightmare. What then was the reaction of the village guardian of the peace going to be?

A cheerful rat-tat on the door announced the arrival of the post and Drummond put his head out of the window.

"Morning, Joe. Anything for me?"

"No, sir," said the postman. "Two for Mrs Eskdale. Be she coming back this morning?"

"She is, Joe."

The postman's glance strayed to the parlour window.

"Good Lord, sir! what have 'ee been doing here?"

"Got angry with it and bit it, Joe," answered the other with a grin. "Chuck the letters through the bottom hole into the parlour."

The postman did as he was asked, still clearly intrigued beyond measure at the broken glass.

"It was all right yesterday evening, sir," he remarked.

"Indigestion in the middle of the night, Joe: eating glass is the best thing in the world for it."

"Strikes me a motorcar had indigestion up the road there, too: I never did see such a pool of oil. Ten times the size of that there one outside your gate."

"What's that, Joe?"

Hugh Drummond, who had slipped on a shirt and a pair of flannel trousers, appeared at the door.

"Oil outside the gate? Let's go and have a look at it."

The dew was still heavy on the grass as the two men strolled down the path, with the dogs behind them.

"B'ain't nothing to pool up further," repeated the postman. "There it be."

"So I see," said the other thoughtfully. "Yes – that's oil right enough."

"Darned near skidded in other patch, I did." The postman prepared to mount his bicycle. "Dratted stinking machines, I calls 'em. Well, good morning, sir."

"Morning, Joe."

For a moment or two it was on the tip of his tongue to ask this reservoir of local gossip if any strangers had been seen in the neighbourhood, but he refrained. If they had, he reflected, Joe would have passed it on by now; and if they had not it would only whet still more that worthy's insatiable curiosity, already strained to bursting point by the broken window.

He watched the postman cycle away; then he again looked at the pool of oil. Nothing very interesting about it, except one thing. It exactly covered and obliterated the pool of blood which had been there a few hours previously.

"Interesting," he muttered to himself. "Very interesting. One wonders excessively."

He whistled the dogs to follow him and started up the road. He did not wonder at all: he knew what he was going to find, but it was better to make certain. And sure enough he had only gone a bare quarter of a mile when he saw a large dark patch in the dust in front of him. There was no mistake about it: beside it was the beaten-down bit of the verge. This was the place where he had overtaken the car.

For a while he stood there smoking thoughtfully. This oil had not been put down at the time – that he was prepared to swear. Therefore someone had been sent back during the night to do it. A clumsy way of covering their tracks: oil does not generally flow from a motorcar quite so prolifically. Besides, this was new oil, and not old stuff from the sump. At the same time it was difficult to see what better method could have been thought of on the spur of the moment. And one thing it proved conclusively: Mr Emil and Co. were desperately anxious to blush unseen.

He strolled back to the cottage, where a loud hissing noise in the kitchen announced that the kettle was boiling, and made himself some tea. As a cook he did not excel, but having raided the local hen he was proceeding to boil the fruit of her labours, when a knock on the front door and a chorus from the dogs proclaimed a visitor.

"Come in," shouted Drummond. "I shan't be long."

"Will the bulldog bite?" asked a very delightful feminine voice.

The chef paused in his work. Who the deuce could this be?

"Jerry – come here, you blighter!" he cried as he went to the front door. "How dare you…"

He paused again. Confronting him was a charming-looking girl of about twenty-five. What she was dressed in his masculine eye somewhat naturally failed to notice, except that it seemed the goods. Also it most certainly was not the raiment one would expect to see at that hour of the morning in the middle of the fen country.

"Forgive me," he murmured, "I was expecting a dear old lady whose dimensions are somewhat similar to those of a steam-roller, and your sudden appearance rather shook me. Won't you come in?"

The girl stared at him in silence for a moment or two, and it seemed to him that a look of surprise flashed across her face.

"My car has broken down," she said at length. "It is just a few yards up the road. I wondered if you had a telephone here, so that I could ring up a garage."

"I'm afraid that's beyond me," he confessed. "The telephone is a *rara avis* in these parts. But perhaps I might be able to help, and if I can't my own car is being brought here shortly by a bloke from a garage. He'll do the necessary if it defeats me. Let's go and have a look."

"So you have a car, have you?" she said. "I should have thought that was even more of a *rara avis* round here than a telephone."

They were strolling along the road towards a small two-seater, which, with its back towards them, was standing motionless a couple of hundred yards away.

"Amongst the inhabitants, you're right," he agreed. "I am only a visitor."

"Are you in that little cottage all by yourself?"

"Until Nanny comes back," he said with a grin. "She is the steamroller I told you I was expecting."

She stared at him with a slightly puzzled frown.

"I don't quite understand," she said. "Where do you live usually?"

"In London – where, I trust, I shall have the pleasure of renewing your acquaintance."

"But why on earth do you come to a place like this?"

"For excitement," he told her, "when London gets too dull. One would never find anyone like you on the doorstep along with the morning milk in the old metropolis."

But her frown was still there, though she smiled faintly.

"You're rather an extraordinary individual," she remarked. "Have you been here long?"

"Two days," he answered. "Now let's have a look at the bus."

He opened the bonnet, and even as he did so he heard a little gasp. He glanced up: the girl, with her eyes closed, was holding on to the door.

"What is it?" he cried. "Aren't you feeling well?"

"Would you get me some water?" she muttered. "My head is all swimming."

"Of course I will. I won't be a second. Get into the car and sit down."

He raced back towards the cottage and got a glass of cold water. Pray Allah she was not going to throw a faint, he reflected. Hugh Drummond's ideas of first aid were most sketchy. But when he got back to the car she seemed to have partially recovered, though she sipped the water gratefully.

"Sorry to be so silly," she said apologetically, "but I have not had any breakfast."

"My dear soul," he cried, "that must be remedied at once. If you can bear a boiled egg, or, better still, can do something in the bacon line, we will do the trick at my cottage."

"I ought to be getting on," she answered doubtfully.

"That's out of the question until you've had some food. Breakfast first; then we'll tackle the car."

She allowed herself to be persuaded, and they walked back to the cottage together.

"Where are you off to that makes a start at such an ungodly hour necessary?" he asked.

"To a house not far from Cambridge," she answered. "My uncle's place. And he wanted me there early to get some wretched tennis tournament fixed up for this afternoon. Good heavens! What have you been doing to the windows? I didn't notice them before."

"A merry Norfolk pastime," he said with a smile. "Some blighter wished it on me last night."

"What *do* you mean?" she cried.

"A fact," he assured her. "Someone threw a brick through the window and nearly hit little Willie in the tummy."

"What on earth did he do that for?"

"The ways of drunks are passing strange," he answered. "But I don't know what the proud owner will say when she sees it."

It was the story he had decided to tell Mrs Eskdale, and since the two women were likely to overlap it saved bother to spin the same yarn to both.

"Are you expecting her back soon?"

"At any moment. And then, providing we've got your car right, I'm off to London."

"Country getting too exciting?"

"That's the idea."

He poured out the tea and went into the kitchen to get the eggs.

"Put some milk in mine, like an angel," he called out. "And two lumps of sugar."

For the fraction of a second he had paused as he spoke; for the fraction of a second he had stood motionless, his eyes glued to the mirror which hung above the little range. For in it he had seen the reflection of the girl seated at the table. And she was putting something into his tea which most certainly was not milk.

He forced himself to continue speaking mechanically, but his brain was racing overtime. He knew his eyes had not deceived him, and the shock was a considerable one. It was such a complete surprise. That the girl was anything but what she seemed on the surface had never entered his mind for an instant. But now as he went on talking he was trying to adjust himself to this new development.

If – and there was no doubt about it – she had put dope in his tea she must be mixed up with the bunch of last night. And at once the reason for the look of surprise on her face when she first saw him was clear. She had been expecting a man of the labourer type, and instead she had met him.

The point to be decided, however, was what to do next. He was convinced that she had not the slightest suspicion that he had seen her, and the essential thing was that she should continue in the same state of ignorance. At the same time the little matter of the tea had to be settled. And so, being a direct person, he disposed of it at once. He tackled the loaf and the knife slipped. Thence his elbow took the cup: his trousers took the tea, and the thing was done save for some mild and suitable blasphemy.

"I am a clumsy devil," he cried. "And, ye gods! that tea is hot. Will you excuse me while I go and remove these garments?"

"Of course," she said. "You poor man! How it must have hurt."

She was all anxious commiseration: not by the flicker of an eyelid did she show any annoyance at the failure of her scheme. And as he changed he wondered what her next move was going to be. Sleep dope – at least he hoped it had been no worse than that; she was such an astoundingly attractive filly. Just something to drug him while she once more searched the house for that paper. It surely must be important – that message that had been wrapped round the stone – for them to take all this trouble to find it. And they could not be looking for anything else.

They were thorough, too, sending this girl as a follow up; they left nothing to chance. So thorough, in fact, that he removed the paper which he had placed for safety in the lining of his hat, and having finally and definitely committed it to memory, he put a match to one corner and watched it flare away to ashes. Not that he saw any possibility of her getting hold of it, but young women who were prepared to dope drink on sight, so to speak, wanted watching. And once again he wondered what to expect next.

The noise of the gate closing made him look out of the window: the girl was strolling up the road towards her car. And for a while he watched her through narrowed eyes. She walked with a graceful swing which met with his entire approval, and the more he thought of the thing, the harder did he find it to reconcile her appearance with what had taken place downstairs. In fact, he tried to persuade himself that the mirror was distorted and that he had made a mistake. Unfortunately the mirror was not distorted, and he knew he had not done anything of the sort, but it was a valiant and praiseworthy attempt.

The sound of wheels greeted him as he went downstairs; Mrs Eskdale was descending from the local carrier's cart.

"Master Hugh," she cried as she saw his clothes, "you're not going away?"

"Afraid I am, my pet," he answered, "but perhaps it will only be for today. Anyway, I'm leaving the dogs with you."

She waddled up the path, to pause aghast at the sight of the parlour window.

"An accident, Nannie," he continued, with his arm round her waist, "caused by a passing drunk last night, from whom I removed two perfectly good Bradburys to repair the damage. And this is a delightful lady whose car has broken down, and who has been having breakfast with me."

The girl had joined them, and the old nurse looked at her suspiciously. Delightful ladies in the proximity of her Master Hugh did not fit into her scheme of things. But the girl smiled so charmingly that she partly relented.

"It was such a mercy that it happened here: I don't know what I'd have done without that cup of tea. And what a sweet cottage you've got."

Mrs Eskdale relented still more: a sure way to her good graces was through her garden or her house. And when, an hour later, Drummond's car drew up outside she had quite taken the unexpected visitor to her heart. Moreover, the hour had mostly been spent in the cottage. As Drummond unblushingly admitted, his knowledge of a car's anatomy was confined to adding petrol periodically and oil when he remembered, and a very brief survey of the derelict was enough to convince him that the matter was far beyond his attainments.

But not beyond those of the mechanic from Sheringham. Briefly, Drummond explained to him what had happened as they walked up the road, and he grunted dispassionately.

"Suddenly conked out, did she? Looks as though she's run out of petrol."

But on that point Drummond was firm; he, personally, with an air of great impressiveness, had performed evolutions and had looked in the tank. Shortage there, at any rate, was not the cause of the disaster.

"Well – we'll see," said the mechanic, removing his coat and bending over the engine. And it was not until half an hour later that the mechanic, with a grunt of astonishment, proceeded to scratch his head and gaze at something in his hand.

"You say, sir," he said at length, "that she was going all right and then she suddenly stopped?"

"That's what the lady told me," said Drummond.

"Most extraordinary thing I've ever known," remarked the man.

"Can't you find out why she stopped?"

"I know now why she stopped, sir," said the mechanic. "But what I can't make out is how under the sun she ever went. Look here, sir – this thing in my hand is the top of the distributor, the thing what's used in the electric circuit."

"I'll take your word for it," remarked Drummond courteously.

"Well, sir, in a motorcar everything depends on the contact points being clean and dry; otherwise you don't get any connection. Now, if you look at these you'll see they're swimming in oil. The whole thing is swimming in oil. And what I can't understand is how the oil ever got here."

"Something must have leaked somewhere?" said Drummond vaguely.

"You couldn't have a sudden leak here, sir; there's no oil pipe anywhere near it. Besides, there's no trace of a leak. Now, from what the lady says, the car was going all right to start with. Well, if she was firing properly this oil couldn't have been here. Stands to reason. Then she stops firing because this oil is here. Stands to reason again. But what don't stand to reason is *how* the oil got here. It couldn't have come of itself."

And with that illuminating phrase light dawned on Drummond. If the oil could not have come there by itself, someone must have put it there. That sudden faint became clearer. And as he watched the girl playing with the dogs outside the cottage a slight smile twitched round his lips.

"How long will it take you to put it right?" he demanded.

"Not very long, sir. I'll just have to take this to pieces and thoroughly clean it and dry it."

Drummond glanced down the road: the girl was coming towards them.

"Put it back," he said quietly, "and follow my lead. I'll make it worth your while. You haven't been able to find out what's the matter. Well, this is a black business," he cried as the girl joined them. "Up to date the expert has failed."

"What am I going to do?" she said disconsolately. "Poor old uncle! He'll get every handicap wrong, bless his heart."

"Not on your life," laughed Drummond. "What's the matter with my bus? I can easily drop you at your uncle's house on my way to London."

The girl looked at him doubtfully, whilst the mechanic hurriedly concealed a grin. So that was how the land lay.

"I couldn't think of troubling you," she said. "It's miles out of your way."

"It's nothing of the sort," he answered. "In any case, the day is yet young. We will leave this warrior here to delve still deeper into the villainies of your machine, and we will push off."

"Well, if you're quite sure it's not a frightful bother," she said gratefully. "It's most awfully good of you."

"Say no more." Drummond waved a vast hand. "The matter is settled save for one trifling detail. Where is he to take the car when he's got it to go? To your uncle's house?"

She hesitated for a moment.

"Let me think," she said. "I think it would be better if he left it in Cambridge. Do you know Cannaby's garage?"

"I don't, miss, but I can find it."

"You see," she explained to Drummond, "my uncle has only just gone there, and it's difficult to describe where his house is. So leave it at Cannaby's garage," she told the mechanic, "and I will ring them up and tell them to pay you whatever it comes to."

He touched his cap.

"All right, miss. I'll leave her there."

He watched the two of them as they strolled back to the cottage, and the grin was no longer hidden. The exact refinements of the case were beyond his ken, but the main basic idea was obvious. And it struck him that the large bloke was no bad judge either, an opinion he had no desire to retract when

Drummond returned alone and gave him a ten-shilling note. To bring the car along in an hour or so, and keep his mouth shut at Cannaby's garage were his instructions and easy to understand. What was a little harder to follow was the meaning of the cryptic telegram he had in his pocket. His orders were to send it if the writer had not arrived at the garage by midday.

Darrell. Senior Sports Club, London. Spider. Parlour. Cambridge. Hugh.

It did not seem to make sense to him. It was not a racing code, so far as he could make out; it had but little to do with love. In fact it defeated him. And not the least perplexing part of the matter was that there seemed to be no reason to prevent the bloke sending it himself.

CHAPTER 3

That he was deliberately walking into the parlour and playing the part of the fly did not trouble Hugh Drummond in the slightest. Too often in the past had he done the same thing for it to worry him. And even when the girl asked him to stop in a village so that she could ostensibly telephone her uncle to say that she would be late, but in reality to warn in about his arrival, he rather welcomed the opportunity for getting things straightened out in his mind.

Her name he had discovered was Venables; and the more he had talked to her the more he had wondered at her being mixed up with his visitors of the previous evening. So much so that he had once again begun to wonder if his eyes had deceived him over the tea-cup incident. Against that however, he had to put the matter of the car. If what the mechanic had said was correct, she must have deliberately put the oil in herself. She had done it the first instant she could after finding out that his overnight guests had made a mistake in putting him down as a local product. And as one who was used to acting on the spur of the moment himself he could only admire her technique.

Without doubt had he tried the self-starter when he first got to the car the engine would have gone perfectly; believing that she had to deal with a labourer who knew nothing about motors she would not have troubled to put the machine out of commission. And then quite unexpectedly she found out her error, and rectified it in a way that showed she was no inexpert

29

driver. But with what object? Answer obvious. So that she could dope his tea and again search the house for the message. There she had backed a loser, and had taken it without turning a hair.

He lit a cigarette as he sat idly at the wheel; the telephone call was a lengthy one. What had been her next move? He recalled her growing anxiety over her uncle's tennis party; her apparent impatience to get started. She had naturally not suggested it, but was she hoping all along that he would take her in his own car? If so it must have seemed to her that he had played right into her hands.

Again, however, came the question: with what object? Why did she want him to meet her uncle? And this time the answer was not so obvious. The idea that it was anything to do with getting her there quickly because of a tennis party he dismissed as absurd. If it was only that, she, having done the damage to her own car herself, could very easily and oh! so cleverly have discovered it herself. Why then did she want him to go to her uncle's house at Cambridge? Could it be possible that certain arrangements were even now being made to greet him in a suitable fashion? Could it be possible that such an unladylike thing as a rough house was looming in the offing?

Drummond grinned happily to himself; life seemed astoundingly good. True, at the moment, the warfare was blind, but he held one very valuable card. He was convinced that the girl had no inkling that he had got her taped. That she suspected him was obvious; the mere fact that he had acted the part of a yokel the previous night, and had lied about the broken window, was sufficient to blot his copy-book.

"I'm so sorry to have kept you waiting all this time," said the girl when she at length appeared. "But my poor old uncle seems terribly worried."

"That's not so good," answered Drummond. "What's the trouble? Has the vicar's wife ratted from the tennis party?"

But she remained dead serious.

"Captain Drummond," she said, "I hate to bother you. But would you be an absolute dear and take me to Norwich?"

"Of course," cried Drummond. "Take you anywhere you like, bless your heart. And it's very little out of our way. Or do you want me to leave you there?"

"No, no; I've just got to find out something. It won't take me a moment."

"The day is yet young," said Drummond cheerfully. "Take as many moments as you like."

He glanced at her out of the corner of his eye and saw that she was in no mood for conversation. She was staring in front of her, and her fingers were drumming a tattoo on the armrest.

"It's damnable," she burst out once. "Utterly damnable."

"I'm sure it is," he remarked soothingly. "What's the trouble?"

But she shook her head.

"The family skeleton," she said bitterly. "And it's driving my uncle into his grave."

And not another word was spoken until they reached Norwich.

"Will you wait for me here," she said as the car drew up under the shadow of the cathedral. "I'll be as quick as I possibly can."

"Here you will find me," Drummond assured her, and watched her till she was out of sight. The idea of following her had crossed his mind, only to be dismissed at once. What significance, if any, was to be attached to this unexpected change of route, at the moment was beyond him. But one thing was certain. If he was still to retain his one trump he must do nothing to make her think he suspected her. And to follow her in the broad light of day, when she clearly did not want his company, would be such an outrageous piece of bad taste that it would give him away immediately. So there was nothing for it but to possess his soul in patience until she returned, and then await further developments.

It was twenty minutes before he saw her coming towards him, and it was obvious her mission had not been a success. Without a word she got into the car, and he started up the engine.

"Cambridge?" he asked. "Or is there anything else you have to do here?"

"No, thank you," she said. "I've found out what I wanted to know."

"I fear the result is not very satisfactory," said Drummond.

"Satisfactory," she cried. "I don't know how I shall break it to my uncle."

"Look here, Miss Venables," said Drummond quietly. "I don't want to barge in, or anything of that sort, but can I be of any assistance? I mean, it's clear that something is up."

For a while she did not answer; then suddenly she seemed to make up her mind.

"Captain Drummond, have you ever heard of *Der Schlüssel Verein*?"

"The – whatever you said. Afraid I haven't. What does it mean when it's at home?"

"Actually it means the Key Club."

"I'm still afraid I haven't," said Drummond. "It sounds pretty harmless."

She gave a short laugh.

"You may take it from me that the name is the only thing about it that is harmless. The Key Club is the most dangerous secret society in Europe today."

Drummond negotiated a cow with care.

"The devil they are," he remarked. "I thought secret societies had gone out of fashion some time ago,"

"Then you thought wrong," cried the girl bitterly.

"Well, well – one lives and learns. Anyway, what do these birds mean in your young life?"

"Nothing in mine actually," she answered, "but a lot in my uncle's."

"Is your uncle a foreigner?"

"Good heavens! no. He's as English as you or I."

Drummond was thinking hard, though his face expressed polite interest. And suddenly it dawned on him that if he still wanted to hold that trump card of his he must, after such an opening, allude to his visitors of the previous night. To keep silent would be tantamount to admitting that he did not trust her.

"Funny you should talk about foreigners," he said casually. "I had a visit from two of them last night. Germans."

"*You* had," she cried, and Drummond gave her full marks for registering amazement. "What on earth did they want with you?"

" 'Pon my soul, Miss Venables, I don't know. They talked a great deal out of their turn, and a gentleman called Emil…"

"Emil," she gasped. "Was he wearing a ring with a blue stone in it?"

"That's the cove. Do you know him?"

"Captain Drummond, he's one of the big men in the Key Club."

"Is he now? He was throwing his weight about all right last night. Took me for a farm labourer, and I did not disillusionise him. He arrived shortly after that drunk I told you about had bunged the brick through the window. It seemed to interest him quite a lot – that brick."

"But I don't understand," she cried. "Why did you let him think you were a farm labourer?"

"Saved bother," answered Drummond casually. "He seemed set on it."

"I can't get this straight at all," she said. "Why should he worry about a brick?"

"Extraordinary what some people's hobbies are," he remarked. "He seemed all hot and bothered about it. Waved a gun in the atmosphere, and frothed at the mouth. Of course it may have been a pool of blood in the road outside that caused the apoplexy."

"A pool of blood!" she echoed. "But was somebody hurt?"

"Presumably. Blood doesn't grow on its own. Though, of course, it may have been some animal."

"Didn't you do anything to find out?" she cried.

"My dear Miss Venables, the mist was so dense you could hardly see your hand in front of your face. Besides, Mr Emil was occupying my attention. He seemed to think I'd got a man concealed about the cottage."

"You mean he was chasing someone?"

"That is undoubtedly the impression he gave me."

"I see," said the girl after a long pause. "Only too clearly, unfortunately."

"I'm delighted to hear it," remarked Drummond. "For I most certainly don't. And if you can explain I shall be very grateful."

"Do you know who it was I went to see in Norwich?" she said, after another long pause.

"Haven't an earthly, bless you. How should I?"

"The man whose blood was on the road. The man they were chasing."

"And did you see him?"

"No. His landlady told me that two foreigners called for him late last night, and that he went away with them. They'd found him, and then I suppose he somehow escaped from them in the mist. And it was then they came to you. Oh! it will break Uncle John's heart."

Drummond stared at her.

"What's Uncle John got to do with it?"

"It was his son; my first cousin Harold."

Drummond whistled thoughtfully.

"Was it, by Jove! And why, if it isn't a rude question, should Mr Emil and Co. be chasing your first cousin Harold?"

"Captain Drummond," she said suddenly. "I'm going to trust you. Whether I'm doing right or not, I don't know, but the whole thing has got on my nerves. And now that this has happened, and you have been mixed up in it in such an extraordinary way, I feel I just can't stand it any more. Three years ago Harold went to Germany…"

"Just a moment, Miss Venables. What sort of a bloke is Harold?"

"A nice boy, but weak. His mother died when he was born, and Uncle John, though I'm devoted to him, has brought him up very badly. He's spoiled him abominably all his life, with the inevitable result that Harold is a waster. Well, as I say, he went to Germany three years ago – his one great gift is that he speaks languages perfectly – and there, in some extraordinary way, he got mixed up with that devil Emil and the Key Club. In fact he became a member of the society himself."

"Did he? Seems strange that an Englishman was allowed to join a German secret society."

"So he ought to have realised," she admitted. "But he didn't; until it was too late. He looked on the whole thing as a sort of joke, till one fine day he discovered his mistake. You'll understand, Captain Drummond, that neither my uncle nor I knew about it at the time; we only found it out quite recently. And though we noticed he was looking haggard and worried, he wouldn't tell us what was the matter. And then one day I got it out of him. They were bringing pressure on him to supply them with confidential information."

"Hold hard a minute," cried Drummond. "What confidential information could your cousin have access to which would be of any value to them?"

"I'm sorry, Captain Drummond; I'm telling it badly. I forgot to say that Harold is in the Foreign Office, and so he frequently has the opportunity of seeing important documents."

"I get you," said Drummond. "Please go on."

"A fortnight ago it came to a head. I was with my uncle at the time, and Harold suddenly arrived one evening in a pitiable condition. And to make matters worse he'd been drinking, which, to do him justice, is not a vice of his. For a time he was quite incoherent, but at last we got some sort of sense out of him. It was terrible, Captain Drummond; terrible. Apparently these devils, who had hitherto contented themselves with threatening him by letter from Germany, had arrived in this country, and were bringing pressure to bear on him in person. There was some document or other they wanted a copy of, and unless he got it for them he knew what the result would be."

"Why didn't he go to the police?"

"Just what my uncle said to him. And then we heard the ghastly truth; he didn't dare to. He had already sent these men certain information which he had no business to, though he swore on his Bible oath that it was of no real importance. For all that the mere fact that he'd sent anything at all was enough to brand him for life. And these brutes knew it, and were bringing the screw to bear, over something that really was vital – something that it really was traitorous to give away.

"He was at his wits' end, Captain Drummond. If he didn't tell them it meant death; if he did he felt he would never hold up his head again. And so he had taken the only course open to him. Somehow or other he had managed to get three weeks leave, and he'd bolted from London. But now arose the difficulty. He couldn't stop in my uncle's house, because they could easily track him there. So he had to go into hiding. And we decided on the rooms in Norwich where I went today."

"But how did you know this had happened last night, Miss Venables?" asked Drummond.

"My uncle told me over the telephone," she said. "You see this tennis party has been fixed for weeks, and both my uncle and I agreed it would be unwise to postpone it. I've been staying with some friends for a few days, and it was when I rang him up to explain why I was late that he told me he had phoned Harold last night and again this morning, and that the only reply he could get was from the landlady to say that Harold's bed had not been slept in. The rest you know. Somehow or other they got on his tracks, and now..."

She was rolling her handkerchief into a ball in her hands.

"Poor old Uncle John! He idolised Harold."

"I'm very sorry for both of you," said Drummond gravely. "In fact it's the devil and all of a business."

"I suppose I oughtn't to have told you, but somehow or other you look the sort of man one can rely on."

"Deuced kind of you to say so, my dear," cried Drummond genially. "But the thing that is worrying my grey matter is why your cousin should have bunged a rock through the window."

"I've been thinking of that, Captain Drummond," she said thoughtfully. "Do you think it possible that he wrapped a piece of paper round it: some message or other, which he hoped you would get?"

"Good Lord!" cried Drummond, "that's a darned brainy idea. Now you mention it, that's probably why our old friend Emil was so interested in the contents of my pockets. And to think I never thought of that."

He stole a glance at her: her forehead was puckered in thought. And once again he gave her full marks for her acting. How much of the Harold sob-stuff yarn was true he had no idea: but he had to admit that it was a very plausible tale, very plausibly told. Further, that *if* he had not seen what he had seen in the mirror; and *if* the mechanic had not made his illuminating remark about the oil, he would probably have believed it. And if he had believed it, there would have been no reason against passing the message on to her.

He was growing more and more intrigued over the whole affair, and increasingly anxious to meet Uncle John. The girl by his side was obviously English: would her relative prove the same? Was he even her uncle at all? And what terms was she really on with the man called Emil? In fact only one certainty seemed to him to stand out in the confusion. They had correctly surmised what the stone had been used for, but after that they were floundering in the dark. Had he received the message, or had he not? And to find that out they were obviously prepared to go to considerable lengths.

He pulled himself together: the girl was speaking again.

"What's that?" he cried. "See any sign of a piece of paper? Not a trace. There was certainly nothing wrapped round the stone when it came into the room, so if there was anything there to start with it must have fallen off earlier. In which case it might be somewhere in the garden, unless it has blown away. Pity you didn't have your brainstorm earlier, Miss Venables: we could have had a look. For if it comes under Mrs Eskdale's eagle eye it will instantly cease to exist. But in any event I don't see really that it could prove of much value. What could your cousin have written which would help matters? You've got to remember that so far as he knew the house was occupied by a labourer."

"He might have found out where they were taking him to, Captain Drummond, and flung the name as a despairing SOS through the first lighted window he saw."

Drummond gazed at her in admiration.

" 'Pon my soul, Miss Venables," he boomed enthusiastically, "it's a pleasure to work with you. Now I should never have thought of that. SOS, by Jove! That's the stuff to give the troops."

"If we're going to save him," she went on, "it's vital we should know where they've taken him to as soon as possible. And I know my uncle won't want to call in the police."

"What about sending a wire to Mrs Eskdale telling her to give the dustbin a once over?" said Drummond helpfully. "The old dear will think I've gone bughouse, but what matter."

"It can't do any harm, can it?" cried the girl. "A very good idea, Captain Drummond."

"Splendid. We'll stop at the first post office we come to. Incidentally, I suppose she'd better send the answer to your uncle's house. What address shall I give her?"

"Hartley Court is the name of the house. Just Hartley Court, Cambridge, is enough."

"And your uncle's name?"

"Meredith: he is my mother's brother."

"Right," cried Drummond. "It shall be attended to. She's a sensible old dame, and if she finds the paper and there's anything on it we shall know. Is that a post office ahead? It is. I won't be long."

He pulled up beside the kerb, and leaving the girl sitting in the car he went inside. A faint smile was twitching round his lips, and he stood for a few moments tapping his teeth with the pencil. Then he suddenly gave a little chuckle and seizing a form he began to write quickly. It was a long message, and when it was completed he reread it carefully. It was perfectly clear: Mrs Eskdale could make no mistake. He tore it off the block, removing at the same time the two next forms which he rolled into a ball and threw into the paper basket.

"If by any chance," he said to the man behind the counter, "any inquiries are made later in the day about this wire by anyone – it doesn't matter who it is – you'll be careful to say nothing, won't you?"

"Trust me, sir," said the operator. "The contents of that there telegram is a secret. Not even the King of England has the right to ask to see it."

"Quite, quite," cried Drummond soothingly. "But it might be put in such a way that it would seem to you that you were doing no harm. But when I tell you there's a big bet at stake you'll understand."

"Think no more about it, sir. I knows my duty, and I does it."

"The deed is done," said Drummond as he got back into the car. "I've asked the old girl to look in the garden for a piece of paper with writing on it, and if she finds anything to wire the contents to your uncle. It should be through in a couple of hours: there's a post office not far from her Cottage."

"Thank you so much," she cried. "It's a shame to give you all this trouble."

"Devil a bit, bless you. But we'd better get a move on, or your uncle will pair off the wrong people."

"He's cancelled the party, so that doesn't matter," she said. "He told me so on the telephone: he felt too worried over Harold, so he's put them off. For all that I would like to hurry: you see, he doesn't know what we know."

"Of course not," agreed Drummond. "I'll stamp on the juice. I make it that we've got about twenty more miles to go to Cambridge itself."

"The house is about three miles this side," she said: a spot where even at that moment an earnest council of war was in progress.

In an upstairs room stood a grey-haired man of about fifty-five: facing him across the table was the German called Emil. And he had only just arrived.

"I don't understand," he was saying harshly. "You say that this farm labourer is motoring Doris here."

"Farm labourer," sneered the other. "Do farm labourers have Rolls Royce coupés? He fooled you to the top of his bent, Emil. He's a man called Captain Drummond."

"So," said the German softly. "What was he doing then in that cottage all by himself?"

"He goes there for duck shooting. But a far more important point is why he pretended to be a labourer. That's what I can't make out. What was his object?"

The German lit a short and dangerous-looking cigar.

"What was his object?" repeated the grey-haired man. "It looks to me definitely as if our friend knew where he was going."

"In that fog?" The German shook his head. "Not possible, Meredith. Besides, he was more dead than alive even then."

"Then it is a very strange coincidence," cried Meredith. "There *must* have been a message round that stone in view of who it was who threw it. He would never have done such a senseless thing as to smash a window for fun."

"Well, I couldn't find it, and from what you say Doris has not succeeded either. And don't forget, Meredith, that all that matters is that no one should find it. Provided it's lost, we're safe."

"But is it lost? So long as I thought this man was a labourer I didn't mind. Now a totally different complexion is put on things."

The German shrugged his shoulders.

"We went through his house with a fine toothcomb," he said.

"What's the good of that?" cried Meredith impatiently. "A message can easily be committed to memory"

"Now look here, Meredith," said the German quietly, "you'd better pull yourself together. If what you're getting at is correct, and this man Drummond is one of them, why didn't our friend here go up to the cottage? Or why didn't he call out for help? It's folly to suppose that he'd have adopted the method he did, if he *knew* who was inside the room. No, no, my dear fellow: you're alarming yourself unnecessarily. Knowing that he'd only got a short time he took a chance with the first house where he saw the owner was still awake. It might have been a genuine labourer: it might have been Jones or Smith, but it happened to be this fellow Drummond. Why he should have pretended to be a farm hand I can't say: possibly my gun frightened him and he thought it was safer."

"Perhaps you're right," said Meredith hopefully. "At any rate we can only wait till we see Doris."

"Which reminds me, Meredith," remarked the German. "There's a question I've long been wanting to ask you. What are we going to do with that young woman when we've finished?"

"The same as with the others, I suppose."

"And you think she'll stand for it? I wonder. I have sometimes thought of late that she has become unduly inquisitive."

He stared at the ash on his cigar.

"Increasingly desirous, shall we say," continued the German, "of finding out what only the Inner Council know. Particularly with regard to the whereabouts of our – how shall I put it – our headquarters."

"Feminine curiosity," said Meredith. "Perfectly natural."

"It is now my turn to say perhaps you're right," said the German. "Anyway, here comes the car. Her wisdom in bringing him here is doubtful, but since she has, I, naturally, must not be seen."

"He is certainly no chicken," remarked Meredith, staring through the curtains.

"He is one of the largest individuals I've ever seen in my life," said the German. "Let us hope his brain is not equivalent to his brawn."

They watched the car drive up to the door and the girl get out. And a few moments later she entered the room.

"Well?" cried both men.

"He's got no message," she said quietly. "Of that I'm certain. But how on earth did you come to make such an idiotic mistake, Herr Veight? I very nearly gave the whole show away this morning when I saw him. And I had to change my entire plan of campaign on the spot."

"Was it wise to bring him here?" said Meredith.

"I had to. First I tried to dope his tea: that failed. Then I had another look in the garden whilst he and the mechanic were tinkering with the car up the road. But the old woman who owns the cottage was with me and I had to be careful. I could see nothing, and so to make perfectly certain I had to concoct a scheme. Now listen, Mr Meredith, because you'll have to go down and see him. You're my uncle, and it's your son Harold in the Foreign Office who has been abducted by the German gang of *Der Schlüssel Verein*."

"Great heavens!" cried Emil, "you haven't told him that, have you?"

"Of course I have. What you don't seem to be able to get into your thick head," said the girl angrily, "is that this man is not a farm labourer. He's a gentleman even if he is a fool. And do you suppose he's going to keep quiet over last night unless something is done about it? The only possible way of keeping his mouth shut is to enlist his sympathy. And that's what I've done: and this is how I did it."

"Upon my soul, my dear, I don't think you could have done better on the spur of the moment," said Meredith when she had finished. "I'll keep the good work going."

"If there is no answer to his wire we can assume that whatever message there was is definitely lost. If there is an answer, well – "

She paused significantly.

"Captain Drummond is certainly entitled to a drink," murmured Meredith, and Emil smiled. "And the nature of the drink will depend on the nature of the message."

"Exactly," said the girl. "And now come on. He'll think it strange if we keep him waiting too long. Don't forget you're the broken-hearted father. Incidentally, how much longer have we got to wait?"

"Three days: four. Certainly a week should do it. He's nearly cracked, so I was told this morning."

"Then for a week at least this man Drummond has got to keep his mouth shut."

"Wouldn't it be far better – " began Meredith tentatively.

"No," she said emphatically. "Only as a last resort. He can be traced here through Cannaby's garage. Let's go down, dear Uncle John."

They found Drummond apparently dozing over the wheel.

"My dear Captain Drummond," said Meredith courteously, "I cannot thank you sufficiently for all you have done for my little Doris."

"Not at all," cried Drummond, getting out of the car and shaking him warmly by the hand. "A pleasure, sir: a pleasure."

"I hear she has told you the whole terrible story."

"About your poor son, George…"

"Harold, Captain Drummond," said the girl with a smile.

"Of course. Stupid of me: I've got a shocking memory for names. Yes, Mr Meredith, your niece has told me, and I can only hope my wire may result in something helpful. Though I confess I am not optimistic. There was a bit of a breeze this morning, and any loose piece of paper would, I fear, have been blown away."

"Still it is a hope which I cling to. I am an elderly man, Captain Drummond, and this affair has shaken me dreadfully: you can understand a father's feelings under the circumstances."

"Only too easily," said Drummond sympathetically.

"And I was wondering if I might trespass even further on your kindness. Are you in a very great hurry to go?"

"My time is yours, Mr Meredith. I must be up in London for dinner, but until then I am at your disposal."

"Not so long as that, I assure you," said Meredith with a deprecating smile. "But if you would not mind waiting till the answer to your telegram comes, it would indeed be a relief to us."

"Delighted," cried Drummond. "It should not be long now."

"I gather that my niece has explained to you our difficulty with regard to the police, though I cannot believe that Harold has given away anything of importance. But even so I would like to keep them out of it. And if, as my dear niece thinks – and I am inclined to agree with her – the dear boy knew where those devils were taking him to and managed to scribble it down, I would so like your advice and help."

"It's yours for the asking," said Drummond heartily. "And of one thing I can assure you. If there is the smallest fragment of paper in her spotless garden, Mrs Eskdale will find it."

He glanced out of the window.

"Great Scott! That's pretty quick. Here's a telegraph boy on a bicycle coming up the drive. The old lady hasn't wasted any time."

"Get it, my dear," cried Meredith. "And see what it is. Captain Drummond," he continued, as she left the room. "I'm so nervous I don't know what to do."

"Bite on the old bullet, Mr Meredith," said Drummond soothingly. "We shall know soon. Here comes your niece now."

The girl came in reading the telegram with a puzzled look on her face.

"Well, my dear: well?" cried Meredith.

"It's from Mrs Eskdale all right," she said. "But it does not seem to make sense."

And for the fraction of a second Drummond's jaw tightened.

" 'Found paper in garden,' " read the girl, " 'on it written S B Z...' Just a jumble of letters. They don't make sense. About ten of them. Then signed 'Eskdale.' "

Drummond's jaw relaxed, and suddenly the girl gave an excited cry.

"Uncle John! I've got it. It's Harold's code – the code he and I used to use when we were children. We wrote letters to one another in it. I've got it upstairs somewhere."

She darted out of the room, and Drummond lit a cigarette. Also he glanced at Meredith, and having done so suppressed a smile. For Meredith's face was a study, and continued as such till the sound of rapid footsteps announced his niece's return.

"I've got it," she cried, waving the form triumphantly. "It *is* the name of a place. How clever of him! Don't you see, Uncle John? Harold saw the light in the window and assumed the owner or whoever was there would take the message to the police. Then it would have come out in the papers, and though no one else would have spotted it, we should."

"And what is the name of the place, Miss Venables?" asked Drummond with interest.

"Kessingland," she said. "I know I've heard of a place of that name."

"There is a place called Kessingland a few miles from Lowestoft on the coast," said Drummond thoughtfully. "So you think that wire means that your cousin has been taken there?"

"What else can it mean, Captain Drummond? There are probably isolated bungalows there and he has been hidden in one of them."

"My poor boy," said Meredith, passing his hand across his forehead. "What shall we do?"

"Look here," said Drummond after a pause, "can I be of any assistance? True, I don't know your son, but I fear we must assume he's been badly hurt. Now would you like me to go to Kessingland and make a few careful inquiries? I will be most discreet, but it's probably not a very big place and the tradesmen or somebody will be sure to know if any foreigners have turned up there."

"But, Captain Drummond, we couldn't think of bothering you. Could we, Uncle John?"

"Of course not. Besides, my dear fellow, you've got to go to London. And it may take days."

"What matter, Mr Meredith? My dinner party in London can easily be put off. And I feel that in a case like this one should sacrifice everything to help. It may, as you say, take two or three days – perhaps more; but that is a trifle compared to your son's safety. I will start at once."

He waved aside their half-hearted protests, and rose to his feet.

"I will keep you posted of anything I find out," he continued. "And all we can hope is that I shall not be too late."

"I wish I could come with you, Captain Drummond," said Meredith, "but I fear my health is hardly equal to the strain."

"I wouldn't hear of it, Mr Meredith," cried Drummond. "Your place is here – with your niece. I hope that very soon I shall have good news to report."

He pressed the girl's hand gently, and her eyes fell before his.

"May I do so in person?" he murmured.

"Of course," she answered. "My uncle and I will be delighted to see you at any time."

"Goodbye, sir." He turned to Meredith. "And don't despair."

They accompanied him to his car, and as he let in his clutch the girl leaned over the side.

"At any time," she whispered. "I think it is too sweet of you to do this for two complete strangers."

"Strangers?" he said reproachfully. "That's unkind of you, Doris."

They watched the car till it turned into the main road; then Meredith turned to the girl.

"What the deuce," he spluttered, "is the game? What is this bunk about a code?"

"Don't you realise what this message is?" said the girl quietly as the German joined them. " 'Found paper in garden. On it written SBZALFTRPTE. Eskdale.' Don't you realise it *is* a code message right enough?"

"But what?... Why?..." cried Meredith, completely bewildered. "Why Kessingland?"

"Oh! you're dense; you're dense. What did I tell Drummond on the way here? That if there was a message it would be the place they were taking Harold to. So any town with eleven letters would do, and Kessingland happens to be not too near and not too far. It will keep him quiet hunting round the sand dunes, whereas if I'd said nothing he would almost certainly have taken this up to London. Or else had it repeated from the old woman."

"Gad! Emil, the girl is quick on the uptake," said Meredith.

"Extremely," remarked the German, studying the telegram. "I wonder what this really does stand for."

"Not a doubt about it in my mind," said the girl. "It's the address of your headquarters."

For a moment or two the German stared at her; then he smiled.

"Well, my dear," he remarked suavely, "if that is so, you've certainly done no harm in sending that bovine individual to Kessingland."

And with the utmost deliberation he tore up the telegram and put the pieces in his pocket.

CHAPTER 4

It was at precisely twelve o'clock that Peter Darrell entered the lounge of the Royal Hotel, and perceived Drummond with his legs stretched out in front of him, and his face buried in a tankard of ale. Periodically during the last half-hour the large form of the drinker had been shaken with gusts of internal mirth, to the evident alarm of an old lady opposite who was knitting some incomprehensible garment. And now, realising that a second was approaching, she rose hurriedly and bolted to cover in the drawing-room.

"Come hither, my Peter," boomed Drummond. "Things is 'appening."

"So I gathered, confound you," cried Darrell. "I was lunching with the Marriot filly. Why the dickens aren't you killing ducks?"

"Draw up, Peter, my boy, and put your nose inside a pint. This is my third, and my confidence in myself is even now not restored. There was a time," he continued sadly, "when I regarded myself as a pretty ready liar – somewhere round about scratch. This morning, Peter, I have been holding converse with a plus two performer."

"Do you mean to say you've brought me down here to tell me that? Who is this bloke?"

"It's a lady, Peter, a beautiful, charming girl with an uncle. And the dear child yearned greatly for a message to be sent her by telegram: a message doubtless of hope and comfort to cheer

49

her maiden heart. But you look bewildered, Peter: let us begin at the beginning."

He hitched his chair closer to Darrell's, and lit a cigarette. The lounge was empty save for the hall porter, and he so far came out of his habitual coma as to wonder once or twice what the big man in the corner was talking so earnestly about to the owner of the racing car outside. For it was twenty minutes later that the owner of the car spoke for the first time.

"But, damn it, Hugh," he said, "I don't understand about this second message. The one they were after, you found in the window. That's clear. What is this other one that Mrs Eskdale found?"

Drummond grinned.

"Peter," he remarked, "I have exercised a little story-teller's licence on you. Mrs Eskdale never found a message. When I told you I wired Mrs Eskdale to send a message I did not add that I told her what message to send. And for a time I wondered what message I should tell her to send. It had to be something mysterious, and yet something that looked genuine. Suddenly – out of the blue, as a gift from the gods – came the idea. A newspaper was lying in the next compartment and I happened to glance at it. And my prepaid wire ran as follows:

Wire Meredith Hartley Court Cambridge following message Stop found paper in garden on it written SBZALFTRPTE Eskdale.

"But what is SBZ and all the rest of it?"

"Coldspur's cipher nap tip for Lingfield in the *Daily Leader*," said Drummond quietly.

Darrell stared at him open-mouthed.

"Then how the deuce has she made Kessingland out of it?" he spluttered.

Once again Drummond grinned.

"Because, old lad, Miss Doris Venables, as I said at the beginning, is definitely rated at plus two and she plays quicker than George Duncan. I take off my hat to that wench."

"More beer," said Darrell decidedly. "This is too obscure for me. I still don't see her object."

"Simple, Peter. To get rid of me. I'm becoming a nuisance: in fact, I always have been a nuisance since I appeared in the picture. But it was quick of her – damned quick. Think it over, old boy: look at the matter from her point of view. Every single move that the other side has made since Emil and his boyfriend paid me their visit last night has been directed to one end – to get the message that was wrapped round the brick. And though I may not be quite up to her form I flatter myself that I'm sufficiently near it to play level. Obviously she believes that I've swallowed her precious Harold lock, stock and barrel. And to tell you the truth, Peter, until the Kessingland episode I wasn't at all certain that Harold was a myth. Now it's plain that he is."

"I don't exactly see that, old boy."

"Don't be dense, Peter. That's Coldspur's cipher: by no hook or crook can you make Kessingland out of it. There ain't such a horse. Therefore all the talk about her code with Harold was a lie. Now she thinks that she's got the genuine message that they've been hunting for, and so the one urgent thing for them to do was to get shot of me. Mark her guile. She believes that I think she's got a message from Harold. So she looks up a town with eleven letters in it, and if I hadn't suggested going there you can bet your bottom dollar she'd have made the suggestion for me. She took care, you see – in the most natural way, I admit – not to let me see the wire. Otherwise I might have wondered why Z and A both stood for S. But as it is she thinks I'm taped for Kessingland, and God forbid she should think otherwise!"

"How are you going to work it?" demanded Darrell.

"After we've had lunch, Peter, we are going to Kessingland. There, with our well-known charm, we will get hold of someone of comparative intelligence to whom we will give stamped telegrams – three or four should be enough. We will concoct them later. The first, which can be sent to the lady this evening, will merely announce my arrival. Tomorrow, in the morning, a hint that I am on the track of foreigners; in the evening, still on the track. The next day, that the trail has died, but still trying, etc., and so forth. I might even go so far as to write a letter to be posted late tomorrow evening, which should convince her that little Willie is still safely buried in that delectable spot. Then, Peter, having done this, we shall return here."

"And what then?"

"A closer inspection of Hartley Court by night seems to me to be indicated."

Drummond beckoned a waiter and ordered two Martinis.

"I can't help feeling, Peter," he continued, "that there are things afoot here which are bigger than ordinary common or garden crime."

"Do you mean political?"

"That's the notion. I'm inclined to believe that there's something in that Key Club business."

"Mightn't be a bad idea to rope in Ronald Standish," said Darrell thoughtfully.

"Not at all bad," agreed Drummond. "He'd know, if anybody did. Go and ring him up, Peter. Tell him that aught is amiss here in the children's kindergarten, and will he kindly report his vile dog's body as soon as possible."

Darrell crossed to the telephone box and Drummond lit a cigarette. Definitely a good idea: if his surmise was right, if by a strange freak of fate he had blundered into deep waters, there was no one who would pull his weight better than Ronald Standish. He knew all the hush-hush men intimately, and what was more, they trusted him implicitly. For the more Drummond thought things over, the more did he feel convinced that this was going to prove a hush-hush job.

"He'll be down in time for dinner this evening," said Darrell, rejoining him.

"Splendid," cried Drummond. "Let's go and have a spot of food, Peter, and then push off. The sooner we lay the Kessingland trail the better."

And at that delectable East Coast watering-place luck proved to be right in. One of the first people they saw was a man they both knew, who was staying there for a few days, and who readily agreed to send the wires for them.

"For Heaven's sake, get 'em in the right order, old boy," said Drummond, "and don't send 'em all off at once or we are undone. And now, Peter – to horse. I propose to go back via Nannie's cottage to warn in the dear old thing that I shan't be back for a few days. It's very little out of our way, and she'll worry herself sick if I don't turn up.

"Still there, you see, Peter," he cried as they approached the cottage some half-hour later. "There's the trampled-down bit of verge; there's the pool of oil. It's dusty now, but you can see the outline clear enough."

"The poor devil must have bled some," said Darrell.

"You're right," remarked Drummond gravely. "Gad! Peter, I wish I could get to the bottom of this show."

He drew up outside the cottage.

"Shan't be a moment," he cried. "The old darling will probably want us to stop to tea, but I'll tell her we can't. Nannie," he shouted, opening the gate, "where are you?"

There was no answer, and he walked up the path. His terrier and spaniel came bounding to meet him, and he stopped to pat them.

"Where," he demanded, "is that lazy devil Jerry?"

And then, on the threshold of the door, he paused, and stood very still.

"Peter," he called softly, "come here."

Darrell joined him: the reason for Jerry's laziness was clear. For the bulldog was lying motionless on the carpet, and it was obvious at a glance that he had been shot through the head.

"By God! old Jerry," muttered Drummond in a voice that shook a little, "somebody is going to pay to the uttermost farthing for this. How did it happen, boy; how did it happen?"

His eyes were roving round the room, and suddenly he gave an exclamation and stepped to the table. Then he bent down and picked up a pair of leather gloves which were lying near.

"Look at these, Peter," he cried. "See that brown and white stitching effect? Can't mistake it. These are the gloves Doris Venables was wearing this morning when I motored her to Cambridge."

"Are you sure, Hugh?"

"Of course I'm sure. Or they're an identical pair, and that is too amazing a coincidence to swallow. What the devil has happened?"

"She must have been back here."

"But why, Peter? What did she want to come back for?"

"Perhaps to make certain the wire was genuine," suggested Darrell.

"But why shoot Jerry?" cried Drummond. "Why, in the name of all that is miraculous, shoot the old chap? He made great friends with her this morning."

Darrell made no answer: he was standing by the door listening intently.

"There's someone asleep upstairs, Hugh. I can hear breathing."

Drummond joined him at the door; there was no doubt about it. Somebody was almost snoring in the room above, and they were up the stairs in a flash. And there an even more amazing spectacle met their eyes.

Lying on the bed fully dressed and completely unconscious was the ample form of Mrs Eskdale. Her face was flushed, and every now and then a strangled snort convulsed her.

"If I didn't know her better, Peter," said Drummond after a while, "I'd say she was blind drunk. But the old dear never touches a drop of anything except an occasional glass of some hell brew of her own. Elderberry wine, or something."

"She's either drunk or drugged, Hugh," said Darrell decidedly. "There's not the smallest doubt of that."

They bent over her, but there was no suspicion of alcohol about her breath.

"That settles it, Peter," said Drummond. "She's been doped."

He shook her gently by the shoulder, and then not so gently, but it produced no result.

"It may be hours before she awakes," he continued with a frown. "This is the devil and all, Peter; I don't like to leave the old lady."

"It's not that that is worrying me so much," said Darrell. "I'm trying to reconstruct the crime as they say. How did she get here? No girl could possibly have carried or dragged an unconscious woman of her weight up those steep stairs."

"Therefore," remarked Drummond, "if the girl was alone Mrs Eskdale must have been up here when she was given the dope. No; hold hard a minute. Let's suppose she was giving the girl a cup of tea, and that little Doris pulled the same stuff on her as she tried to do on me this morning. Then the old dear began to feel queer, but still managed to get up here under her own steam. How's that?"

Darrell nodded.

"It fits. But what about Jerry? If all that happened was that Mrs Eskdale came upstairs more or less normally, why should he get excited? And surely no one would shoot a dog just for the fun of the thing."

"You think the girl was not alone."

"I don't know what to think, Hugh; the whole thing is baffling. But the only solution that seems to fit Jerry having been killed and Mrs Eskdale being up here is that some sort of a rough house took place below. What it was about the Lord only knows."

"She's loyal to the core, is that old dear. It's just possible they wanted to see the message itself, and she wouldn't show it to them. And it would have been a bit difficult seeing that she hadn't got one to show."

He broke off abruptly, staring out of the window with narrowed eyes.

"Do you see that clump of bushes, Peter, one finger left of that stunted alder?" he said softly. "There's something just moved in them."

Darrell picked up the target a hundred and fifty yards away on the other side of the road.

"I'll take your word for it, old boy," he answered. "Your sight is so damned uncanny... No, by Jove! you're right. I saw it myself."

"It's a man; I can see his face, just to the right of the middle."

Drummond rubbed his hands gently together.

"Stay here, Peter; I'm going to stalk that gentleman. And in this flat country it'll mean a big detour starting from the back of the cottage. But if I can manage to get under cover of that hedge running by the alder, I'm home. Show yourself every now and then at the window."

And then followed for Peter Darrell an interval of pure joy. An ardent stalker himself, it was an education to watch Drummond at work. Conditions naturally were different, but the principles were the same, and as an object lesson in how to make cover where none existed it could not have been beaten. He had forgotten Mrs Eskdale, who still snored placidly on her bed; his whole attention was riveted on a blurred white face peering out of the undergrowth, and the slinking figure away to the right.

At last Drummond reached the hedge which was his first objective and scrambled through it. Then out of sight of his quarry he straightened up and started to run. Nearer and nearer he got, and now he was moving cautiously. Ten yards; five yards, and then in a flash it was over. Came a sudden spring; a shrill squeal of fear and the next moment Drummond emerged into the open field with his prisoner. And his prisoner's gun.

Darrell met them at the gate, and studied the captive with interest. And somewhat to his surprise he saw that he was of a very different type to what he had anticipated. The man was well dressed, and on the surface at any rate appeared to be a gentleman. He was dark and clean shaven, and his nationality was not obvious. But his English when he spoke was perfect.

"May I ask," he remarked icily, "the reason for this incredible outrage?"

"Get inside," said Drummond curtly. "A pretty weapon this, Peter; compressed air. And you will kindly remember, my friend, that any attempt on your part to escape would cause it to be used on your right knee. And that's a painful wound."

"I shall have the law on you for this," said the man in a voice that shook with rage.

"By all means," cried Drummond affably. "But just at the moment my friend and I are the law."

The man went slowly up the path, and as he came to the door he paused for a second. The sound of Mrs Eskdale's snores still came rhythmically from above, and Darrell watching his face saw a faint look of relief flash for a moment across it. Then it became as mask-like as ever.

"Now, sir," he remarked, "once more I insist on an explanation."

"Are you the man who did that?" said Drummond quietly, pointing to the dead bulldog.

"I am not," answered the man. "This is the first time I have been in this cottage."

And Jock, his teeth bared, snarled in a corner.

"You lie," said Drummond softly. "You lie, damn you, and there's the proof." He pointed to the terrier. "However for the moment we will leave that. Why were you lying up in those bushes watching this house?"

The man lit a cigarette.

"I'll buy it," he remarked with a yawn.

"I wonder," said Drummond pleasantly, "if you have ever read a book called 'Stalky and Co.'?"

The man stared at him in blank surprise.

"I ask for this reason," continued Drummond. "In that immortal classic there is a story which tells of the way Stalky and two low companions of his dealt with a pair of bullies at their school. And it is most efficacious."

Once again the man yawned.

"I suppose your remarks have some point," he said languidly. "But if so I fear it has eluded me."

"Then I will endeavour to make it plainer," said Drummond. "They dealt with these bullies in their own coin. They bullied them even worse than the bullies had done to their victims. And the result was an unqualified success."

His eyes were boring into the man opposite.

"Am I getting clearer?" he continued. "At the present moment my friend and I represent Stalky and Co.; you represent the bullies. People who shoot my dogs, and drug harmless old ladies may be justly regarded as bullies. And since you've taken the gloves off I propose to do the same. Ah! would you, you swine."

His arm shot out as the man's hand came out of his pocket, and a knife clattered on to the floor.

"Peter, get me that rubber strap out of the car, and the rope."

"What are you going to do?" muttered the man, writhing helplessly in Drummond's grip.

"You will see in due course," said Drummond. "It is not a treatment I would recommend for the sick and ailing, but that doesn't apply to strong and hearty men like you who lie about on wet grass and go big game shooting. Who knows – you might even beat the record."

"The record," stammered the man. "What record?"

"Twenty minutes," explained Drummond, "is the longest time known up to date that the patient undergoing this treatment has lasted without praying for death. Got 'em, Peter? Good. Here's a good stout chair; let's lash him to that."

The man let out a wild shout, and began to struggle desperately, but in the hands of two past masters of the art of rough housing he was like a child. In half a minute he was trussed up like a fowl, and two scientifically arranged handkerchiefs almost prevented his breathing.

"Now," said Drummond, balancing a piece of rubber belting about eighteen inches long in his hand, "before we begin I wish everything to be quite clear. What my friend and I are doing now is quite illegal. But as I told you before for the time being we have taken the law into our own hands. How long we continue to keep it there depends entirely on you. When you have had enough, and decide to tell us exactly what happened this afternoon in this room, just nod your head."

The man's eyes, sullen and vindictive, were fixed on Drummond, who had raised the strap shoulder high.

"The essence of this means of persuasion," explained Drummond, "is not to hit too hard, and at the same time to leave no part of the area selected untouched. In your case I propose to take the right leg from the knee up. So, and so, and so."

Steadily, almost gently the belting rose and fell travelling from the knee up to the thigh and then back again.

"It's been used in the third degree frequently," went on Drummond conversationally. "Also in other cases where confession is good for the soul. The only time I have actually seen it employed myself was in Australia in a mining camp. One of the miners had committed the unforgivable sin of stealing another miner's gold. And he'd hidden it. So in order to find out where, they tried this method. It succeeded, and then there was no reason to delay shooting him any longer."

The sweat was beginning to pour down the man's face.

"It's generally about the tenth journey," continued Drummond, "that you think your leg is going to burst. About the fifteenth you wish it would, and near the twentieth you're sure it has. We've just got to six now, so there's still plenty of time to go. And I should like confirmation of those figures."

But the man had had enough; his head was nodding furiously. And at a sign from Drummond, Darrell removed the handkerchiefs.

"So you have decided to speak," said Drummond. "Good. But let me warn you of one thing. If I detect you in a lie I'll continue this treatment up to thirty."

"What is it you want to know?" said the man sullenly.

"What took place here this afternoon. Why has Miss Venables been here? Who drugged Mrs Eskdale? Who shot my bulldog?"

"I can't answer the first one, and that's straight. A girl was here, and her name may have been Venables, but why she was here I don't know. Two of us got orders…"

"Who from?" snapped Drummond.

The man hesitated, and Drummond half raised the strap.

"Look here, if I tell you all I know will you promise to let me go?"

"I won't promise, but I will give it my favourable consideration," said Drummond. "I should hate to see more of you than I need. Now, who gave you your orders?"

"I don't know his name; none of us do," said the man. "I've never even seen him."

"How do you get your orders?"

"Either by telephone, or in a typewritten letter. This time it was by telephone."

"Go on," said Drummond curtly. "What were your orders?"

"To go to a certain hotel near Cambridge and await further instructions."

"What happened then?"

"We were joined by a man I'd never seen before, and we got into his car and came here. The girl's car was standing outside the door, and the man led the way into this room, where she was talking to the old woman upstairs. She turned as white as a sheet when she saw him, and clung to the other woman who tried to protect her. It was then the bulldog turned nasty and the man shot him with that rifle. The girl tried to run away, but the man caught her by the gate and brought her back. Then while we held her he gave her an injection with a hypodermic syringe in her arm. And the old woman, too. In a few seconds they were both unconscious, and we carried one to the car and the other upstairs."

"What a pretty party," said Drummond quietly. "Go on."

"That's about all," said the man. "My friend drove the girl's car away; the man took her at the back of his own. And I was told to lie up in those bushes and watch the cottage."

"With that gun?" remarked Drummond dryly.

"That had been forgotten, so I took it with me."

Drummond lit a cigarette and turned to Darrell.

"What do you make of it, Peter? Do you think this mess is speaking the truth?"

"His story fits, old boy," said Darrell. "But what I would like to know is this. Do you usually go round acting blind on the instructions of a man you've never seen before, when they entail drugging women and trifles of that sort?"

"My orders were to obey him," answered the man.

"You mean the orders you received over the telephone from your other boyfriend," said Drummond. "I should like to hear a little more about him. You said none of you knew his name. Am I to understand that there are many bits of work like you about the place?"

"There are several."

"My God! you shake me to the marrow. Is it a sort of secret society?"

"We do what we are told," said the man.

"Charming; charming," remarked Drummond. "You aren't by any chance members of the Key Club, are you?"

The man stared at him blankly.

"I don't know what you are talking about," he said.

"That's either very good acting, Peter, or it's the truth. And so either the Key Club is a further invention of this lovely lady, or we have two societies. Aren't we lucky chaps? To return, however, to your own private one, my friend. The motives that actuate it are, I take it, entirely criminal."

For the first time a very faint smile flickered round the man's lips.

"They would hardly stand an appeal to the House of Lords," he said.

"Excellent. And do you receive adequate remuneration from this man you've never seen and who presumably is your Lord High Mukkaduk?"

"We don't do it for love," remarked the other.

"You surprise me," said Drummond. "Now there's another question. Could you describe the man in whose car you came here, and who drugged the two women?"

"Medium height; dark eyes; rather saturnine face."

"A description which might fit my visitor of last night, Peter. On the other hand it fits numbers of other men. Well – the mystery increases. If it was him it goes to confirm his story to me in the car. However we'll go into that later. The first thing to decide is what to do with this blighter."

"For God's sake, gentlemen, don't give me up to the police," cried the man earnestly. "I swear that what I've told you is the truth so far as I know it, and you half promised you'd let me go if I spoke."

"And yet the police would be highly edified," said Drummond. "A young army of people like you all doing what you're told. And they would let you off nice and light if you turned King's Evidence."

"It isn't what the police would do," answered the man. "If it came out that I'd told even you what I have my life wouldn't be worth a moment's purchase. But that damned strap would make a deaf mute speak."

"It is certainly an aid to conversation," agreed Drummond cheerfully. "Well – I'll think about it. You can stop here till I'm sure Mrs Eskdale is comfortable, and then we will decide on your immediate future. Peter, come upstairs with me."

"Well," he said as they entered the room where the old lady still snored peacefully, "what are we going to do with him? My own reaction to the swab is that he has been speaking the truth."

"Same here, Hugh. I don't think anyone could have invented that story on the spur of the moment. It accounts for everything that was puzzling me before."

"Except the girl's object in coming over," objected Drummond. "You say to confirm the telegram. But what could have made her suspect it in the first instance?"

"We can't positively settle that till Mrs Eskdale wakes up," said Darrell. "And it looks to me as if that wasn't going to be for some time."

"Which raises another small point. What are we going to do with her, poor old dear?"

"Nothing we can do, except cover her up with an eiderdown and leave her to sleep it off. Write her a note, Hugh, saying we'll be along tomorrow morning, and that until then you don't want her to say anything to anybody."

"Her pulse is normal," said Drummond. "I think she'll be all right here."

"My dear old lad," cried Darrell, "we can't cart an unconscious woman of her bulk round the country. If you warn in one of her neighbours to come and look after her there's not a single one of her pals who won't believe she's not dead drunk. And she'd hate that. Honestly I think she's perfectly safe here. She can't be of the smallest importance to the bunch we're up against."

Drummond pulled out his pocket book and began to scribble a note while Darrell strolled to the window and looked out.

"Hullo!" he cried softly. "It would seem that the tall gentleman is in a hurry. And he hardly looks like a local resident."

Drummond joined him, and together they watched a man in a dark suit striding rapidly along the road away from the cottage. He was fully a hundred yards off, but even at that distance his great height was noticeable. Then he disappeared round a corner and the sound of a self-starter came faintly to their ears.

"More motorcars," said Drummond, pinning the note to the pillow. "They'll have to have an AA man here soon to regulate the traffic. Well, Peter – let's get on with it. We'll allow this bloke to come with us, and we'll drop him somewhere. After all, he's only one of the small fry, and I did more or less promise we'd let him go."

"What about the dogs?"

"Leave them here. And incidentally that swab below can damn well dig poor old Jerry's grave. Go and find a shovel, Peter, and then set him free, while I tuck up Nannie."

And he was just wrapping the eiderdown round her when a wild shout came from Darrell.

"Hugh! For God's sake, come here."

Drummond dashed downstairs and into the parlour. Lolling forward in the chair, and only kept in position by the rope which bound him, was the man. And a dagger had been driven up to the hilt in his heart.

CHAPTER 5

For a while they stood there too stunned to speak. The thing was so utterly unexpected. Not a sound had they heard upstairs, and yet during the ten minutes they had been out of the room this unknown man had been murdered.

"Must have been that tall man we saw striding up the road," said Darrell at length.

"Whoever it was he must have struck from behind," remarked Drummond. "This fellow would have shouted if he'd seen him."

He went into the kitchen and looked round. The back door was open; and on the stone floor were marks of earth.

"He must have come over the fields and stood here," continued Drummond.

"Where he heard every word that was said," remarked Darrell.

"Which confirms the story. There would have been no object in murdering that man if he had been lying. At the same time, Peter, there are one or two rather rum points about this. The mischief was already done: the beans were already spilt. That poor devil could do no more harm, and he certainly wasn't going to the police himself. Why then do the one thing which under normal circumstances is going to get the whole yarn to the police through us quicker than anything else?"

"Vengeance," suggested Darrell. "The murderer saw his chance and took it."

"Perhaps," said Drummond. "But vengeance loses much of its force if the victim doesn't know it is coming. And I refuse to believe that any man would sit in a chair and let another man stab him without raising Cain."

"Condign punishment then."

"Which could be meted out at any time. Why run the appalling risk of murdering this man knowing that we were upstairs? Knowing that he might not kill instantaneously, and that there might have been a cry which would have brought us down? Why take such a chance, unless…"

"Unless what?"

"Unless," said Drummond slowly, "the murderer *wants* us to go to the police."

Darrell stared at him.

"Wants us to," he echoed. "Why the devil should he want us to?"

"To force our hands: to find out exactly what we know. It sounds far-fetched, I know, but if you look into it it's not quite so fanciful as it appears at first sight. Supposing this afternoon, either here or at the post office down the road they got hold of the actual wire I sent Mrs Eskdale. The instant they read it they realised that I'd been fooling them, didn't they?"

"That's so," agreed Darrell.

"Step two. If I fooled 'em there, the strong probability is that I fooled 'em before. In other words I had received the original message. Now if we go to the police about this I shall have to tell them the whole story, which includes the contents of that original message. And how long do you think it will be in a place like this with local constables and hordes of journalists before that message is public property?"

"That's the last thing they're likely to want," objected Darrell.

"Is it? That's just where you may be wrong, Peter. Having failed to get what they really wanted – namely the message to themselves alone – isn't it possible that the next best thing is to share it? Even if they can't prevent A5's message reaching the people it is intended for, at any rate they will be wise as to what it is."

"You think they'd murder a man for that?" said Darrell doubtfully.

"If they thought the contents of the message were sufficiently important – yes. And judging from their whole line of action they *do* think that."

"There's something in it," said Darrell. "But what are we going to do, old boy? We must report this, or we'll get into the most frightful row."

"Admittedly, Peter, we must report his death. But is there any necessity to report anything else – anything else, that is to say, that is true? We arrived here to find Mrs Eskdale unconscious, the bulldog dead – this man murdered. The other side will know that is a lie, but they will think we are telling it because our own actions when we bound him would hardly bear cross-examination. In other words that we are frightened of mentioning that part. Further, because Joe the postman will certainly do it if I don't, we must account for the hole in the window. And, by Gad! Peter, if Coldspur's tip for Lingfield has gone wallop, we'll give the blighters another one to bite on. There's big stuff on here, old boy, and we've got to take a chance. We'll tell the truth in London, but if we tell it down here we're going to be detained and the Lord knows what. And what we want to do is to fade away as unostentatiously as possible. But if we're going to have a shot at fooling these swine again we must do the obvious thing first, and report to the local police."

"What about Mrs Eskdale?" remarked Darrell.

"She complicates matters a bit, poor old darling. For now that this has happened we certainly can't leave her here. Tell you what, Peter: we'll have to get her up to my house in Town. And you must take her and the two dogs. We'll wedge her up with cushions in the front of the car, and you can drop me at

Belmoreton down the road where the nearest police station is. I'll tell 'em the tale: you go on to London and leave her in charge of Denny. Then come back to the Royal at Cambridge."

Luckily the road was deserted as they carried her down the path, and with great difficulty got her into the car. And having removed the note from the pillow, and taken one final look round, they left the cottage with its grim contents.

"You'll have the devil of a job to prevent her rolling off the seat, Peter," said Drummond, as he got out in Belmoreton. "But if she does she's on the floor for keeps, so do your best."

He stood watching the car till it was out of sight: then he accosted a passer-by.

"Police station," said the man. "Down the street and first on the right."

He found it without difficulty, and with growing amazement the sergeant in charge listened to his story. Two constables drifted in and stood gaping: a dog fight outside went the full number of rounds unchecked.

"So there you are, my brave fellow," cried Drummond in conclusion. "Murder and sudden death are loose upon your smiling countryside."

"It's the most amazing story I've ever heard," remarked the sergeant, scratching his head. "Have you your car here, sir?"

"I have not," said Drummond. "My friend has taken Mrs Eskdale up to London in it. So you'll have to raise another."

The sergeant gave an order to one of the constables, who left the police station; and returned five minutes later in a taxi. In some inexplicable way the news that something was afoot had filtered round, and a small crowd of listeners had collected in the street outside. And the instant Drummond appeared a young man, with eagerness shining all over his face, detached himself from the others and approached him tendering a card.

JOHN SEYMOUR
Eastern News

"I'm a reporter, sir," he whispered excitedly. "Just started. Is there anything big on, sir? It will mean a lot to me if I can get in first."

Drummond regarded him thoughtfully: a pleasant-faced lad quivering with keenness.

"There is something very big on, Mr Seymour," he said with a smile. "But as the matter is now in the sergeant's hands I'm afraid you must ask him."

The boy's face fell.

"Can't you give me a hint, sir?" he pleaded.

"Didn't I see you standing by that perfectly good Norton over there?" said Drummond.

"That's mine, sir," cried Seymour.

"There is your hint," said Drummond. "My knowledge of motor bicycles is not profound, but I would hazard a guess that you might be able to keep pace with this antiquated box on wheels that we are going to go in. Now, sergeant," he added, as that worthy appeared. "Are you ready? Because I want to get on as soon as I can."

It took them about twenty minutes to reach the cottage, and only once during the whole drive did Drummond catch a glimpse of the Norton. A point which pleased him: evidently John Seymour was not unintelligent. And the possibilities of having a tame journalist in his bag had struck him immediately.

The cottage was just as he had left it, and he led the way up the path followed by the sergeant and a constable. Then, having flung open the door he stood stock still. There lay Jerry as before, but of the man who had been stabbed there was no trace.

The chair was empty: the man had gone. So had the gun and Doris Venables' gloves.

It was the sergeant who broke the silence.

"Not much sign of the corpse, sir," he remarked a little sarcastically.

"Very little," agreed Drummond, still looking about the room.

"And you left the body lashed up in that chair?"

"I did," said Drummond.

"I suppose you felt the dead man's pulse?" asked the sergeant mildly.

Drummond stared at him: so that was his reaction.

"I did not," he said. "It hardly seemed necessary when he had a dagger sticking into his heart. My dear sergeant, do you really imagine that I've invented this story?"

The sergeant lifted his eyebrows.

"No, sir – not entirely. What I do think is that the man was alive all the time and fooled you."

"In what way was that possible?" demanded Drummond.

"Well, sir," said the other kindly, "I can think of one way at once. Suppose he was just an ordinary sneak thief who came along to see what he could steal. You wouldn't believe, sir, the amount of money some of these cottage folk keep hidden in their stocking. While he's drugging the old lady, the bulldog goes for him: so he shoots it. Then as he's searching the house he sees you and your friend arrive, and realises he's caught. So he lashes himself up as well as he can, and sticks the dagger sideways through his clothes so that it looks as if he was stabbed."

"A damned ingenious fellow," remarked Drummond enthusiastically. "Though I should have thought it would have been simple to do a guy through the back door."

Drummond was thinking hard. Not having done so already, it was impossible to tell the sergeant the whole truth, which, of course, put the worthy officer's theory out of court.

"The only other theory is that he was murdered, as you say, and that the murderer has since returned and removed the body," continued the sergeant. "My objection to that is – why not have removed it in the first instance? Why leave it here at all?"

"Possibly," suggested Drummond mildly, "he had nothing to remove it in."

The sergeant continued to expound, but Drummond hardly listened. How did this new development affect the situation? He *knew* what had happened: he *knew* the man had been murdered. But was it worth while endeavouring to convince the sergeant? Or did it suit his book better to let that officer continue to think that he had made a mistake? And the more he thought about it, the more did he incline to the latter course. It would save bother and prevent any possibility of his being requested to remain at hand in case of further developments.

A shadow fell across the floor: John Seymour was standing by the open window.

"Here's something for your paper, young man," cried the sergeant cheerily. "Who killed the bulldog and why? Well, Captain Drummond, I can assure you I will not let the matter drop. And should we by any chance catch anyone answering to your description of the man we'll get in touch with you for identification purposes. Can I give you a lift anywhere?"

But an idea had been forming in Drummond's mind, and he turned to the reporter.

"Have you got a carrier on your machine?"

"I have, sir."

"Then I wonder if you would give me a lift later? I want to bury poor old Jerry."

"Of course; only too delighted," cried Seymour.

"And possibly," added Drummond, "I might be able to supply you with a paragraph for your paper. All about those holes in the window and trifles of that sort."

"Funny you should say that," said the constable, speaking for the first time. "Other people seem interested in them 'oles."

"What do you mean?" asked Drummond.

"When I was getting the car, sir," explained the man, "bloke came up to me in the garage who seemed to know all about you. Leastwise, he knew you'd been here last night, and that a stone had been thrown through your window. 'Funny thing to do,' says he. 'Must have had a message wrapped round it.' 'Maybe it did, and maybe it didn't,' I answers. 'Anyway, I reckons it ain't no business of yours.' "

"Did he say any more?" demanded the sergeant.

"He asked me point blank if there was a message," said the constable, "so I told him to go to hell."

"Excellent advice," remarked Drummond. "Well, sergeant, I'm sorry I haven't been able to supply you with a corpse. I'll try and do better next time. And if you get hold of the blighter I'll come along and give him a thick ear."

"Now, young feller," he said to Seymour when the two policemen had gone, "you and I have got to do a job of work."

"What's that you were saying about a corpse, sir?" cried the reporter, open-eyed.

Drummond laughed.

"Bad break on my part, wasn't it? If you advertise that you've got a corpse about the house it's always advisable to produce it when called on. But before we go any farther we'll bury this poor old chap. There are a couple of shovels outside."

It took them half an hour, during which time Seymour earned several medals for suppressing his curiosity. But when the ground was finally smoothed over he could contain himself no longer.

"There must be a story here, sir," he cried. "Couldn't you let me have it?"

"Have some beer," said Drummond. "You don't drink! Excellent. Nor do I when there is none. Now, Seymour, I've been thinking things over while we buried Jerry, and I've come to the conclusion that you may be of considerable use to me. Not only that: you may be of considerable use to yourself. In other words, if you follow my instructions implicitly I may be able to put you in the way of a thundering big scoop."

The youngster's eyes gleamed.

"Unless I'm much mistaken, Seymour, there are some very big doings afoot," continued Drummond; "doings which by an extraordinary freak of fate started last night when a stone came through the window out of the fog. A message was wrapped round the stone – a message which certain people in this neighbourhood are very anxious to get hold of, as you may have gathered from what the constable said. That message has been destroyed, but I have it memorised in my brain. To keep them quiet, however, this morning I decided to fool them. So by methods which I won't go into now I got another message through to them – a false message, which I hoped they would think was the real one. Well, whatever they may have thought of it at the time, subsequent events have left no doubt in my mind that they know the second message was a fake. And so I propose to plant them with a third. Which is where you come in, for you are going to do the planting."

The reporter leaned forward eagerly.

"Now you've got to get one thing into your head: you will be dealing with some very clever and dangerous men – men whom it is extremely difficult to bluff. So the thing must be done in the most natural way possible. And this is the way I suggest. Can you get a small paragraph into your paper tonight?"

"If it's worth it, sir – of course."

"You must see that the sub-editor does think it's worth it. Head it: 'Extraordinary Story of Fen Cottage. Message from the Night.' And then – darn it, I can't do journalese. What I want you to imply is that this message came, and that you know the contents, but that you're not allowed to divulge them as yet."

"I get you, sir," cried Seymour, scribbling rapidly in a notebook. "How does this sound?

" 'From our special correspondent. Belmoreton.'

"Your headings are good – then…"

" 'I have just heard a most mysterious story from Captain Drummond of London, who has been staying in a small cottage near here…' Why were you staying here, sir?"

"Duck shooting," said Drummond briefly.

" 'For the duck shooting. The night before last, during a period of dense fog, a large stone was flung through his window, with a piece of paper wrapped round it. On the paper was written a message. The fog was so thick that Captain Drummond was unable to find the man who did it. At first he thought it must be a practical joke, but yesterday afternoon, on returning to the cottage, he found his favourite bulldog shot dead on the floor. He at once got into touch with the police, who are investigating the matter. At present I am not at liberty to disclose the nature of the message.' How's that, sir?"

"Excellent," said Drummond. "Now we come to the next and more important point. And here I've got to rely entirely on you. Within an hour of that appearing – or I'll eat my hat – you will be got into touch with by ingratiating gentlemen who will treat you as their long-lost brother. And then, young feller, it's up to you. You've got to divulge the contents of that message, so that they really believe you're speaking the truth. Register outraged indignation to start with at the bare thought of passing it on; then weaken gradually and sting 'em for a pony at least. And, above all, don't let 'em think I told you: pretend you heard it from the police. Get me?"

"You bet I do," cried Seymour. "And what is the message?"

" 'Rosemary. BJCDOR,' " said Drummond. "That will do as well as anything."

"And what was the real one?"

"That, perchance, in due course you shall know. But not at present. It isn't that I don't trust you, Seymour, but in a case of this sort the fewer people there are in the secret the better."

"And where am I to get in touch with you again?"

"The Senior Sports Club, St James's Square, will always find me," said Drummond. "Drop me a line there if anything happens. And now get me to Norwich as quick as you can. I'll hire a car there to take me to Cambridge."

"Aren't you going back to London, sir?"

"Not till tomorrow. So if anything happens before lunch, get on to the telephone to me at the Royal. Or, better still, come over on your bike and see me personally."

He took a last look round the room; then, having closed the front door, he walked down to the gate. The road was apparently deserted, but for a long time he stood under cover of the bushes, peering up and down it, while Seymour stared at him in surprise.

"Never forget, young feller," said Drummond, "that there are games in this world where one mistake is one too many. And this particular game comes into the category. We go to the right, don't we, to get to Norwich? But before we finally decide we'll just try a little experiment. If we get the gate open, can you start the bike on the path here?"

"I can," said Seymour.

"I have a hunch," continued Drummond, "that in a moment or two we are going to have some fun. Hold the gate, and I'll get the bike in."

He was out in the road, and back with the bike in something under a couple of seconds, and Seymour gazed at him open-mouthed. For Drummond was smiling grimly, and in his eyes was a queer look of excitement.

"As I thought, Seymour. Was it my sudden appearance that frightened those birds in that small tree down the road there, or was it someone who moved on the ground underneath them?

Moved when he saw me. Now, look here, my lad, are you game to take a risk?"

"Of course I am. But what sort of risk?"

"The risk of being shot. Because, unless I am much mistaken, you will shortly have what is generally alluded to in all romantic literature as your baptism of fire."

"I'm on, sir. What am I to do?"

"Stout feller. Start your engine, and when I'm up behind you, go out through the gate and turn *left*. Then swerve. Keep on swerving from one side of the road to the other till we are round the bend. Then go all out. Ready? Let her rip!"

The bicycle shot into the road, with the two men up on it.

"Swerve!" shouted Drummond as something spat through the air close to their heads. "And again."

Phit! Phit! Two more bullets pinged past them, and then they were round the bend.

"Now all out," said Drummond quietly. "Well done, boy, well done. There aren't many fellows of your age who can say they've been under fire."

"But this is grand," cried the youngster as the bike touched sixty miles an hour. "What next?"

"See that barn in front of us? Turn in there. We'll wait and see."

The Norton slowed down, shot through an open gate and into an empty barn.

"Quick!" cried Drummond. "Out of sight, and stop the engine."

And the instant he had done so they both heard away in the distance the roar of a racing engine. It was rapidly coming nearer, and through a chink in the wall they both peered out. Rocking from side to side like a thing possessed, a long, low, black car hurtled past the barn. The driver was crouching over the wheel, and the man behind him seemed to be urging him on to even greater speed.

"Just as well we pulled in," said Drummond calmly. "They've got the legs of us. Now back the way we've come, and stamp on her again, Seymour."

And twenty minutes later Drummond found himself in Norwich for the second time that day.

"Cheery little bunch, aren't they?" he said with a grin. "It's lucky for us I had that hunch at the cottage. Otherwise I'm afraid there would have been a little advertisement in the paper: For Sale: 1933 Norton. Property of the late Mr John Seymour."

"How dared they do it, sir? It would have been murder on the high road."

Drummond laughed.

"You'll see quite a lot of that before you've finished this trip," he answered. "But don't forget: no mention of what's happened in the paper."

When suddenly Seymour gripped his arm.

"Look, sir, look!" he stuttered; "there's the car itself!"

Drummond glanced across the square: there was no mistaking that long black body. The two occupants were just getting out, and he noted that the one who had sat beside the driver was immensely tall, even as the man Peter and he had watched striding away from the cottage had been. And at that moment an impulse that could not be resisted overcame him. Straight across the square toward them he sauntered, and they met in the middle. And meeting, stopped dead in their tracks while a man may count thirty. Then Drummond spoke.

"You exceedingly damnable swine," he drawled. "Unless you'd proved it to me I wouldn't have believed it possible that anyone could be such an incredibly lousy shot. Do you want a stationary hayrick at five yards?"

Not a muscle moved in the tall man's face; for all the effect it produced the remark might never have been made. He just stared fixedly at Drummond with a thoughtful look in his eyes, whilst past them drifted the sleepy afternoon traffic. Then, still in absolute silence, he signed to his companion and the two of them continued on their way.

Drummond watched them till they were out of sight, then he lit a cigarette. And being perfectly fair with himself he had to admit that that round was the tall man's. Though absolutely without nerves himself, there was something far more ominous in that complete silence than in any threats he might have used. And since he never made the fatal error of underrating an opponent, it was in a somewhat contemplative mood that he rejoined Seymour.

"What did he say, sir?" cried the youngster eagerly.

"He didn't," said Drummond shortly. "I rather wish he had. And you can take it from me, young feller, that it's going to be a case of watching your step from now on. There's a phrase about sticking at nothing, which is generally more metaphorical than literal. In his case it isn't."

His eyes strayed across the square to the big black car, and he grinned faintly.

"Why not?" he murmured. "Why indeed not? I must now get a taxi – or its equivalent. Follow me in a few minutes towards Cambridge. But wait a bit and see if anything happens."

With fascinated eyes the young reporter followed Drummond as he leisurely crossed the square. Saw him approach the black car and glance round. Heard the sudden roar of the engine instantly throttled down. And then, to his unspeakable and unholy joy, watched it disappear round the corner.

"Golly! what a nerve!" he muttered ecstatically to himself. "What gorgeous brass! And here, as I live, is the ruddy shover."

The man crossed the square to where he had left the car, and then stared about him bewildered. Until what had happened dawned on him, and he retraced his steps at a run. The tall man had just appeared and the two met not twenty yards from where he was standing. Cautiously he edged closer, only to halt abruptly at the sight of the tall man's face. For it was set like a frozen mask, but through that mask there gleamed such concentrated rage that it was as if the devil himself stood there. Then the look vanished, but the youngster was still standing motionless five minutes after the two men had disappeared. It seemed to him that he had seen the naked essence of evil.

After a while he pulled himself together and started his engine. He knew the road to Cambridge by heart, and his brain was full of other things as he rode along. What an amazing adventure he had blundered into! Sheer luck, too, that he had happened to be in Belmoreton that afternoon. What a glorious scoop it was going to be! And he had just visualised himself choosing which offer from countless London editors he would graciously accept when he saw Drummond standing in the road ahead, and pulled up.

"Had they found out when you left?" asked Drummond.

"They had. And I've never seen such rage incarnate on a man's face."

"I don't expect he was pleased," said Drummond happily. "And he'll be even less so when he finds the car."

"Where is it, sir?"

"Just in there. On top of a nice little disused chalk pit. When we've finished it will be at the bottom. Ever seen such a car go over a cliff, Seymour? You haven't? Nor have I. I think it ought to be great fun."

"Won't there be an awful stink about it?"

"I think not," answered Drummond. "You see, as I view the matter, Mr Longshanks is hardly in a position to raise even the smallest aroma, let alone a stink. And so we are quite safe in making his shoot this afternoon as expensive as we can. I admit that it rather goes to my heart to smash up such a perfectly glorious bus, but in this weary world one can't have everything."

He switched on the engine as he spoke.

"I'll keep the clutch out with my hand," he continued, "and you get in and put her in bottom. Then pop out and we'll let her go."

The car was standing two yards from the top of the quarry, with a few small bushes between it and the edge. It shot forward, seemed to hang in space for one dizzy instant, and then with a dreadful rending noise it crashed downwards out of sight. Came a last coughing grunt from the engine, then silence.

"That will give some of your fraternity a chance to do a bit of Sherlock Holmes work," said Drummond as they walked back. "Though it may be some days before it is discovered; you can't see it from the road as you go past."

"Shall I take you to Cambridge now?" said Seymour.

"You shall not," remarked Drummond with a grin. "Your girl friends must be a deuced sight more adequately protected than I am if they can stand that carrier of yours. I've still got partial paralysis of the spine. Run me to Thetford and I'll get a car there."

And it was just on eight o'clock when Drummond, with the pleasurable feeling of something accomplished, something done, paid off his driver and once again entered the hospitable doors of the Royal to find Peter Darrell and Ronald Standish waiting for him.

"Splendid, old boy," he cried to the latter. "Delighted you could come."

"I brought him along," said Darrell. "I've already told him the main points."

"He has indeed," remarked Standish gravely. "You've bought it this time, Hugh, with a vengeance."

"Do you know anything about these blokes?" asked Drummond eagerly.

"Enough to assure you that your chances – and Peter's, too – of celebrating your next birthday were a hundred per cent better this time yesterday than they are at the present moment."

"Don't 'e talk lovely, Peter?" laughed Drummond. "As a matter of fact," he continued seriously, "I realised we were up against a pretty tough lot. You remember that good-looking, tall man we saw in the road walking away from the cottage?"

"The fellow who stabbed our bird?"

"That's the gentleman. He's let drive at me three times already with, I should imagine, the actual gun we got hold of. Listen, boys – for I'm telling you."

"Mad," grinned Standish when he had finished. "Mad as a ruddy hatter."

"Can you place him, Ronald?"

"Not at present. Six feet six, you say?"

"At least. And with a pretty powerful punch I guess if he knows how to put 'em up."

"And you pinched his car and dropped it over a precipice. Gorgeous. Maybe a trifle crude, but nevertheless definitely creditable."

"But look here, Ronald, if you don't know the bird, why so morose over Peter's and my next birthday cake?"

"Because I do know the Key Club," said Standish quietly. "Or, at any rate, of them."

"Splendid," said Drummond. "Let us gargle together, and then you have our ear."

CHAPTER 6

Ronald Standish glanced round the lounge, then he led the way into a small alcove.

"Not," as he explained, "that I think anyone here is likely to be interested in our conversation, but I want to keep you two fellows out of sight as much as possible. I don't matter – yet; but you are known.

"The Key Club started a few years after the War in Central Europe. The members used to wear a tiny key as a badge in the lapels of their coats, which was supposed to signify the unlocking of the door leading to a more satisfactory world. Things were in a shocking state, especially in Germany and Russia, and quite a number of similar societies sprang up, flourished for a time, and then they died painlessly of their own utter futility. For some reason or other, however, the Key Club survived. Branches began to appear in France, and finally in England, and it became, in fact, an international organisation. Members were pledged amongst other things to abolish war, and so long as it remained at that nobody cared. They talked the hell of a lot and there it ended.

"And then about four years ago there occurred a very startling development. At the time I was on a special job which entailed me being for the greater part of the day at the War Office. And one morning a peculiar-looking bird rolled up and asked to see someone to whom he could impart information. He hadn't any appointment; he didn't seem to know anyone by name, and so one of the messengers decided to send him to me. He got through on the phone and I told him to send the man up. All sorts of crazy blokes come along with useless schemes, and I was prepared for him to be one of them. And when I saw that little key in his buttonhole I was certain of it. To my amazement, however, he produced from his pocket the formula of a new high explosive which he told me had just been perfected by the French. Now, we happened to know that the French had been experimenting on those lines, and therefore the information, if true, was of value. But since, so far as I was concerned, it might have been the formula for a new baby food, I passed the word along for an expert to come and vet it. And his report was that, though he could not possibly say what value there was in it without practical experiment, it undoubtedly was an explosive of sorts.

" 'How did you get this?' I asked my visitor.

" 'That,' he answered, 'is nothing to do with you. There it is, and good day to you.'

"I stared at him open-mouthed.

" 'But look here,' I cried, 'don't you want any payment for it? We shall have to make a few inquiries first, of course.'

" 'Make any inquiries you like,' he said. 'The thing is yours.'

"And he stalked out of the office, leaving the chemical wallah and me gaping at one another. Birds with worthless stuff to sell I had met, but a man with valuable information to *give* was a bit of an eye-opener. And when we discovered that it undoubtedly was the genuine formula of this explosive our amazement increased. The man had vanished, and I'd been too thunderstruck at the time to have him followed. I'd got his card but there was no address on it, and at that the matter rested for a few weeks, when the next extraordinary development took place.

"Through devious channels we discovered that Germany, Italy, Japan, America – in fact every Power that counted – had been presented with the same formula, free, gratis and for nothing. Which, as you can imagine, caused a positive riot of joy amongst the French military authorities.

"However, that was their funeral; what was intriguing us was the reason for such an apparently pointless thing. That the secret must have been obtained by bribing some Frenchman was obvious, but why *give* it away? More than that, why give it to everybody? And at last we were forced to the conclusion that the motive underlying it was a sort of perverted idealism. These people realised it was impossible to stop research work: that first one country and then another would be bound to get hold of something which would place that country temporarily at an advantage. Their notion, therefore, was that if they could find out what that something was each time and pass it on to everybody else, the temporary advantage would be gone and we'd all start level again. Crazy – if you like – and yet there, staring us in the face, was the actual proof of the pudding. The composition of the new French high explosive was public property.

"Now, all this is, of course, stale news. But I think it's rather important that you should get hold of things from the beginning. And so we've got to the point where the members of this club ceased being a harmless hot-air factory and began to act. Still more or less harmless, it is true: since everybody was put wise, nobody gained. But a new agency had definitely arisen, though no action could be taken against it: it had done nothing wrong or criminal. So the powers that be held a watching brief and waited.

"For two years nothing more happened. Reports came in from time to time showing that the members were still holding meetings, but at that it remained. And then one day – I don't know if you remember the case in the papers – a man was found dead in his bunk in the Harwich–Hook of Holland boat. At the first glance it looked as if death was due to natural causes, but when the steward turned him over he saw to his horror that a dagger had been driven up to the hilt in his heart. It was a tiny weapon, but quite large enough to kill him."

"Are we getting a line here, I wonder?" said Drummond thoughtfully. "It was quite a small one this afternoon."

"Quite possibly," said Standish. "To resume, however. The strange thing about the man on board was that there was literally nothing by which to identify him. There were no letters in his pockets; his passport had disappeared. His clothes and underwear were not marked, and beyond the fact that his overcoat and hat had both been bought at Harrods there was no indication whatever as to who he was, or even as to his nationality. He looked English, but that was about all that could be said for it.

"Naturally there was the devil of a commotion when the boat reached Harwich. The murderer was on board, but it was manifestly impossible to detain over three hundred people. And so, after the police had taken every passenger's name and address, the boat train proceeded to London, and the stewards and everyone else on board were put through the hoop.

"The results were meagre. The cabin steward stated that the man spoke English, but was not prepared to say whether he was an Englishman or not. He also stated that he was carrying with him an attaché case. Of this he was positive; he had seen it lying on the bunk whilst the man had been out of the cabin just after leaving the Hook. To the best of his belief the man had turned in about half an hour after they sailed, but he couldn't swear to it. And more than that he couldn't say.

"The bar-room attendant was the next man to be questioned. He said that the man had ordered a whisky and soda and some ham sandwiches before the boat started, and that he had remained in the bar for about twenty minutes. He had not actually seen anyone speak to him, but that did not of necessity mean that no one had, as several men had been in the bar at the time and he was busy serving them. He, too, was not prepared to say if the man was English, though he rather thought it.

"And then a rather significant fact came to light. About a quarter of an hour after they had sailed, and so presumably after he'd finished his sandwiches, the man had gone to the lavatory to wash his hands. The boy in charge was certain of that fact because he had stood beside him holding a towel in readiness. And while he was standing there, and the man was leaning forward over the basin, the boy noticed that a small key was fixed to the back of the lapel of his coat. That key was not found on the dead man.

"At the time the local police attached no importance to it: they had never heard of the Key Club. And it wasn't until the information reached headquarters that its significance was realised. The boy was questioned over again and stuck to it, and since it wasn't the sort of thing anyone would be likely to invent it was accepted as a fact. The man had been a member of the Key Club.

"The point, however, that occupied us was whether there was any special significance in this; did it give a clue to the motive for the murder? Robbery was ruled out – the man's money was intact. If it was revenge, or if a woman was at the bottom of it, would the murderer have bothered to remove the key? But if there was a connection between the crime and the badge it was obvious that he would take it off. It was by the merest chance that the key had been seen at all; and but for the boy in the lavatory no one could have known anything about it. Had the dead man, therefore, been guilty of treachery or something of that sort, for which death was the penalty? The trouble was that from what we knew of the Club up to date, it was not an institution that patronised murder. It was almost as baffling as if it had been the Salvation Army involved.

"In due course the man was buried, still without any clue to his identity. And since the affair had considerable publicity in the

English Press, it seemed probable that the man was not an Englishman. A full description of him had been given, and it was almost incredible that he should have no kith or kin. And then one day about a week after came the next development. An extraordinary letter was received at Scotland Yard, which the authorities at first believed to be a hoax."

Standish took out his pocket-book.

"I made a copy of it at the time, and after I'd seen Peter this afternoon I looked it out. Here it is."

He passed a sheet of paper over to Drummond.

With reference to the recent murder in the Harwich boat, why was Mario Guiseppi stabbed at the corner of the Strada Marino in Genoa two days before it happened? What was in the lost attaché case? The Key Club still maintains its ideals, but there is treachery at the top.

"There was no signature," continued Standish, "and the postmark was Kensington. The handwriting was an educated one; the paper was the ordinary stuff you can buy anywhere in a penny packet. So the police, not thinking anything would come of it, got into touch with Genoa, and somewhat to their surprise found that a man named Mario Guiseppi had been stabbed at the corner of the Strada Marino two days before the murder in the boat. And further inquiries elicited the very important fact that Guiseppi was a skilled draughtsman in the employ of the Italian Navy who had been working on some extremely confidential drawings with regard to their latest submarine.

"Things were moving, though they were still pretty dark. Had the man who was murdered in the boat brought copies of these plans from Guiseppi, and the transaction been discovered? Had Guiseppi been killed as a punishment for being a traitor to Italy, and the man in the boat been murdered in order to get the tracings back? It seemed possible, and the list of passengers was scrutinised. There was no Italian in it, though that, of course, didn't prove anything.

"So the Yard advertised and broadcasted for the anonymous writer of the letter. They were discreet in what they said, though naturally it was necessary to be explicit enough for the man to know whom the advertisement was intended for. And that, I fear, is what did it. The morning after the broadcast a man was found with his neck broken, lying in some bushes in the small garden of a house in Kensington. It transpired that he occupied the fourth story of the house, which was let as rooms, and that the preceding night he had had visitors who had stayed late. So much the lodger underneath him could say, as the visitors were still talking when he had gone to bed.

The extraordinary thing was that no one seemed to have seen these visitors. The landlady had not, but she had been occupied in the basement. And, since no one could get in without a latch-key, it seemed clear that the dead man, whose name was Johnstone, had brought them in himself. Apparently he was a quiet sort of bloke, who went out very little, and his main hobby was reading. And at first the sergeant who was called thought it might have been an accident, until an examination of certain marks near the window convinced him that there had been a struggle. The lodger below had heard nothing, but he was a sound sleeper and his bedroom was at the back. At any rate, the sergeant phoned the Yard, and Inspector McIver went down. And the first thing he noticed was that a specimen of the dead man's handwriting on his desk corresponded with the writing in the letter.

"Now they thought they really had something to follow up, but once again they were disappointed. The only relatives they could run to earth were two elderly female cousins who lived down in the West Country and hadn't seen the dead man for ten years, and an uncle who lived up North and hadn't seen him for fifteen. Nor did he seem to possess any friends; at least nobody volunteered to come forward. There was nothing to help them in his correspondence, and the discovery of the familiar small key in a drawer only confirmed what they already knew from his letter.

"In fact – an *impasse*, and the Yard authorities were annoyed. They dislike unsolved murders, and here were two in the course of a few days. That there was a connecting link between them and the death of the Italian in Genoa was obvious: that that link was the selling of secret information with regard to the new submarine was likely. But beyond that stood a blank wall, from which there emerged during the next few weeks only one further bit of evidence. It transpired that Guiseppi had been seen during the week before his death in the company of two men both of whom had a key suspended to their watch-chains. This information came from the proprietor of the small restaurant where the draughtsman used to have his lunch, but he could give no description of them that would not have fitted a hundred middle-class Italians.

"And so for the time the matter rested. The official theory was that Guiseppi had sold information to the Key Club; had been discovered and murdered. That the emissary of the Key Club had in his turn been murdered in order to obtain that information. And that finally the man Johnstone had been done to death too, to prevent him passing on what he knew to the police. But as to whether the same criminal or bunch of criminals were responsible for all three, or what had happened to the tracings there was no means of telling. Certainly no offer was made of them to the British Government as had been the case before with the French high explosive.

"Six months elapsed before anything more was heard. And then a very remarkable fact came to our knowledge, which though it bore out in part the police theory, also put the activities of the Key Club in a somewhat different light. You may remember that the time before they had *given* the secret to *all* countries; this time they had sold it to one. Through devious channels we found that the French had bought for a large sum of money the actual submarine details on which Guiseppi had been working at the time of his death. Abstract idealism had been replaced by concrete realism."

"There was damned little idealism about my bloke this afternoon," said Drummond with a grin.

"Just so," continued Standish. "I'm getting to that now. When this last bit of information came to light we began making some pretty searching inquiries. It was all done on the quiet, naturally: there was nothing criminal to take hold of. And after a while, by piecing together little bits from here and little bits from there, a much more sinister aspect began to emerge; an aspect which bore out the letter written by Johnstone. He had called it treachery at the top; we called it by another name. For, in short, the Key Club had become a criminal organisation, which was all the more dangerous in view of the fact that ninety-nine per cent of the members were totally unaware of any change. They were being exploited by a small nucleus of international crooks – crooks who did not stop at murder.

"At first sight it seemed surprising; at second the only surprising thing about it was that we hadn't thought of it before. Here was a society capable of getting at times highly confidential information. And this society was insane enough to be inspired by ideals. Why, some of the big men must almost have fainted with horror at the thought of what they were missing! This milch cow already to hand, and nobody doing anything about it. The situation had to be remedied, and it was at the trifling cost of three men's lives.

"When exactly the criminal element got in we couldn't find out, and it was immaterial. Obviously some time after the episode of the French high explosive, and before the Guiseppi affair. How many were actually posing as members of the Key Club we didn't know – we don't know now. One man in the inner councils would be enough to pass on information to his pals outside. But what we could do was to throw more light on the Harwich boat murder, or at any rate the reasons for it.

"The man had been killed by some member of the nucleus who knew what he was carrying in the attaché case. At the time of his death he was undoubtedly on his way to the English Admiralty, from where the same procedure would have been followed as before with the explosive. Johnstone had been thrown from his window because by some means he had found out more than it was advisable for a mere member of the rank and file to know. And Guiseppi had been stabbed – this was only surmise on our part, but it fitted in – he had been stabbed to prevent any possibility of his again passing on the information to some other absurd idealist of the Key Club. In fact the cat had pulled a very plump chestnut out of the fire for the monkey to sell to France."

"How long ago was all this?" asked Drummond.

"About eighteen months. Since then, as far as I know, they have done nothing. Now it looks as if they were on the warpath again."

"Any idea what they can be after?"

"Not an earthly. I chucked the job I was on over a year ago. But I know all the boys who are still at it, and if – which is very unlikely – they are wise to anything, we may be able to help each other mutually."

"Why unlikely?" queried Darrell.

"If they're still hunting the same line of country, if as they did in the case of Guiseppi they've bribed one of our people to give away some secret, we shan't know anything about it till it's sold to a foreign Power."

"Guiseppi was killed," said Drummond thoughtfully. "Do you know if anyone who would have been in a position to pass on information of value has gone west? There can't be a frightful number of 'em."

"Not that I know of," answered Standish. "But that can easily be found out. In fact I'll do so now."

He rose and went to the telephone, to return a few minutes later.

"Definitely no one," he said. "The Yard people were a bit curious as to why I asked, but I rode 'em off. I want to be on rather firmer ground before bringing them in."

"Do you think the brick bunger is the Guiseppi of the piece?"

"It's possible. Though it makes it difficult to follow. They got him back: that you saw with your own eyes. So what more did they want?"

"The message he threw through the window."

"True, old boy. But why, *if* he's the Guiseppi this time, should he throw a message through the window? If he was the traitor, already badly wounded, and trying to get away with his life, why bung a cryptic and incomprehensible message into a cottage? Surely on seeing the light his first instinct would have been to come to the occupants for sanctuary."

"But that's what defeats me whoever the bird was," cried Drummond. "In any event why didn't he come inside?"

Standish lit a cigarette thoughtfully.

"The point has been puzzling me ever since I first heard it from Peter," he said. "And I can think of only one solution. We must assume that the man was sane: the message, though we can't understand it at present, was not gibberish. This man, then, by some means which we don't know escaped from Emil and Co., and was wounded in doing so. He knew they were utterly unscrupulous and would stick at nothing. And so he reasoned as follows: 'If I go into that cottage and am found there they will think nothing of killing the occupants of the cottage in order to prevent the smallest chance of those occupants passing on the information which they will assume I have told them. And there goes my last hope of getting that information through. I will therefore throw a message in and go on myself in the hope that it will be found by the occupant and not by Emil and his friends.' Which incidentally is just what happened."

Drummond nodded.

"That's so. Through a sheer fluke."

Standish shrugged his shoulders.

"One has always got to take a chance," he remarked. "It came off, and that's all that matters. And it's not he who worries me most: it's the girl. I can't place her. She tries to dope your tea; she makes every endeavour she can to get hold of the message. OK so far. Nothing inconsistent up to date. On the way back she tells you about the Key Club."

"Reviling the institution good and hearty," put in Drummond.

"That may or may not mean anything: the point is that she brought up the subject. Why? She could have put up her little fairy tale about Harold without mentioning the Key Club at all. And if she is on their side…"

He relapsed into silence and the other two stared at him.

"Surely she must be," cried Drummond.

"Something to it, Hugh," said Darrell. "You know what that bird told us this afternoon: she was drugged as well as Mrs Eskdale."

"It's this way," said Standish. "Her actions to start with don't tally with her later ones. To begin with she seems to be on the side of this man Emil; subsequently she seems against him."

"Always provided it was Emil who did the drugging," put in Drummond.

And at that moment the hall porter put his head round the corner.

"One of you gentlemen named Captain Drummond?" he asked.

"What do you want, porter?" said Drummond.

"Telephone call from London, sir."

"How the devil does anyone know I'm here?" cried Drummond in surprise.

"May be Denny, Hugh," said Darrell. "I told him to put a call through in case the old lady came round."

Drummond nodded and went off to the box.

"It's a puzzler, Peter," remarked Standish. "Why did that girl go back to the cottage this afternoon?"

"All Hugh and I could arrive at was that she wanted to verify the wire," said Darrell.

"But why? What should have made her suspicious? She must have believed it to be genuine when she got it, or she wouldn't have acted as she did. What made her change her mind? And stranger still. If she was allowed to receive it in the first instance without anyone bothering, why should there be this feverish excitement over her getting it repeated?"

"Ask me another. The whole thing has got me guessing. Where does this tall bloke come in? It must have been him who stabbed that wretched devil. Is he one of this criminal bunch at the top that you were talking about? Because unless that man he killed was the world's best actor, I'll swear he'd never even heard of the Key Club."

"It oughtn't to be difficult to get a line on him," said Standish. "What was it, Hugh?"

"Denny right enough," said Drummond, rejoining them. "Nannie has recovered. It was the telegram the girl went back about. I've just been talking to Nannie herself."

"How is the old dear?" asked Darrell.

"She's all right. Still got the twitters a bit. It seems the girl arrived about five minutes before the men did. Nannie was upstairs changing her dress, and the girl waited in the parlour."

"Where presumably she read the wire as you sent it to Mrs Eskdale," said Standish.

"No," answered Drummond. "I specially asked her that. The old lady had torn it up. All the girl wanted to see was the original message that had come through the window. Which put Nannie, somewhat naturally, in a quandary as she hadn't any message. And then, before the old lady realised what was happening, the man appeared on the scene, and she remembers nothing more."

Standish started to pace up and down with his hands thrust deep in his pockets.

"This beats me," he said. "Why should the girl have wanted to see the original message? If, which is extremely unlikely, she had discovered it was Coldspur's tip she would have realised that you had been fooling her, Hugh, from the word 'go.' What possible object could there be in that case of her going back to the cottage? If, on the other hand, she still believed the wire to be genuine, why bother to confirm it? You think, Peter, to make sure there was no mistake in it. Perhaps you're right. But then – why drug her? It doesn't make sense to me. She was allowed to handle and read the wire in the morning, and she is doped when she tries to see the original in the afternoon. By Jove! chaps, there are some mighty rum points about this show. Is this man Meredith really the girl's uncle? Where does he stand with regard to Emil? Where do both of 'em stand with regard to Hugh's tall friend? Are they two separate gangs, and where does the Key Club come in? Is the girl with one and against the other, or is she against them both? If so, what is her game?"

"There's another thing, too, that I can't understand," said Drummond. "No one is fonder of a thick-ear party than I am, but one doesn't go about slaughtering people unless there's a good reason. Why then is that tall swine so matey? Particularly with me. If they think…"

He broke off abruptly.

"Hullo! young feller, what do you want? Ronald – this is my friend Mr Seymour of journalistic fame."

The youngster gave a sheepish grin.

"Well, sir," he said, "I remembered what you'd said about passing on that information. So after I'd handed in the stuff to the sub-editor I went into a pub in Belmoreton. And I heard Tom the barman talking about Mrs Eskdale, and saying what a funny thing it was she'd taken to racing. So I pricked up my ears and asked a few questions. And it turned out that the man in the post office, who always has a bit on every day, had been in there at lunch and had remarked on Mrs Eskdale having sent a wire containing a racing tip. Joe wouldn't have thought any more about it but for the fact that a stranger in the corner seemed very interested, and asked a lot of questions. The man from the post office got suspicious and shut up, but the stranger went straight away into the telephone box, and put through a long-distance call. At least Joe thought it must have been long-distance owing to the time it took."

"What time was this, Seymour?" said Drummond.

"I suppose about midday, sir, or half-past twelve."

"How do you fit that in, Ronald?"

"What time did the wire arrive at Hartley Court?" asked Standish.

"Just about midday too," said Drummond.

"So that you had left Hartley Court before there was any possibility of this telephone message saying the wire was a fake reaching the other side."

He turned to Seymour.

"Did your friend Tom, the potman, happen to mention any specific question the stranger had put?"

"Apparently he was very anxious to find out whom the wire had been sent to."

"And did the post office man tell him?"

"I couldn't tell you, sir. But I know that he did say it was a *Morning Leader* tip, and that Coldspur was dead out of form just now."

Standish rubbed his hands together.

"Things became a trifle clearer, Hugh," he said. "They saw at once that the only person who could possibly have inspired the worthy Mrs Eskdale to send a bogus wire was you yourself. And therefore they realised you had been fooling 'em. Hence the target practice this afternoon. What, however, is not so clear – in fact this information has increased the fog – is their treatment of the girl. It's difficult enough to see why they should have drugged her when they thought it was all genuine. But why they should do so if they knew it was a fake is beyond me. If what Seymour tells us is correct – and from the activity over there this afternoon I'm sure it is – they must have known there was no message at all at the cottage."

"So must the girl," objected Darrell.

"I wonder," said Standish slowly. "I wonder. Supposing she didn't know anything about it: supposing she believed the wire to be genuine. She goes back to the cottage to make sure, and for some reason or other that action arouses their suspicions. Alternatively, suppose they don't want her to find out the message is a dud… I know it's difficult to follow, but when you come across an apparently inexplicable fact, you must be prepared to accept an equally inexplicable solution. If it fits… In short, have we a parallel with the Guiseppi case? Is this girl the counterpart of Johnstone? If so…"

He paused and his face was grave.

"You mean she may be in danger," said Drummond.

"Exactly. And I don't like it. Not one little bit. Men who indulge in gun practice on an open road are not likely to entertain many scruples over a mere girl. Look here, Seymour," he continued, "you'd better get back, and do exactly what Captain Drummond told you. You did excellently in bringing us this information; it's most valuable."

The youngster's face flushed with pleasure and Drummond smiled at him.

"You shall have your scoop, young feller," he said. "Keep your ears open and your mouth shut. A good boy," he went on, as the roar of a motor bicycle announced his departure. "He may prove useful. What's the next move, sergeant-major? So far as I can see, everything we've done up to date has been a waste of time."

"Let's adjourn to the abode of drink," answered Standish, "where in the intervals of lowering a couple we might hear some local gossip."

The three men crossed the lounge and entered the bar, which was deserted.

"Good evening, bright eyes," said Drummond. "Will you with your own fair hands decant some sherry?"

"Dry or sweet?" asked the barmaid.

"Dry, darling. Tell me, have you ever in the course of your peregrinations round the smiling countryside gone past a house called Hartley Court?"

"Hartley Court," cried the girl, "belongs to Doctor Belfage."

"I had an idea that a man called Meredith was living there at present," said Drummond.

"Very likely. The doctor often lets it to the racing set. Two and six, please! At least, I suppose he didn't ought to be called a doctor no more."

"Dear, dear," cried Drummond. "Has he blotted his copy-book?"

"Not half he hasn't. Got struck off the register about a year ago. Fair scandal there was, I can tell you."

"How very reprehensible," remarked Drummond.

"Nasty little man he was, too," continued the girl. "I wouldn't have had him near me: him and his beastly animals. Had a sort of zoo, he did. Taken 'em with him to his other house."

"And where might that be?" asked Drummond idly.

"Good gracious me," muttered the girl. "Talk of the devil..."

A short, stout man had entered the bar. His face was round and puffy; his appearance oily and smug.

"Good evening, my dear," he said, washing his hands with invisible soap. "I think – yes, I think – a little drop of auntie's ruin with some Angostura bitters in it. Been a lovely day, gentlemen."

"Very," answered Drummond curtly, and glanced at Standish, whose face was expressionless.

In the lapel of Doctor Belfage's coat was a small bronze key.

CHAPTER 7

"Funny, isn't it," remarked the barmaid, "that you should have been saying... Now then, clumsy, look where you're putting your great fat hands."

"A thousand apologies, my dear," cried Standish, picking up the glass he had knocked over. "Let's have the other half. It is strange, sir," he continued affably, "that just before you came in we were remarking on the fact that outside the Navy one so rarely sees the good homely pink gin being drunk. Cocktails, yes: gin and French: sherry."

He rambled on, and the barmaid after one quick look of surprise took her cue.

"And, by the way, sir," Standish was saying, "if it's not an impertinent question on my part, may I ask if that badge you are wearing in your coat has any special significance?"

"It certainly has, sir," answered the other. "It is the badge of a society to which I belong, and a meeting of which I am actually attending tonight."

"Indeed," said Standish politely. "Some local organisation, I suppose?"

"Far from it, I assure you. I don't think I am exaggerating when I say that its ramifications extend all over the world. The Key Club, sir, so called because it symbolises the unlocking of the door into an improved world. Many of the undergraduates here belong to it; there is no entrance fee, and membership is open to all regardless of social position."

"Most interesting," remarked Standish. "Some time I must make further inquiries about it."

"Would you care to come to the meeting this evening – you and your friends?" asked the doctor. "There will be no difficulty about it at all. Strictly speaking each member is allowed only one guest, but I can easily arrange for other people to sponsor two of you."

"That is very good of you," said Standish. "Where is the meeting being held?"

"At a house of mine called Hartley Court. It is at present let, but the tenant is a keen member of the Key Club himself."

He glanced at his watch.

"We shall just be in nice time if we start now," he continued. "The house is about three miles out of Cambridge."

He looked at them inquiringly, and Drummond shook his head.

"I'm afraid I shan't be able to avail myself of your kind offer," he remarked. "I've got to be pushing off for London shortly. But why don't you two fellows go? It ought to be rather interesting."

"Peter can't very well," said Standish. "You've got that bloke coming in at ten, old boy."

"So I have," cried Darrell. "Forgotten all about him till you mentioned it."

"But I'd like to come very much," said Standish, lighting a cigarette. "I suppose it won't be a very late show?"

"About eleven o'clock. And then we have an informal talk, with light refreshments. Well, good night, gentlemen." He bowed to Drummond and Darrell. "I'm sorry you can't come."

The door closed behind him and Standish, and immediately the barmaid became agog with excitement.

"What's the game?" she cried. "What are you boys up to? Be sports and tell. I played up over that pink gin."

"You did indeed, my dear," said Drummond. "And I'd tell you like a shot what we were up to if I knew myself. I mean it, really; I promise you."

"Tell that to the marines," she scoffed. "Why didn't you want that little horror to know you'd been asking me about Hartley Court? Him and his improved world! I nearly gave the show away then by laughing. Look here," she said shrewdly, "is there something crooked on? Are you guys detectives?"

"We are not," laughed Drummond. "But…"

He paused as a page-boy came into the bar with a letter.

"Given me by a gent, sir, what's just left."

Drummond opened it, and found a hastily scrawled note from Standish.

Safer neither of you come: even Peter might be recognised. Don't know if clumsy trap or pure coincidence. Be on hand outside. Keep that barmaid's mouth shut. Am taking Peter's car. RS.

He read it and handed it to Darrell.

"No, my dear," he said, "we are not detectives. At the same time, you can take it from me that there is a bit more in this than meets the eye. And I want you, please, to promise me something. It's really very important. I want you to promise that you won't say a word about it to a soul. There's a big bet on, and if you keep quiet there's a spot of money in it for me, and a fiver in it for you."

"A fiver! Big boy, for a fiver an oyster would deafen you compared to me. For all that, I wish you'd tell."

"Honest, kid, there's nothing to tell as yet. Thumbs crossed. Later on there may be lots, and you're for the front row of the stalls… A bit rum, Peter," he went on thoughtfully, "having a debagged doctor in a moral uplift society."

"Probably joined before he got the bird," said Darrell. "May have been useful to him in his practice."

"I've seen other guys wearing that little key," announced the barmaid. "Undergraduates mostly. I thought it was some University club. Pretty pimply-looking lot they were."

"Do you know where that little man lives now?" asked Drummond.

"I don't," said the girl. "He went right away from this part of the country when the trouble took place."

"And one rather wonders, Peter, what brings him back," remarked Drummond. "I can't think that a meeting of his darned club, finishing up with light refreshments at eleven, would prove a sufficient inducement... Give me some sandwiches, my pet," he continued, as some men came into the bar. "We will get down to 'em in that corner."

"What's the plan of campaign, Hugh?" said Darrell as they sat down.

"We'll have to be guided by events," answered Drummond. "Personally, I don't think Ronald is likely to find anything out that's going to help us. This meeting can't have been arranged today, so presumably it's just in the ordinary course of affairs: part of the general smoke screen which covers the doings behind. In which case those attending it will be perfectly harmless."

He glanced at his watch.

"No good our starting for at least another hour," he remarked. "I'm going to have a spot of shut-eye. Wake me if I snore."

It was one of Drummond's most remarkable traits – his ability to snatch forty winks almost at will, and in a couple of minutes he was sound asleep. Darrell, on the other hand, had never felt so wide awake in his life. Vaguely he heard odd remarks from the bunch gathered round the bar, but his brain was busy trying to get some semblance of order into the existing chaos. What

Standish had told them certainly threw some light on the matter, but in all conscience light was needed.

That their trip to Kessingland had been a complete waste of time was obvious, but what would have happened if they had not gone back via the cottage? Doing so had only been a last-minute decision and could not have been anticipated by the other side. And yet they had left a man to watch the cottage. Taking no chances evidently… Even so, to murder him for a trifling indiscretion seemed a bit drastic.

And the attempt on Drummond's life. True, when it was made they knew he had fooled them: true, they suspected even if they did not *know* that he had been in possession of the genuine message the whole time. But murder seemed out of all proportion when the contents of the message were considered. On the other hand, admittedly they could not know what those contents were.

Mary Jane. Urgent. G G Pont. A5.

What the devil did it mean? Could it be that Mary Jane was the girl herself – Doris Venables? A nickname or something of that sort. That the message was actually intended for her? In that case she must have known there was something badly wrong, when she got Drummond's faked wire. A point; a definite point… *Did* she know? Was she playing some very deep game – deeper by far than the unfortunate Johnstone in the Guiseppi affair? And the more he thought of it, the more did he become convinced that if Miss Doris Venables could be found and made to talk, many things would become clearer.

The bar was getting more empty. Drummond was still asleep, and Darrell himself was beginning to feel drowsy, when, happening to glance at the door, he saw something that instantly made him wide awake. Not that he gave any outward sign of it – Drummond had trained him far too well for that – but every sense was on the alert. Save for a narrow horizontal strip at the top the door consisted of frosted glass. And in the centre of that strip was the face of a man. He was looking straight at their corner, and after a while he turned and spoke to someone who was out of sight. Then he disappeared, and Darrell touched Drummond on the arm.

"Sorry to disturb your slumbers, old boy," he remarked, "but a guy has been peering through the top of the door and giving us the once over. He's gone now, but in case he comes back you'd better have a look at his dial."

"Sure it was us he was interested in?" asked Drummond.

"Absolutely. He was looking straight at us."

They waited a few minutes, but there was no further sign of him. And when at length the bar closed and they went into the lounge they could see no one about the place who looked even remotely interested in their doings.

"You can see that corner perfectly," said Darrell, and then he gave a sudden exclamation. "Come here, Hugh. I'm six foot, and I can only just see over the frosted glass. I saw that bloke's whole face; I saw his chin."

"Our tall friend?" queried Drummond thoughtfully and beckoned to the hall porter. "Has a very tall gentleman been in here recently?" he asked.

"Yes, sir, there has. He went about five minutes ago."

"Do you know his name?" asked Drummond.

"No, sir. I ain't never seen him before."

The page-boy had drawn near and now spoke.

"Asked for you, sir, he did. Captain Drummond. I said as 'ow you were in the bar, and I thought the gentleman had joined you."

Drummond nodded and turned away.

"Seems hard to shake 'em off, Peter," he remarked. "Do we perceive in this the hand of the unfrocked doctor?"

"He didn't know your name," said Darrell.

"No. But with a face like mine I'm not hard to describe. I'm open to a small bet, Peter, that there are other activities on at Hartley Court tonight, besides that fatuous meeting. And it's on account of these that Doctor Belfage has appeared on the scene. It's unfortunate he should have chosen to lower his pink gin at this pub, but it can't be helped. Of course the instant he arrived at the house he was told about us, and realised he'd been talking to the very men who had caused all the commotion. Longshanks was there and came down to make sure."

"I hope old Ronald's all right," said Darrell.

Drummond laughed.

"I don't think we need worry our heads about Ronald," he answered. "His only danger is the possibility that the light refreshments at eleven may prove to be non-alcoholic. No, Peter, it's you and I who have got to watch it just at the moment. And what I'm wondering about is their next move. Officially I'm going to London, and you're seeing a man about a dog here. But do they believe it? If so, are they going to take any steps to alter our plans?... Good Lord! Cabbageface, what on, earth are you doing here?"

A tall, somewhat languid man had just entered the hotel, followed by a positive lorry-load of suitcases.

"Hullo, Hugh!" he drawled. "The surprise is mutual. Can one get a drink?"

"If you're staying in the hotel, sir," said the hall porter.

"Clarence," remarked the newcomer, "I fear you will not rise high in your profession. Do you imagine I have taken those bags out of the car merely to put them back again?"

"Peter," said Drummond, "meet Cabbageface, otherwise known as Major Humphrey Gregson. This is Darrell."

The two men shook hands.

"Often seen you playing at Lord's," said Gregson, "in the intervals of my onerous duties at the War House."

"Are you travelling in underclothes or what, old boy?" demanded Drummond, eyeing the pile of suitcases.

"Not exactly," said the other with a grin. "But honestly, Hugh, what are you fellows doing here?"

"Investigating a spot of bother, Cabbageface," answered Drummond guilelessly.

Gregson looked at him steadily over the rim of his glass.

"Ever the same old Hugh," he remarked quietly. "Can it be possible, I wonder, that this meeting is not quite so fortuitous as it appeared at first sight?"

"Ronald Standish is here," said Drummond, with apparent irrelevance.

"The devil he is! When did he come?"

"This afternoon."

"Is he in the hotel now?"

"No, Cabbageface, he is not," said Drummond deliberately. "He is at the present moment attending a meeting of a society known as the Key Club."

Gregson stared at him blankly.

"Standish at a meeting of the Key Club!" he remarked in amazement. "What in the name of all that's marvellous is he doing that for?"

"He was asked by a nice kind gentleman," said Drummond. "So incidentally were we, but Peter and I wouldn't play. By the way, have you ever heard of a doctor called Belfage?"

"No. Why?"

"Or a man called Meredith?"

Gregson shook his head.

"Or a German named Emil?"

"Emil! Medium height: dark: dangerous-looking customer."

"The description serves."

"That might be Emil Veight," said Gregson half to himself. "Hugh," he continued, "this is the most amazing affair. Quite obviously we are mixed up in the same show. How on earth did you get pushed into it?"

For a few moments Drummond did not reply. Then: "What's your job at the War House, Humphrey?"

"Intelligence – though you might not think so."

"Hush-hush business you mean."

Gregson nodded.

"You can call it that if you like."

"If you were sending a report, or getting a message through, would you always sign yourself by your own name?"

"I don't know that I'm quite prepared to answer that question, Hugh," said Gregson. "A bit near the confidential, you know. And we must pretend to be hush-hush."

"You wouldn't perhaps sign yourself A2 or A3 or something like that?" pursued Drummond imperturbably.

Gregson stared at him.

"Without committing myself," he said quietly, "let us assume for the moment that I should."

"Good," remarked Drummond. "You asked me how I got pushed into this performance. The reason was that someone who signed himself A5 – "

"Ginger Lovelace!" cried Gregson involuntarily.

"Bunged a message through the window of a cottage I was staying in last night," continued Drummond, ignoring the interruption.

"But why did he do that?" cried Gregson, utterly bewildered.

"Because he was wounded unto death," said Drummond gravely, "and Emil and his damned bunch were after him."

"My God!" stammered Gregson. "Ginger wounded! Where is he now?"

"I can't tell you," said Drummond, "for I don't know. Before I could get hold of him he'd vanished into the fog. And then Emil and Co. appeared on the scene."

"What was the message, Hugh?"

Drummond looked round; there was no one near.

" 'Mary Jane. Urgent. G G Pont. A5,' " he said in a low voice. "Can you make head or tail of it?"

" 'Mary Jane,' " repeated Gregson. " 'G G Pont.' What the devil was the old lad talking about?"

"It means nothing in your young life then?" said Drummond.

"Absolutely nix," answered Gregson. "Ginger wounded! Have you been to the police?"

"Yes and no, Humphrey. It's much too long a story to go into now, but rightly or wrongly I decided not to last night. The cottage is not on the telephone: you couldn't see your hand in front of your face: and I had no idea who the bloke was. In fact at the time the whole thing completely defeated me. But today's doings have produced one certainty. The gentlemen on the other side are prepared to go literally to any lengths to get hold of the message I've just told you. Now even if that message is beyond you, can't you throw some light on things? Why was Lovelace down here? What's brought you down here?"

Gregson lit a cigarette.

"One at a time. Lovelace has officially been on leave for a matter of two months. And with us, as you may know, that does not mean leave. I'm not clear what he's been on: the Chief is a firm believer in not letting the right hand know what the left is doing. All I can tell you is that he has been in Poland, and until now I thought he was there still. So much for Ginger. Now for my show. I was to come here prepared for any eventuality; hence" – he grinned gently and waved a hand at the suitcases – "a few props in the change-of-appearance line. I was to meet a woman round about ten o'clock, and after I'd heard what she had to say, I was to act entirely on my own initiative. And it being about ten now, the lady may shortly materialise."

"And she may not," said Drummond thoughtfully. "It's beginning to fit a little more, Peter. Have you any idea what sort of a woman she is, Cabbageface?"

"Not the slightest, old boy. No more, I gather, had the Chief. In fact he was even less communicative than usual. But he did mention the Key Club, which proves that we are both chasing the same hare."

"Do you employ any women on your job?" asked Drummond.

"Certainly. But none, so far as I'm aware of, actually in England."

"Your boss would know if this woman you're meeting was one of them?"

"Yes. But that doesn't mean he'd of necessity tell me."

He looked at Drummond keenly.

"From the general tenor of your remarks, Hugh," he said, "you would seem to have encountered a lady during the day's toil. Have you?"

"Yes," answered Drummond. "I'll make it as concise as I can, Cabbageface, because Peter and I have a date."

Gregson listened without comment, and it might have been noticed that the languid expression had completely disappeared.

"Doris Venables," he said, when Drummond had finished. "She is a new one on me, though that means nothing. And you think it may be she who got in touch with the Chief?"

"It looks possible. She is obviously mixed up in this show, and she's the only woman we've butted into up to date."

"In that case," remarked Gregson thoughtfully, "I doubt if I shall have the pleasure of making the lady's acquaintance tonight. They must have found her out."

"Yes," said Drummond gravely. "I'm afraid they have. And if that is so, from what I've seen of 'em I doubt if you'll ever make her acquaintance. Could I possibly get on to the Chief tonight?"

"Possibly: at his private house. I can try."

"I wish you would. It won't take you long to get through at this hour. I'd like to know before we start."

"Where are you going?"

"To the house where the meeting of the Key Club is in progress. Are you coming?"

"I'd like to, but I'll tell you for certain when I've phoned the Chief."

"I like it less and less, Peter," said Drummond as Gregson entered the telephone box. "I know she tried the dirty on me this morning, but the more I think of it the more do I believe that Ronald's right. I believe that girl is fighting a lone hand; I believe that even if she's not on our side she's against the others. And they've got her – the swine... Well, Cabbageface?"

"Got straight through to him," said Gregson, as he joined them. "He does not know anyone called Doris Venables. The woman who rang him up gave no name. But she mentioned the Key Club and Emil Veight: so I was right there. I'm to use my own discretion as to what I do."

"He didn't happen to say what time she rang him up, I suppose?"

"After lunch."

"So if it was little Doris, she must have done it on her way to the cottage. She went there to confirm the wire by seeing the original: she then proposed to pass it on to you tonight and fixed an hour when she knew this meeting was taking place, and she could slip away undetected. Is this bird Emil Veight well known?"

"Only to the select few, old boy. High up in the German Secret Service during the War, and since then a cosmopolitan spy."

"Cosmopolitan!" Drummond raised his eyebrows.

"International, if you prefer it," said Gregson. "If the cash is there he is prepared to work for anybody. A thoroughly dangerous customer, but if any blood-letting has to be done he generally leaves it to other people."

"One other point, Cabbageface," remarked Drummond. "I wonder why she rang you up, and not Scotland Yard. As a rule you blush unseen so far as the outside is concerned."

"Only the lady herself can tell us that," answered Gregson. "And since it is now half-past ten I'm thinking there is not much use waiting for her to do so here. How far is this house you've been talking about?"

"About three miles. Are you coming?"

"You bet your life I am. I'll address the gathering if you like."

"Look here, Humphrey, we'd love to have you, but I don't want you to come under false pretences. Holding His Majesty's commission and all that sort of stuff. It's not the meeting I want to see: it's the other activities – if any. We're going to break into that house, and if we're caught there's going to be trouble."

"My dear Hugh," said Gregson with a faint grin, "if one half of what you have told me is correct, I can't quite see the proud proprietors ringing up the police whatever we do. So let's get on with it."

"Good for you," answered Drummond. "But I thought I'd better warn you."

He crossed the lounge to a map that was hanging on the wall.

"The house is there," he said, "so we'll start in the opposite direction and make a detour. The betting is a fiver to an orange pip that this hotel is being watched, and it may help to put 'em off. Let's go in your car, Humphrey, as it is outside."

The cinemas were emptying as they left the hotel, so that the street was fairly crowded. But they were clear of the town in a few minutes, and Gregson let the car out.

"I'd like to see the type of bird who attends these meetings," said Drummond. "I should think Ronald must be having a gorgeous time. Go left here, Humphrey."

They got into a network of smaller roads as they circled round Cambridge, and it was Darrell who first noticed that they were being followed.

"No one who isn't loopy would come this way for fun," he remarked. "There's been a car about two hundred yards behind us ever since we left."

Drummond looked up from the map he was studying and turned round.

"I saw one of those little wasp effects standing near the entrance to the hotel garage," he said. "If it's the same you'll never get away from it, Cabbageface. I vote we stop and see. We're in plenty of time for the party. Pull up round this corner, old boy, and switch off your lights. Stay in the middle of the road."

Gregson did so, and Drummond was out in a flash and into the ditch followed by the other two. The car behind them was just approaching the bend, and he heard a sudden screech of brakes as the driver realised that the headlights he had been following were no longer there. Then it pulled up with a jerk some ten yards from the deserted car.

"Good evening," said Drummond placidly. "I trust we are in fine fettle."

The two occupants swung round, as a torch shone on them from behind. They could see nobody, only a vague outline leaning over the back of the car. And then suddenly the outline was joined by two more.

"What the devil is the meaning of this?" spluttered the driver.

"Motor bandits, my dear boy," remarked Drummond. "And now tell me all that is in your heart. Why, for instance, have you been following me all over England?"

"You're mad, sir," cried the driver. "Why should I want to follow you?"

"You're very pimply, Narcissus," said Drummond thoughtfully. "And so is your friend. I once cured a man of pimples, but the treatment was too drastic and he died. So if you want to retain your pimples, and I can quite realise you'd be unrecognisable without them, you will answer my question. Why have you been following me?"

"Go to hell," said the youth furiously. "I've taken the number of your car. My friend and I are undergraduates, and you'll hear from the police about this. Do you imagine you've bought the blasted road? Why can't we drive where we like?"

"Not on your bath night, Narcissus. I see you are members of the Key Club."

"What's that to do with you?"

"Strange, isn't it, Peter?" remarked Drummond. "They are certainly a peculiar institution. Unfrocked doctors, and half blues for cat's cradle. Well, my dear boys, you are shortly going to be the victims of an abominable outrage. England will ring with it: questions will be asked in Parliament. But I don't like your lights behind me at all. And as your car is undoubtedly faster than ours there's nothing else for it. Do you mind my extracting you from your seats?"

Two large hands seized the driver and his companion by the coat collar, and drew them out as a cork is drawn from a bottle.

"Have you any rope in your car, Cabbageface?"

"I have," said Gregson in a shaking voice.

"Good. Then we'll just tie these two back to back in the middle of the road, and if anyone comes along they can pretend to be perfect strangers. And if no one comes along, Narcissus, you can hold converse with one another through the small hours on the infinite blessings of peace and disarmament. Also the stupidity of following another car quite so closely in a flat country. No, no: there's no good in struggling. Your state of fitness might just enable you to last for a couple of rounds of spillikins, but you mustn't tax yourselves more until you've had your Ovaltine. Finished, Peter?"

The two youths were almost crying with rage and fury. They were standing back to back each with his right wrist lashed to the other's left, whilst round their waists ran one strand of rope.

"Unspeakable cads," spluttered Narcissus.

"Not at all," said Drummond genially. "Personally, I think we've let you off very lightly. You mustn't go following people round the country. And if I may give you a word of advice it is this. Don't fall down. If you do, not only will the one underneath leave a lot of his face in the road, but you'll find it practically impossible to get up again. Come on, chaps: we mustn't delay any more. Good night, my little ones."

"You'll be getting me cashiered, Hugh," said Gregson, still weak with laughter, as they drove away. "Of all the outrageous assaults I have ever seen perpetrated, that wins in a canter, and the blighters have got my number."

"They won't do anything, old boy," answered Drummond. "They would never hear the last of it if they did. Anyway I'm the culprit. But have you ever seen such a pair of maggots?"

"What do you expect from a bunch of crazy pacifists?" cried Gregson. "The Lord knows – I don't suppose any of us three want another war, but we don't get hysterical about it. And we know what war is; they don't."

"I take it there can be no doubt that this is another Guiseppi affair," said Drummond after a while.

"Not the slightest, I should say, if Veight is mixed up in it."

"Do you know of anything particularly secret which we've got at the moment?"

"There are always a lot of confidential things knocking around," said Gregson. "But I can't say I know of anything that is a super secret. The Chief might. And tomorrow I, at any rate, must get to him as quickly as possible. Jove! if only one could get a word with Ginger... What was he on the track of?"

"One thing is pretty clear, Humphrey. Whatever the game is, it isn't over yet. If they'd already got their information, they wouldn't still be playing round here. No one would run the risks they have run today without some very powerful incentive."

"That's true," agreed Gregson. "And that's what I don't quite understand. You either get information or you don't. If you're going to get it, it presupposes that the individual you are getting it from is willing to sell it. In which case why the Wild West show?"

"Supposing the individual wasn't willing to sell it and they want to make him?" suggested Drummond.

"Keeping him a prisoner, you mean. Possibly. But if anyone in a position to sell big stuff had disappeared we should know about it. And, so far as I know, no one has."

"It's a teaser, Cabbageface. Anyway, we may discover more tonight. There is Hartley Court in front of us, and the party is still going on. Let's leave the car here and walk."

CHAPTER 8

A row of cars drawn up in the drive proclaimed that the meeting was a popular one. The front of the house was in darkness save for the hall, and light on the lawn at the back showed that the Key Club was airing its views on that side of the house. Luckily the undergrowth was dense, and the three men had no difficulty in finding a spot from which they could view the proceedings, which in all conscience were harmless enough.

A large and somewhat pompous-looking individual was holding the floor at the moment. They were too far off to hear what he was saying, but the audience, in which there was quite a sprinkling of women, was obviously becoming restive. And since it was ten minutes past the time for light refreshments the fact was not surprising. At last he sat down and after a little perfunctory applause Meredith got up.

"Evidently the end of a perfect day," whispered Drummond. "That is Uncle John. And the little blighter on Ronald's left is Doctor Belfage, Humphrey."

More hearty applause this time and everybody rose to their feet, extending their hands palm upwards in front of them.

"The Key Club!"

The words came clearly to the listeners through the still air; then there was a general buzz of conversation as the party broke up into little groups.

"Here comes Ronald," said Drummond as Standish appeared at the window. He was talking to Doctor Belfage, and after a while he stepped out on to the lawn, and lit a cigarette. Then he turned round facing the room and they could see a small light moving behind his back. He was signalling with a torch in Morse.

"Short: long," muttered Drummond. "Check me, you fellows. R.U.T.H.E.R.E.H.O.O.T. 'Are you there? hoot.' Go on, Peter: you're better than I am at that game."

The mournful cry of an owl came from Darrell, and at once the signals started again.

W.A.I.T.W.I.L.L.J.O.I.N.U.

"'Wait will join you,'" said Drummond. "And something more. D.A.N.G.E.R."

The signalling stopped, and Standish stepped back into the room. The party was beginning to break up; from the front of the house came the sounds of self-starters.

"Hope he won't be too long," remarked Drummond. "He'll have to park your car somewhere, Peter: he can't leave it in the drive."

"He's saying his last tender farewells now," said Darrell. "Have you blokes noticed that there's not another solitary light in any room in the house? There must be some servants surely."

The last of the guests departed, leaving Doctor Belfage and Meredith alone. That some heated argument was in progress was obvious: the ex-doctor being excited, while Meredith seemed to be trying to pacify him. And then one sentence reached the listeners' ears.

"Madness! Why wasn't I told?"

It was almost a shout, and Meredith laid a soothing hand on the little man's arm.

At last the conversation finished and Meredith came over to the windows and shut them. Then he drew some wooden shutters across, and there came the sound of bolts being pushed home.

118

"That's torn it," said Drummond. "No getting in by that room."

The light still filtered out through the chinks, and Drummond turned to the other two.

"Wait here," he muttered. "I'm going to do a bit of keyhole peeping. If Ronald comes give a hoot, Peter."

He faded into the darkness like a great cat and a few moments later he was crouching outside the window peering in. Most of the room was outside his range of vision. He could see the table with the drinks and empty glasses, and some of the chairs pushed back in disorder just as their late occupants had left them. And then Doctor Belfage came into view, walking backwards and forwards with a worried look on his face. He was muttering to himself and every now and then he shook his fist in the air angrily. Clearly Meredith had not succeeded in calming him.

Suddenly the little man halted. He swung round facing in what Drummond knew was the direction of the door, and a shadow fell across the floor. Then came a second shadow which materialised a moment later into a dark swarthy man with high cheekbones and a hooked nose, who might have been a Spaniard. In his hand he held a small package which he gave to the doctor, who put it in his pocket.

"Well, Doctor," came a deep voice, "how do things progress?"

It was the unseen man who was speaking.

"As well as can be expected," answered Belfage. "But I tell you that man is a devil: he has a will of iron."

The dark man smiled evilly.

"Others have had that will before," he said softly. "It is only a matter of time."

"But we have no time," shrilled the doctor. "This man Drummond, of whom I learn for the first time when I arrive here tonight, may know everything. It was the act of a lunatic not to have warned me. My God! I actually asked him to come here."

119

"And what would it have mattered if he had," rejoined the deep voice. "True, he might have died of boredom had he attended your ridiculous meeting, but that would have saved a lot of bother. Your nerves do not seem to be all they might, my dear Doctor."

"They're shot to hell," cried the other. "I had no idea it would take so long. And now, after what happened last night we may be interrupted at any moment."

"Calm yourself, Doctor. It was, I admit, unfortunate that our good friend Emil allowed that interfering soldier to give him the slip. It was still more unfortunate that he mistook Drummond for a farm labourer. For all that I don't think much damage has been done."

"How can you possibly tell," demanded the doctor. "This man Drummond has deliberately fooled us from what Meredith tells me. And what he's done over one thing, he may very easily do over another."

"He is certainly a nuisance," agreed the unseen man. "But, as I said before, I don't think we need worry overmuch. Had he discovered anything really vital, he would not still have been in Cambridge."

"That's true," said the doctor. "I hadn't thought of that. But I shall be thankful when this is over."

He lit a cigarette with a hand that shook a little.

"I frankly admit," he continued, "that this latest development has shaken me badly."

"One can't expect plain sailing all the time," returned the other contemptuously.

And at that moment there came the hoot of an owl from across the lawn: Standish had arrived.

"If only we could find out what Drummond knows," said the doctor.

"Maybe we shall shortly," answered the other softly. "But from what I overheard this afternoon I don't think he knows much."

The speaker came into sight: it was the tall man, and Drummond studied him thoughtfully.

"My God!" he heard a whisper from behind him. "It's Gregoroff."

Drummond turned round: Standish was peering over his shoulder.

"The most cold-blooded murderer unhung," muttered Standish. "Russian Secret Service: I ought to have thought of him when you mentioned his height. May the Lord help you, Hugh, if he ever gets you at his mercy."

"Tell me the old, old story," whispered Drummond with a grin, as Gregoroff helped himself to a drink. "What are we going to do, Ronald?"

"Wait and listen," answered Standish. "We may learn something."

"No, I don't think he knows much." Gregoroff was speaking again. "But I had to take steps this afternoon to prevent any possibility of his learning more. Well, Doctor, there is a good deal to discuss. Shall we adjourn?"

The light went out: the door closed, and Drummond straightened up.

"Not going to learn anything more here," he muttered. "What about having a council of war?"

They skirted round the lawn, and joined the other two.

"You signalled danger, Ronald," said Drummond. "What did you find out?"

"It was by way of being a general warning, old boy," answered Standish, "inspired by the personnel of the household. The people who attended the meeting were, as I expected, genuine and harmless. I've seldom heard more concentrated bilge talked quite so continuously, but that is neither here nor there.

Mine host, Mr Meredith, was the first gentleman to attract my attention. The last time I saw him he was being sentenced to seven of the best at the Old Bailey for forgery, under the name of Ferguson. The two men who took our coats and hats are both old lags, and another swine I saw on the stairs is a white slave merchant. And so I thought it wise to let you know, in case you hadn't realised it already, that the party wasn't entirely hot air and elderberry wine."

"Did any of these blokes recognise you, Ronald?" said Drummond.

"Not on your life. I blush unseen, so far as gentlemen of that kidney are concerned. Now except possibly for Meredith, those are all small fry. But there is also Emil Veight, who I didn't see, and now – Gregoroff."

"Our tall friend, Peter," explained Drummond.

"Well, as I was saying to you, Hugh," continued Standish, "if anything more was necessary to prove what we're up against, the presence of that devil does it. In fact, I can't imagine how he got into the country. It's true that so far as I remember he has never done anything criminal actually in England, but our people know all about him."

"What do you make of the whole thing up to date?" said Darrell.

"Just what I said to you at the hotel. This is a second Guiseppi case. But whom they have got hold of: what they have stolen: where the key to the mystery lies, I know no more than you. Is it in that house in front of us, or is it somewhere else? There are three cars still left in the drive, which seems to show that others may be leaving besides that doctor."

And at that moment a woman's scream, instantly stifled, rang out. It came from the house and the four men stiffened.

"That settles it," said Drummond quietly. "I'm going in. Are you fellows on?"

"Sure," answered Standish. "But we keep together. The strange thing is that there's not a single light in any window."

"There may be an inside room," said Drummond. "Come on. And keep your guns handy."

They crossed the lawn, and began skirting round the walls to find a suitable window to break in at. But they were saved the trouble: a small side door was unlocked, and a moment later they were all inside the house.

Absolute silence reigned, and the darkness was intense as they crept forward.

"I'm going to switch on a torch," breathed Drummond. "Stand well away from me."

The beam shone out and circling round picked up the staircase. Then darkness again as they felt their way towards it. And now a murmur of voices came from above, and a faint light which grew stronger as they advanced. A door was ajar on the first floor: it was through it that the light was filtering. Then the voices ceased, and they could hear the sound of a woman's sobs.

"The penalty," said a harsh voice suddenly, "is death."

It was so unexpected that they halted abruptly; then once again they tiptoed forward and paused by the room with the light. The sobs were coming from inside, and Drummond flung open the door, to stand motionless on the threshold. The room was an operating theatre.

The walls were pure white, so designed that no corners existed to catch dust. The light was brilliant without being dazzling, and was thrown from a powerful reflector up on to the ceiling. Cases of gleaming instruments stood against the wall, and in the centre was the table and various basins.

For a while it seemed as if the room was empty, and then as their eyes grew accustomed to the light they saw a woman lying on the floor on the far side of the room. Tears were streaming down her face, but her sobs had ceased, and she was staring at them in bewilderment. Young and dark, she was obviously a

123

foreigner, and after a while she put her finger to her lips, as the sound of voices came from across the passage.

"Save me," she whispered. "Save me, for the good God's sake."

"Then get up," muttered Drummond. "We'll save you, but there is no need to lie there."

"But I'm bound," she answered.

In two strides Drummond was across the room, and had picked her up. Her ankles were lashed with rope, but there was no time to free them. At any moment the owners of the voices might return, and their situation with a helpless woman on their hands was not too good.

"Hop it, boys," he said tensely. "We can come back later."

And even as he spoke the door closed with an ominous clang.

For a space they all stood motionless staring at it; then Drummond deposited the woman on the table and crossed the room.

"Trapped," he said at length. "By all that's holy! What complete, utter, congenital fools we are. A steel door with a Yale lock."

The woman started to whimper again, and with a short laugh Drummond returned to her, and taking out his knife he cut her free.

"Well, my dear," he remarked, "that appears to have torn it for the moment. This delightful apartment doesn't seem to go in for windows, and nothing short of a ton of dynamite would break down that door."

"It is terrible," she moaned. "Terrible. This is, how you say, ze doctor's room where he do things to people. And ze walls, no noise go through."

"Soundproof, is it," said Standish curtly. "Still, there must be some ventilation somewhere. By the way, this isn't your pal, is it, Hugh?"

"Great Scott! no," said Drummond. "What's the trouble, my dear? Why had they lashed you up?"

"Because I find out things zey do not want me to know. Because I say I will tell ze policemen."

"What sort of things?" cried Drummond eagerly.

"Zey have ze men captured – *prisonniers*. But what does it mattaire?" she burst out wildly. "We are *prisonniers* ourselves. And ze big man he is a devil. He will kill us all."

Drummond patted her on the shoulder reassuringly, and produced his revolver.

"We may have something to say about that," he said. "Now listen, mam'selle, do you know who these men are who are prisoners?"

"No, m'sieur, *non*. I do not know. One, he is old; the other is of your age. But I do not know who zey are."

"Do you know where they are?"

"In a big house, m'sieur." She passed her hand over her forehead. "A big house... M'sieur, I feel so funny."

"So do I, by gad!" cried Gregson. "I feel as if I was tight."

Drummond sat down suddenly in a chair; he was feeling tight, too. He looked at Standish, and two Standishes were swaying by the wall. Came the sound of a fall behind him, and he tried to turn his head. But he could not, and even as he made a last desperate effort the two Standishes collapsed and lay still.

His revolver was still within reach, and he tried to pick it up. But his arm would not move: it felt as if it was bound to his side with iron bands. He tried one leg: the same result. So he gave it up, and just sat there inert and helpless.

He could think, though sluggishly; he could see, though his vision was blurred. And after a while he became aware of a very faint, sweet smell. Gas, he thought hazily; some sort of paralysing gas.

Suddenly he realised that a man was bending over Standish, a man with a hood over his head. He was doing something to

Standish's hands and feet, and just then he found he was being attended to also. And the amazing thing was that though he could see his hands being lifted and put together, though he could see rope being lashed round them, he could feel absolutely nothing. It was as if his whole body had gone to sleep.

The men disappeared and Drummond lost count of time. Like a drunken man he stared at Standish lying motionless on the floor, and wondered dully what had happened to the other two. And then, starting in his feet and fingers and spreading gradually up his legs and arms, the most agonising pins and needles set in. It was the return of feeling, but while it lasted he felt as if he was going to burst out of his skin. At length it was over; he found he could turn his head. But he also found that his ankles had been lashed to the legs of the chair, though he had been totally unaware of the fact.

"Are you all right, Hugh?"

Standish was regarding him from the floor.

"I think so," said Drummond. "How are the others?"

"I'm OK," came Darrell's voice from behind his chair. "But Gregson's still a bit woozy. The lady appears to have deserted us."

"They carted her out," said Standish, "after they'd lashed me up. Boys, we deserve kicking. We've fallen head foremost into one of the most palpable traps I've ever thought of, and if what that woman said is right and this room is soundproof, so far as I can see we're likely to remain in it."

"Do you think she was a wrong 'un?" said Drummond.

"I'm thinking it doesn't matter much. Right or wrong, she baited the cage all right, and when we suckers were nicely inside they shut the door."

"Where did the damned stuff come from?"

"I don't know. But there's a ventilator high up in the wall behind you, and that's presumably where it's gone. And since the air seems clear now there must be some inlet. The point is, what the devil are we going to do? Can anybody move?"

"I can't for one," said Drummond. "What's the time? How long were we under?"

"Ask me another," answered Standish. "I should say about half an hour. Look out; the door is opening."

"Put them in a row," came a deep voice that Drummond instantly recognised as Gregoroff's. The man who had driven the car the previous afternoon was with him, and the Spaniard, and a moment or two later they were joined by Emil Veight.

"That one," said Gregoroff, pointing to Darrell, "was with Drummond this afternoon at the cottage. Who are these other two?"

"I seem to recognise your face," remarked Veight to Standish. "Who are you?"

"That is a matter of supreme indifference to everyone except myself," said Standish casually.

"Been doing any more shooting, Pansyface?" asked Drummond pleasantly.

For a second Gregoroff's eyes rested on him; then they passed on.

"And that fourth one, who doesn't seem to have quite recovered. He wasn't with them at the hotel. However, it is of no consequence."

His glance came back to Drummond.

"It is strange, is it not, how frequently the simplest traps are the most efficacious," he remarked. "Though I must confess I hardly thought I should bag four of you. By the way, where is the car you stole from me? "

"I swapped it for some peppermint bull's-eyes," answered Drummond with a grin.

The other's face remained as mask-like as ever, and he lit a cigarette with great deliberation.

"You are an extremely foolish man, Captain Drummond," he said. "I suppose you realise that the four of you are completely in our power."

"At the moment it looks like it," yawned Drummond.

"I suppose you further realise that you have been annoying me. And I dislike being annoyed. However, since, owing to your unbelievable stupidity, you have afforded us a very valuable test on a matter we are interested in, we have decided to spare your lives under certain conditions. Last night, when you were in your cottage, a stone was thrown through your window. Wrapped round that stone was a message. What was that message? Your chances of life depend entirely on your giving me the correct answer."

"Is that so?" said Drummond quietly. "Let us get this matter clear. Assuming for the moment that there was a message wrapped round the stone, and that I tell you its contents, am I to understand that you will release us and that we are free to go?"

"My dear Captain Drummond," said Gregoroff with a pitying smile, "you always seem to judge other people's mentality by your own. You must remember that your veracity on the subject of messages is under a definite cloud. No; you will not be free to go. You are far too much of a nuisance when you're at large. And so you will remain here until we have finished what we came over to do in this country. It is for you to decide whether your residence in this charming room is for that period or for – perhaps ever is too strong a word, but shall we say for some months or even years? I trust I make myself quite clear. If you give me the correct message, I will give you my promise to notify the authorities where you are to be found. It may not be for some days, but you are four strong men and a little fasting will do you no harm. In fact, I should think you ought easily to last a fortnight, and I can guarantee to have finished by then. If, on the other hand, you do not give me the correct message, I shall not notify the authorities, with results that may, I fear, prove most unpleasant for you. In fact, as I said, it may be months before you are found. You realise, don't you, that this room is to all intents and purposes soundproof. You further realise that it is impossible to open that door without the key or suitable tools. And so you see your position."

"You've overlooked one small point," remarked Drummond. "The people at the hotel know we're here."

"Apart from the fact that if that was the truth you certainly wouldn't have mentioned it," said Gregoroff, "do you really think that that affects matters? Of course you've been here, Captain Drummond, and you've left. One of my minions will specially inquire for you at the Royal, and will mention that you left here before midnight. I assure you everything has been thought of."

"And so you propose to stop on in this house while we starve in here," said Drummond.

"Wrong once more," remarked Gregoroff genially. "When we leave you tonight, we lock up the house and go – elsewhere. So you will be all by yourselves."

"Unpleasant for Meredith when we are found."

"Why? Unknown to him, you must have returned to the house, and in the course of your unjustifiable exploration shut yourselves in here by mistake. An accident, a terrible accident and a parallel, my dear fellow, to that delightful old tale which I seem to remember. Wasn't it called the 'Mistletoe Bough'? About a charming girl playing hide-and-seek who popped into a chest, and being unable to open it from the inside, remained there so long that she died on the rest of the party."

"With her feet and hands lashed together!" sneered Drummond.

"Captain Drummond, you positively pain me. Before we desert you we shall unloose one of you, who will then perform the same office for the rest. You will be perfectly free to move about; to shout, if you wish to, as much as you like. In fact, the only point which you have to decide is the duration of your visit. Is it to be for a few days only, in which case the ill-effects will not be lasting; or do you propose to be foolish?"

Drummond stared at him thoughtfully; the situation was only too clear. Of the four of them, prisoners in that room, there was only one whose disappearance was likely to cause any comment – Humphrey Gregson. As a serving soldier his absence would be noticed very quickly, but even if it was, what then? He could be traced as far as the Royal; after that the trail vanished. Worse still, if the two undergraduates who had followed them did complain to the police, and gave the number of Gregson's car, the trail was leading directly away from Hartley Court.

"I cannot afford to wait all night, Captain Drummond." Gregoroff was speaking again. "I will give you another two minutes in which to decide. And please be under no delusions. If it was not for the fact that I want to know the contents of that message, I should leave you here to starve like the rats that you are without the smallest compunction. In case, too, that you have hopes in another direction, your two cars will not remain where they are at present."

Still Drummond said nothing: his brain was racing feverishly to try and see some loophole of escape. His eyes sought Standish, who shrugged his shoulders.

"Seems to me they've got two to one the better of us, Hugh," he said.

"An excellent judge of odds," remarked Gregoroff.

"If I do give you the contents of that message," said Drummond, "what guarantee have we got that you'll keep your word?"

"None," answered Gregoroff calmly. "But, then, you're hardly in a position to demand guarantees, are you? You've just got to chance it."

"Very good," said Drummond after a pause. "I will chance it. And I hope for your sake that the contents of the message mean more in your young life than they do in mine. For none of us has been able to make head or tail of it. It runs as follows: 'Rosemary BJCDOR.' "

"Where was the message when I searched you?" demanded Veight.

"Where I found it afterwards: between the two window-sashes."

"And where is it now?"

"In my head; I burnt it."

For a few moments the German and Gregoroff conferred together in low tones; then the Russian swung round on Drummond.

"Rosemary BJCDOR," he repeated. "And you don't know what it means?"

"I do not," said Drummond. "It is presumably a code of some sort."

Again the two whispered together, and Drummond glanced at Standish. And Standish was studying the Spaniard with a thoughtful look in his eyes.

"You have no idea who the writer is?" said Gregoroff.

"Not the slightest," answered Drummond.

"Why did you cause that fake message to be sent?"

"My merry disposition," said Drummond calmly. "I don't like you or any of your friends, so I thought I'd have a spot of fun at your expense."

"How many other people know of this message?"

"So far as I know, only the police at Belmoreton. I told them when I reported the death of the wretched bloke who was murdered at the cottage."

Gregoroff turned to the chauffeur.

"Verify that tomorrow," he said curtly. "And now, Captain Drummond, one or two more questions. What do you know of the girl Doris Venables?"

"Nothing at all, except that she's no beginner at telling the tale."

"I have no doubt in my own mind, Paul," remarked the German, "that her story was the truth. What is of more interest is that I have at last remembered who that man is."

He pointed to Standish.

"You were in the British War Office on the Intelligence side. Your name is Standish. How did you get mixed up in this?"

"That again is a matter of supreme indifference to everyone except me," answered Standish.

Emil Veight whispered to the Russian, who gave a low whistle of surprise.

"That puts a different complexion on matters," he remarked. "I thought we were only dealing with meddling fools. Are you still at the War Office, Mr Standish?"

"I am not."

"But you were there a year ago. Things become clearer. So your attendance at that meeting tonight, even if not professional, was at any rate inspired by inside knowledge."

"I haven't the faintest idea what you're talking about," said Standish. "I attended the meeting of the Key Club at the invitation of Doctor Belfage."

"And then remained in the garden spying with your three friends. What did you hear at the meeting that caused you to do that?"

"Nothing," remarked Standish. "We heard a woman scream."

"Twenty minutes after the meeting was over," said the Russian harshly. "You lie, damn you! That scream was the bait to catch you, if you were there. And I knew you were there. Why? I'll tell you. Because you wanted to find out things that don't concern you."

"My dear Hugh," drawled Standish, "the man is a veritable genius. How does he think of it?"

"I don't know, old lad," answered Drummond. "Must have some asset, I suppose, to make up for his ghastly shooting."

Gregoroff stared at him in silence. And the utter lack of concern in Drummond's face seemed suddenly to madden the Russian.

"You damned Englishman," he said at length. "And you really imagined you could come blundering in on my plans with impunity! Well, you've learned your lesson." He turned to the Spaniard. "Cortez, pick up that revolver and search them all for guns."

He waited whilst his order was carried out; then he threw back his head and laughed.

"You fools," he cried. "You unutterable fools! And did you really imagine you were going to get away? Here you are, and here you remain till you die. You won't be able to expedite matters by shooting yourselves; you'll just die the slow, agonising death of starvation. Don't sneer at me, damn you."

With all his strength he struck Drummond in the mouth.

"You'll die," he shouted. "And my only regret is that I shall not be here to see it."

The man was beside himself with rage. A strange red light was glowing in his eyes, and his teeth were bared in a snarl.

"And now I am going. I shall leave the light on, so that you may watch one another growing weaker and weaker. Untie that one."

He pointed to Gregson, and the Spaniard cut the ropes that bound him.

"How long to Horsebridge?" he asked Veight.

"Two hours," answered the German.

"Goodbye and good luck." Gregoroff from the door bowed ironically. "I fear I've spoilt your beauty somewhat, Captain Drummond, but it will be all the same in a fortnight or so. And I owed you one for stealing my car. Not quite so chatty as usual? Well, well – it's quite understandable."

And with one final mocking laugh the door clanged to behind them.

"One man and one man only has done that to me before." Drummond broke the long silence. "And later I killed him. You'd better unlash us, Cabbageface."

"I'm glad you didn't give him the real message, Hugh," said Darrell.

"I thought you blokes wouldn't mind, and I was certain the swine would have crossed us, anyway."

Drummond rose and stretched himself.

"Is there any way out, chaps?"

"If this room is to all intents soundproof," answered Darrell quietly, "and it must be, or he wouldn't have left us here – none, so far as I can see. It will be days before anyone starts looking for us at all, and then they won't dream of trying an empty house. What do you say, Ronald?"

"That I ought to be dropped into boiling oil," answered Standish. "That my brain would shame a louse. Who is A5, Humphrey?"

"Ginger Lovelace. What's stung you, Ronald?"

"That Spaniard wasn't a Spaniard, but a Mexican," was his unexpected answer.

The other three stared at him in amazement.

"What the devil has that got to do with it?" cried Drummond.

"Only that I've solved the real message," cried Standish savagely.

He got up and shook his fists in the air.

"Solved it," he muttered. "And we're helpless. Absolutely helpless."

CHAPTER 9

"I trust that everything is to monsieur's satisfaction?"

The head waiter bowed obsequiously as an underling replaced the gold-foil bottle in the ice bucket. The silver gleamed in the shaded light; a big jar of caviare shone like black velvet in the centre of the table. From outside came the dull roar of the Strand by night; save for that, no sound disturbed the occupant of the suite in the Ritz-Carlton.

"Thank you, Henri. All is excellent as usual. Let my friend be shown up the instant he arrives."

"I will see to it personally, m'sieur."

With another low bow befitting a man whose wealth was reputed to be fabulous, and who, unlike some others of the millionaire variety, dispensed *largesse* freely, Henri marshalled his attendants and left the room, leaving the diner alone.

For a while he ate with the quiet deliberation of a man used to feeding by himself – sparingly and yet with the appreciation of the true epicure. Every now and then his eyes rested on the ormolu clock which occupied the centre of the mantelpiece. They were strange eyes – almost repellent. Very light blue in colour, they protruded slightly, giving the impression of a fish. But what was most noticeable about them was their unwavering stare: they never seemed to blink. Hypnotic, frightening, eyes to which it would take a bold man to lie; eyes which made women turn away with a shudder; eyes which had done more than anything else to make Ivor Kalinsky one of the most powerful forces in Europe.

He finished the caviare, and pouring himself out another glass of champagne, he lit a cigarette. He smoked as he had eaten, slowly and with deliberation, using an amber holder. And after a time he rose and began to pace slowly up and down the room. The clanging bell of a passing fire-engine grew to a crescendo and died away in the distance, but he scarcely heard it: his mind was engrossed in other matters, for Ivor Kalinsky was confronted with the biggest problem of his career. On which side should he tip the balance – for or against another European war?

To the countless thousands hurrying through the streets of London to their favourite cinema it would have seemed fantastic that such a thing could be possible. Had they been asked to swallow such a situation even in their most hectic melodrama, they would have poured scorn upon the mentality of the producer of the film. Governments and politicians made wars – not one lone individual pacing to and fro in a dim-lit sitting-room. Who wanted a war, anyway? Hadn't the last one been bad enough?

For or against! For or against! Ceaselessly his brain was working, weighing factor against factor, as coldly and analytically as a chemist conducting an experiment. To the moral side of the issue he gave no thought; it simply did not enter into his calculations. To him the matter was a game of chess, and it was imperative that he should not make a false move.

He drew back the curtains and stared out over the city. As always, his room was high up: he preferred it because of the increased airiness. Below him lay the river, grey and sombre, with the reflection of countless lights gleaming from the Surrey side. A tug went past drawing some barges down to the Pool, and he watched it till it was hidden by Waterloo Bridge. For or against! That would not be the only bridge that would have to be reconstructed if the answer was "For."

In the distance signs shone and glittered – red and white and blue. One showed a glass of port being filled and emptied; another extolled a boot polish. Red and white and blue: was it symbolical? And in imagination Ivor Kalinsky saw another scene. The lights were extinguished, save for beams piercing the sky like pencils from different directions. The noise of the traffic was stilled; another sound had taken its place, and that came from overhead. It was the roar of countless aeroplanes, punctuated every few seconds by the crash of bursting bombs. And in the streets mobs of screaming men and women rushed frenziedly about, trampling, fighting, mad with terror. The tube stations were full – too full; already people were being suffocated to death. And on the platforms below those in front were being pushed on to the lines unable to withstand the pressure of those behind.

Still the bombs came in ever-increasing numbers. Great blinding flashes stabbed the night as houses crashed in ruins, and then, utterly inadequate, came the staccato crack of bursting shrapnel. The anti-aircraft guns at work, manned by the few volunteers who had reached them in time. And suddenly, like a flaming meteor, one stricken aeroplane shot downwards through the night. A pitiful, ragged cheer, and then it crashed, and the bombs it still carried burst in a roar so titanic that the aftermath was silence. The droning above died away; the raiders had departed, the shambles were left. And war had not yet been declared; only a state of tension existed.

A knock came at the door, and Ivor Kalinsky turned round, letting the curtains swing to behind him.

"Come," he called, and the head waiter entered.

"Sir James Portrush," he announced, and a portly man of about fifty came in. He was dressed in the conventional morning coat, and he carried his top-hat and a dispatch-case.

"Ah! my dear Mr Kalinsky," he cried, coming forward with outstretched hand. "I am delighted to welcome you once more to our shores. You had a good crossing, I trust."

"One or two air pockets, Sir James," said the financier. "Otherwise quite comfortable. You will have a glass of wine with me?"

Sir James held up a protesting hand.

"Thank you; I never touch it. My digestion, you know. I have to be careful – very careful."

"A cup of coffee, then?"

"Again no. Just a little weak whisky and water before I go to bed is all I allow myself."

"Quite a Spartan diet, Sir James," said Kalinsky with a smile. "That will do, thank you, Henri, and see that we are not disturbed under any pretext whatever."

"Very good, m'sieur. I will give the necessary instructions."

The door closed; the two men were alone. And for a space Kalinsky watched his visitor as he settled down. The top-hat was placed carefully on a chair, the dispatch-case on the table. Then, with trousers slightly hitched up and plump legs crossed, Sir James Portrush beamed on his host from his chair. And restraining with an effort a strong desire to say, "Now we're all ready for a nice cup of tea and a good gossip," Kalinsky sat down too.

"I am very glad indeed, Mr Kalinsky," began Sir James urbanely, "to have this opportunity of a chat with you so soon after your arrival. Indeed, the Prime Minister himself would have liked to be present, but an extremely important measure dealing with the totalisator at greyhound racing tracks is occupying all his time at the moment. You cannot perhaps realise the great volume of public opinion in this country that is opposed to betting in any form, and it is very essential to effect some suitable compromise that will prove acceptable to all schools of thought."

The faintest perceptible smile twitched round his listener's lips, but Sir James was busy opening his dispatch-case and it escaped his attention.

"At the same time, my dear sir," he continued, "you must not imagine for one moment that our entire attention is centred on these pressing domestic problems to the exclusion of other matters. And we should indeed be foolish if we were to blind our eyes to the fact that the temper of Europe at the present moment leaves much to be desired: much – ah – to be desired. You agree with me, Mr Kalinsky?"

"I do, Sir James."

"Good. And though we have, of course, our recognised channels of information, and are closely in touch with the whole situation, it struck me that a little private and confidential chat with you might help matters considerably."

"You flatter me, Sir James."

"Not at all, not at all. Your interests are worldwide: you have a finger on every important pulse. Now, in brief, what is your view of the situation? I need hardly say that any remarks you may care to make will be for the ears of my colleagues and myself alone."

"Since you have done me the honour of asking me my opinion, Sir James, I presume you want a candid answer."

"Naturally, naturally."

"You do not, for instance, want me to prophesy smooth things, so that, with an easy conscience, you can return to your legislation for totalisators on greyhound tracks."

Sir James ignored the veiled sarcasm, though it did not escape him.

"I am sure that anything you may care to say, Mr Kalinsky," he remarked with quiet dignity, "will be of great value."

"I doubt it," said the financier quietly, "because the gist of what I have to say may be summed up in one question. Why have you gone out of your way to make another European war inevitable?"

Sir James sat up with a jerk.

"Inevitable!" he stuttered. "Inevitable! My dear sir, we have led the way in every disarmament conference that has been held."

"Which would have been quite admirable if any other country had followed you. Unfortunately they haven't. They – forgive my saying so, Sir James – have merely laughed."

"What else could we have done? It was essential to follow the trend of public opinion in this country."

"Follow! Surely a novel method of regarding your steward-ship."

"You misunderstand me, Mr Kalinsky. It is essential that leaders should sense the temper of those they are called upon to govern. And I say frankly that this country would not stand for another war."

"I can quite believe you. Which is why, as I said to start with, it makes it even more unfortunate that they have brought it on themselves. Sir James, let us be perfectly frank. You, to day, are in the invidious position of a small boy telling two bigger ones not to fight. And the result in that case is that he gets kicked in the seat of his pants by both."

Ivor Kalinsky lit another cigarette, whilst Sir James fidgeted in his chair.

"Unpleasant," continued the financier, "but you asked for the truth. Governments today can be divided into three categories: dictators, knaves and fools. You have no dictator in England, and... Well, what would be the result, Sir James, if I offered you half a million down, here and now, if you would pursue some line of action dictated by me?"

"I should be shocked and horrified, sir."

"Precisely. But there are many other countries where a man in your position would be shocked and horrified if that offer was *not* made. And so we are only left with the third category."

Sir James flushed angrily.

"You speak bluntly, Mr Kalinsky."

"In God's name, why not?" cried the other, thumping the table. "If you'd thought bluntly these last few years this situation would never have arisen. England would still have been the deciding factor in Europe. As it is, you are negligible. And your funny little men who preach pacifism, though they have never heard a shot fired in anger in their lives, flatter themselves that they deserve well of their country. No one wants war, Sir James, but the only way to prevent it is to take the line you have *not* taken. To stop two strong men fighting you must at least be as strong yourself."

"Come, come, Mr Kalinsky, there is such a thing as an alliance."

"Who would deny it? Let us, however, look on your value as an ally. Your army is negligible, and there will be no time in the next war to expand it as you did in the last. Your navy is still a magnificent striking force, but, to be perfectly frank, what is it going to strike against? A few sea forts; another fleet? Who cares? The results in the big scheme of things would be negligible. And as a means of defence, out of date. Command of the seas is still important, but command of the air is infinitely more so. And there you simply fade right out of the picture. Just before you arrived, Sir James, I was standing in the window looking out over this great city of yours, and in my imagination I heard the drone of an attacking air fleet. I saw the holocaust below. It was no trumpery raid such as you experienced in the last war, and by which, so it would seem to the onlooker, you still set your standard. They were up there by their hundreds and the raid itself was the actual declaration of war."

"Really, Mr Kalinsky, it sounds like an extract from the alarmist press. I can hardly believe that you are serious."

"My dear Sir James, your countrymen never have believed that anything was serious until it actually happened. But in the past you have had time to repair your mistake, and somehow or other to muddle through. In the future you won't have that time."

"There certainly wouldn't be much time if what you have described took place," agreed Sir James tolerantly. "And should any nation be so inconceivably barbaric, I don't see how we could prevent them."

"By one method and one method only: fear of reprisals. And that presupposes *existing* strength in the air as great if not greater than they possess themselves. Which is what you have not got."

"But what good would such a senseless act do, my dear fellow? If London was flattened out no other nation would be a penny the better off. Surely the utter futility of war as a road to material gain was amply proved by the last one."

"And you think that lesson has been learned? I envy you your complacency, Sir James. Further, if that is your considered opinion, why did you come here tonight? Our discussion is purely academic."

"*Touché*, Mr Kalinsky, *touché*. I admit that I fear the lesson has not been learned; and I also admit that we have cut down our fighting forces to the nearest minimum. But the country simply would not stand any large increase in the estimates."

The millionaire shrugged his shoulders.

"That, of course, is entirely your affair, Sir James, and one on which it would be presumption on my part to express an opinion. If you are right there is no more to be said."

"But surely you agree with me that another war on a large scale would be an irreparable disaster to the world?"

"Possibly; possibly not. Who can tell? Just as there was no criterion to judge by before the last war, so there is none today.

For the next war, Sir James, will be as different from 1914 as 1914 was from your war in South Africa. But in any event, whether it proves an irreparable disaster or not has got no bearing whatever on its coming."

"You seem to have definitely made up your mind that sooner or later it is unavoidable."

For a while the millionaire did not reply; then he nodded.

"Yes, I think I may safely say that my mind is made up. Sooner or later war is inevitable. And the whole point, Sir James, is whether it is to be sooner or later."

Sir James lay back in his chair with a worried look on his face.

"I must confess, Mr Kalinsky," he said at length, "that such a very definite opinion coming from a man in your position is most disquieting. But surely you and the other big financial interests are against such a catastrophe."

"Certainly. But we are not all-powerful. Whether we like it or whether we don't, we can't stop it. The irresistible urge is there. At the moment it is under control, but believe me that control is very precarious. One spark, and the whole of Europe will be a roaring bonfire. And all that we can do is to try and control the direction of the flames."

"Grave words, Mr Kalinsky."

"The situation is grave, Sir James. And England's unpreparedness makes it all the graver."

For a while there was silence in the room, then Sir James rose to his feet.

"I must thank you, Mr Kalinsky," he said quietly, "for the frank way in which you have spoken. Needless to say I shall put your opinions before my colleagues. And I can only utter a pious hope that you may be wrong. Is there no limit to human madness?"

"If there is I fear I have not plumbed it," answered the millionaire. "Good night, Sir James; I hope to see you again before I leave England."

The door closed behind his visitor, and Ivor Kalinsky sank back in his chair. From many points of view the conversation had been a valuable one: it had enabled him to crystallise his own thoughts, though it had still not solved his problem. He had said nothing that he did not believe to be the truth; and if he had not said everything that he might have, that was nothing to do with Sir James. One spark *would* be enough: it was no business of the Englishman if his was the hand that kindled it.

He got up and once again began to pace restlessly up and down the room. Was the time ripe? A hundred different factors had to be weighed in the balance; a hundred conflicting interests taken into consideration – interests which overlapped and interlaced in a way that made their mutual reactions well nigh incalculable.

There came another knock on the door, and his second visitor was ushered in. It would have been hard to imagine a greater contrast to the one who had just left. The newcomer wore a heavy fur coat, though the evening was warm. A silk scarf was wrapped round his neck; an opera hat was on his head. His face was swarthy; his dark eyes gleamed with vitality. And his booked nose proclaimed his race.

"Some more wine," said Kalinsky as the other flung his coat in a chair, revealing immaculate evening clothes.

"I see you're a pillar of society, Morgenstein," he continued with a faint smile.

"I've just come from Covent Garden," said the other. "Carmenita was in perfect voice, and I waited to hear the Swan Song."

Again the smile flickered round Kalinsky's lips.

"I, too, have been listening to a Swan Song," he remarked. "Sung by the excellent Sir James Portrush."

The Jew eyed him keenly, and then murmured some banality as the waiter returned with the champagne.

"Was he in good voice also?" he asked when they were once more alone.

"He croaked a little towards the end, when he left me to continue vital legislation on greyhounds."

Kalinsky lifted his glass.

"Well, Morgenstein, and what conclusion have you come to?"

"I have not as yet come to any. It is a grave issue, Kalinsky."

"That was the croak in Sir James' Swan Song. He admits, quite frankly, that this country is not prepared for war. Of course that fact is well known to both of us. At the same time it is illuminating when a man in his position says so openly."

The Jew lit a cigar before replying.

"Are they contemplating taking any steps to remedy the state of affairs?"

Kalinsky shrugged his shoulders.

"How can you ever tell with these people? I drew him a picture of the air raid of the future carried out before war was declared. He merely smiled. And yet the man is uneasy."

"Are you prepared to put your cards on the table, Kalinsky, and give me your views of the situation?"

"I certainly am. And I can express it in a nutshell. Unless England increases her fighting forces, war is absolutely inevitable. Nothing can stop it. The point, therefore, that we have to decide is whether we precipitate the crisis now, or whether we wait. If we wait, it is possible that this country may again become the dominating factor in the situation. If we act now, Europe as we know it ceases to exist. Which suits our book best?"

"Absurd though it may sound, I am still frightened of England," said Morgenstein. "She has such an astounding way of pulling her weight at the last moment."

"I think it is far from absurd. More, I may be illogical, but I agree with you. And I can assure you that that very point has weighed largely in my calculations. Could I but find some method of weakening her still more, or alternatively of strengthening others whom we need not name, so that the disparity of power was greater, I would not hesitate for one moment."

"You mean you would favour immediate action."

"Precisely. Would that suit you?"

"It would. But is there any possibility of such a thing occurring?"

"That I shall know more about a little later in the evening. Have you to return to your guests, or would you care to remain and hear for yourself?"

"I will certainly remain. You are expecting some fresh information?"

"I am. What its value will prove to be I cannot say: my correspondent was guarded in his letter. But hitherto I have found him a most reliable man. Emil Veight is his name."

"I cannot recall it," said Morgenstein. "A good man, is he?"

"First class."

Kalinsky smoked in silence for a time; then he changed the conversation abruptly.

"Have you ever come across a peculiar institution known as the Key Club?"

"I have heard of them," said Morgenstein, looking slightly surprised. "Are they to be taken seriously?"

"They take themselves very seriously indeed. Their principal aim is world peace, and the brotherhood of man. And though their aims may be idealistic, their methods are severely practical. They consist, in short, of buying confidential information on armaments from whoever they can bribe and then publishing it broadcast so that all the world shall know. And if you think into the matter it is quite an efficacious way of preserving equality between nations."

"You amaze me, Kalinsky. Have they done it often?"

"On two or three occasions to my certain knowledge quite successfully. And it was in connection with them that I first met Veight. On that occasion, I fear, they were not quite so successful, though they were very useful to me. An Italian, whose name I forget, sold to one of their agents the plans of a new submarine, and Veight, by some means, heard of it. He acted with commendable promptitude. The Italian and the agent, who was returning to England with the plans, were both murdered, and Veight brought the tracings to me on the chance of my buying. I did, and they came in very useful."

"Really! Most interesting. But what exactly has your story got to do with the present situation?"

"That we shall know in a few minutes: Veight said he would be here at half-past ten. And since he mentioned the Key Club in his letter, I can only conclude that something of the same sort has happened."

"He is a reliable man?"

"When it pays him to be. As it does with me. And of one thing I am sure. He would not waste my time or his own unless he thought it worth while. Whether what he has to tell us is sufficiently worth while is for us to decide."

The sound of voices came from the lobby outside and Kalinsky glanced up.

"The man himself, I think. Good evening, Herr Veight," he said affably as the door opened. "You are punctuality itself. You know Herr Morgenstein?"

"By sight and name only," said Veight with a bow, coming into the room. "I trust you are well, m'sieur."

"Quite, thank you. Waiter – bring another bottle of wine. Now, Herr Veight," he continued, as the man left the room, "I gather from your letter that you have something of interest to report. You can speak quite freely in front of Herr Morgenstein."

Once again Veight bowed; then he sat down and lit a cigarette.

"Am I right in supposing, gentlemen," he said "that the state of tension in Europe is acute?"

"Let us proceed on that assumption," remarked Kalinsky.

"Am I further right in supposing," continued Veight, "that confidential information on military matters would be particularly valuable today?"

"That would be for us to decide," said Kalinsky curtly.

"Normally, m'sieur, I would agree. In this case, however, I must have something a little more definite. Naturally I am not asking you to pledge yourselves blindly in any way. But if I guarantee to deliver to you within forty-eight hours, or at the utmost seventy-two, the most closely guarded military secrets in England, what will it be worth to me? Let me make myself quite clear. You remember, m'sieur, the Guiseppi affair?"

"Guiseppi! That was the name, Morgenstein. Yes, Veight, I do. I was discussing it before you came tonight."

"Good. Well, each of these secrets, gentlemen, is as valuable as those submarine plans."

The two financiers looked at one another.

"If that is the case," said Kalinsky after a pause, "I think we would be prepared to guarantee you twenty-five thousand pounds."

Veight shook his head.

"Not enough, gentlemen," he said decisively. I have to split with a man who has been working with me. The risks we have already run are enormous, and the greatest are still to come. Will you make it twenty-five thousand each?"

Again Kalinsky glanced at Morgenstein, who gave a barely perceptible nod.

"All right, Veight," said Kalinsky. "Fifty thousand in all. But we must be the judges."

"Of that I have no fear," said Veight quietly. "You will be satisfied with your bargain."

He paused as the waiter re-entered the room, and there was silence till he had finally withdrawn.

"No fear at all, gentlemen," repeated Veight. "Does Herr Morgenstein know anything about the Key Club, m'sieur?"

"I told him a certain amount when discussing your letter," said Kalinsky.

"Then I will not waste time in explaining that part of it to him. Because, I fear, gentlemen, a certain amount of explanation is necessary over what has happened already. I will make it as short as I possibly can, but it is essential that you should understand the situation.

"The story starts in Warsaw, two months ago, with a man named Gregoroff – Paul Gregoroff – as the chief character. The business which had taken him there was completed, and as he was sitting in the lounge of his hotel after dinner, listening to the band, he became aware of two men who were talking English at the next table. One was clearly an Englishman, the other was a Pole, and both of them were wearing the badge of the Key Club. At first he paid but little attention. Their voices were low; their general appearance was consistent with the fatuous imbecility which one expects in members of that ridiculous organisation. And then one word caught his ear very clearly. That word was 'Gas.'

"He endeavoured to listen more closely, but as luck would have it the band was making such an infernal din that it was quite impossible for him to hear what they were saying. But bearing in mind the recent activities of their society, he deemed it advisable to make some further inquiries. So he squared the police to have the Englishman arrested later on some trumped-up charge connected with his passport, but to treat him with the utmost consideration. Then, wearing a key himself, he went round to the police station.

"The young man was, of course, overjoyed to meet a fellow-member; and when that fellow-member procured his release on the spot, accompanied by voluble expressions of regret from the police, his gratitude knew no bounds, In fact within half an hour Gregoroff was in possession of the whole story.

"It transpired that this youth was by way of being a chemist. And he had been acting as assistant to a man in England who for some months past had been working on a new form of gas. At first Gregoroff was not greatly interested: new gases come and go, each one bringing its own antidote. But when he began to realise the properties of this particular gas, matters assumed a different aspect.

"It seemed, then, that this young fellow had been experimented on himself, not once but many times, by the man he had been assisting. The gas was colourless, odourless, and a fraction lighter than air. It was also harmless – after its effects had worn off. But it was the effect that was interesting: complete paralysis of the limbs, absolute inability to move or speak, though hazily conscious of what was going on around, and finally loss of all feeling. According to the amount administered the duration of this condition lasted. The dose could be graded so as to produce effect for ten minutes or half an hour. But, and this was the vital fact, you were in the grip of the gas before you realised you were. And then it was too late to save yourself.

"I will not insult your intelligence, m'sieur," continued Veight after a pause, "by stressing the marvellous possibilities which opened out in front of Gregoroff if what this man told him was true. Moreover, since it was unlikely that he would have come all the way to Poland merely to tell a stupid lie, Gregoroff decided to proceed on the assumption that he was speaking the truth. And so, still keeping up the role of an enthusiastic member of the Key Club, whose aim was universal peace, be proceeded to pump him dry.

"He discovered that the inventor of this gas was a man called Waldron. He was a Territorial officer in the English Royal Engineers, and in addition to being a chemist he was also a very keen soldier. It was clear, of course, that the military value of this gas was great. It could be used alone, or mixed with something else, and in either case its presence would not be detected until too late. And Waldron, being a patriotic Englishman, proposed to place his discovery so soon as it was perfected at the disposal of the British military authorities – an idea abhorrent to his assistant, though that was a fact of which Waldron was naturally unaware.

"He blathered on about ideals – their common ideals, since he assumed Gregoroff thought as he did. And Gregoroff let him talk, though he hardly heard what he said. Because, M'sieur Kalinsky" – the speaker leaned forward in his chair. – "his mind was busy with the potentialities of this gas apart from its military value. If it was all that this boy claimed for it: if it could be manufactured without too elaborate a plant: if – well, there were many ifs, but the germ of a stupendous idea was there. Imagine the position if one was able to render a man powerless in a room in an hotel without using force, and without the slightest risk of detection from outside. No other gas would do it: it would be smelt in the passage. The same objection applied to an anaesthetic such as ether. Here, then, was the possibility of the ideal weapon. Do I interest you?"

"Go on," said Kalinsky quietly.

"So Gregoroff started on the practical details, and the more he heard the better it sounded. It was cheap to make, and was easily compressible in steel cylinders. These could be of any size desired, from the massive ones suitable for work in war to smaller cylinders which could be moved by hand. Moreover, the respirator was not at all complicated, and could be carried unnoticed in a man's pocket till it was required. In fact, there was only one hitch. This miserable youth did not know the formula. A great deal of the process he was conversant with, but there were one or two points of which he was ignorant. They were known to Waldron *and Waldron only*. A definite setback, as you will agree, but it had to be faced. Because by now Gregoroff was fully determined to go on with the matter.

"The first problem was the young man himself. He was, so he told Gregoroff, in accordance with their custom, and acting on the orders of one of the leaders of England, paving the way for the secret of this gas to become worldwide. He was arranging for a Key Club representative from every country to come to England in a month or so, by which time he would have the full details at his fingertips, and he would then pass the information on to them. Fortunately he had started in the east and was working west through Europe, so he'd been caught in good time. He had given Gregoroff Waldron's address in England, and therefore there seemed no possible object in his continued existence. And so he – er – fell in front of an express train and passed out of the picture."

A faint smile flickered round Kalinsky's lips.

"This Gregoroff of whom you speak: whom is he acting for?"

"Himself, m'sieur," answered Veight promptly.

"And is he the man you mentioned at the beginning, with whom you have to split?"

"He is," said Veight, and paused, listening intently. Then like a flash he crossed the room and flung open the door.

"What are you doing here?" he snarled.

"Tidying up, sare," came the aggrieved voice of a waiter.

"Then get out, damn you. This place is quite tidy already. My apologies, gentlemen," he said, coming back into the room, "but in my work one develops a sort of sixth sense. And tidying up can cover a multitude of keyholes."

CHAPTER 10

"Such was the situation," continued Veight as he resumed his seat, when Gregoroff got into touch with me. He did that for two reasons. First it struck him that it would probably not be a one-man job; and secondly because I have worked in England and knew the ropes far better than he did. And the instant I heard what he had to tell me I threw over everything else on the spot.

"The problem that confronted us was obvious; the solution was not. This man Waldron was a bachelor, living in a small house on the outskirts of Surbiton. He had one old woman servant who did all the work of the house. Further – and this was important – he was of independent means, and did no work beyond his chemical research. If, therefore, it became necessary to abduct him, there would be no office from which he would be missed and which would start a hue and cry. And it seemed to us, when we discussed the matter in Amsterdam, that in all probability abduction would be necessary.

"Our reasoning was as follows. Here was a presumably patriotic Englishman, since he was serving in their Territorial army, and a man of sufficient wealth to do no work. It was therefore very improbable that we should be able to bribe him, especially as he would realise that we were both foreigners. Moreover, if we attempted to and failed, it would at once put him on his guard. And so we decided that our only chance was this. Study the house, study his ways, and at a suitable moment visit him with the definite intention of knocking him on the head and removing him to some safe place where suasion, moral and otherwise, could be brought to bear on him. Which necessitated our finding a suitable *pied à terre*. An hotel or lodgings were obviously out of the question: it had to be a private house.

"And there I came in. During the course of that little job I did for you, m'sieur, I had come across a certain Doctor Belfage. He was an unpleasant little specimen, but he was a prominent member of the Key Club. And since then I had heard that he had got into trouble and had had his name removed from the medical register. But what was important from our point of view was that he had a house near Cambridge which was most eminently suitable for our purpose. It contained a central room which was practically soundproof, which the doctor used as a laboratory, and which would form an admirable prison for this man Waldron should he prove obdurate. That settled, we crossed to England by a route not usually taken by passengers, and successfully eluded the authorities. Gregoroff, in particular, might have had considerable difficulty in landing.

"The first thing to do was to get in touch with Belfage, and I travelled up to Cambridge while Gregoroff lay low in London. And there we got our first setback: the doctor had let his house and was living elsewhere. But though I didn't say anything at the time, I wondered very much who and what this man Meredith, who had taken the house, might be. I was tolerably convinced, shall we put it, that he had never been a candidate for Holy orders. However, he gave me the doctor's address, and I left him.

"The doctor, I am afraid," continued Veight, "was not overjoyed at seeing me. But on my reminding him of a certain incident in his past he decided it would be better to overcome his reluctance and give me some of his valuable time. And so we adjourned to his study.

" 'Still a member of the Key Club,' I remarked on seeing the badge in his coat. 'I hear you've had a little trouble with the medical authorities, Doctor.'

" 'Purely professional,' he assured me. 'What can I do for you, Herr Veight?'

" 'I wanted the temporary loan of your other house, Doctor,' I said. 'Who is that man Meredith who has it?'

"A glance at his face told me that I had taped Meredith correctly, and we both fenced for a while. Then I took the bull by the horns and told him what I wanted.

"Gentlemen, I don't think I have ever seen a man look so completely dumbfounded. He positively goggled at me.

" 'Waldron!' he stuttered. 'Waldron! What do you know about Waldron?'

" 'Evidently just what you do,' I said. 'I want the secret of that gas, and I'm going to have the secret of that gas. Do we work together or do we not? Waldron has got to be made to speak. Are you going to help me, or do I work on my own?'

" 'What do you propose to do?' he asked at length.

" 'That, at present, is nothing to do with you,' I answered. 'But this much I will tell you. I know his address in Surbiton, and he is going to be put through the hoop.'

" 'You propose to abduct him?' he said.

" 'Put it that way if you like,' I remarked.

" 'Then there's mighty little good your going to Surbiton,' said the doctor.

" 'Why not?' I cried.

" 'Because you won't find him there. He's been abducted already.'

"Well, m'sieur, it was my turn to do a bit of goggling now; it was the last remark I'd expected. Somebody had got in in front of us. Who was it? I dismissed the possibility of his lying; the matter was so very simple to verify. So I let him talk, and it soon became obvious he wanted to get rid of me.

" 'I fear, therefore, there is no good your wasting your time, Herr Veight,' was the line he took up.

" 'Don't worry about my time, Doctor,' I said. 'I'll look after that end of the business myself. Am I to understand that this man Waldron is being held a prisoner by the Key Club?'

"It took some time for him to answer; in fact, gentlemen, everything to start with had to be dragged out of him with a corkscrew. Bat after a while he admitted that that was the case. Waldron had been a captive for more than ten days.

" 'In order to make him reveal the formula of his gas, or to prevent him making any more?' I asked.

" 'In order to get the formula,' said the doctor. 'There is one step in the process known only to him.'

" 'And when you have the formula, what is your next move?' I remarked.

"He hesitated and stammered, and finally stated that the next move would be what the rules of the Key Club ordered. The secret would be passed on to everyone interested.

"Well, m'sieur, I knew that was their rule, but I also knew my doctor. He had pocketed a wad over the Guiseppi affair, and I couldn't see him in the role of an altruist. So I tackled him fair and square.

" 'Are you a liar or are you a fool?' I asked. 'For you must be one or the other.'

"He wasn't offended. As you must have guessed by now, he's a pretty poor specimen. So when he found I wasn't going to be bluffed he came out with the whole thing. And a very pretty little business it was.

"By some ruse or other Waldron had been decoyed to the house where he was now held prisoner. This house belonged to a man called Hoskins who, the doctor informed me, was a genuine Key Club idealist, and a man whom no one would suspect for an instant of anything crooked. A telegram had been sent to the servant saying that he would be away for a few weeks, and during that period the secret was to be extracted. Then Waldron would be free to go.

"What was going to happen to Mr Hoskins when Waldron went to the police about it was entirely Hoskins' affair. And according to the doctor, Hoskins was such a complete fanatic that he wouldn't mind.

" 'And where, my dear Doctor,' I remarked at this juncture, 'do you come in? You most certainly are not a complete fanatic, and I can't see you going to prison for the doubtful pleasure of passing the secret of this gas on to the nations at large. Can it be possible that you are hoping somehow or other to get away with the formula yourself and pass it on to *one* nation?'

"And it was obvious that that was exactly what he had been hoping to do. He hadn't made any definite plan, but that was what the little rat had in his mind.

" 'Excellent,' I said. 'We now know where we stand. And since this thing is much too big for you to handle on your own, think how lucky you are that you now have me to help you. Is Waldron at that house of yours near Cambridge?'

"No, he was not. He was at a house called Horsebridge, belonging to Hoskins.

" 'What,' I demanded, 'is the exact place in the jigsaw filled by the Cambridge house?'

"It was to act as an alternative prison in case Waldron was traced at Horsebridge.

"Who was Meredith?

"Meredith was a gentleman with a pretty taste in handwriting, who would come in useful if any letters had to be written purporting to come from Waldron.

"Did Hoskins know that he was consorting with a forger, amongst other people? Hoskins believed Meredith to be truly repentant, and anxious to do his bit in the great cause. 'But where and how,' I persisted, 'do you propose to double-cross Hoskins?

If Waldron is persuaded to tell his secret there is only one possible method of doing so. You've got to murder him.'

"No; a thousand times – no. Nothing of the sort. He was quite pained at the mere thought.

" 'Then what is your idea?' I cried furiously. 'You're not a half-wit. Unless you murder Hoskins, how can you prevent him passing on this formula?'

"He looked everywhere except at me, until I could have struck the little devil. And finally I issued an ultimatum. I told him that unless he was absolutely frank with me, I would send an anonymous communication to Scotland Yard giving the whole thing away. It was bluff, of course; if the miserable worm had called it I hadn't a leg to stand on. But he didn't.

"I wonder, m'sieur, if I might have a glass of that excellent wine. Much talking is making me dry. And I am now coming to the *bonne bouche*. Thank you a thousand times."

Veight drained his glass, and replaced it on the table.

"The *bonne bouche*, gentlemen. Doctor Belfage was far from being a half-wit. I told you. did I not, that I had two military secrets to sell you. You have heard the first; I am now coming to the second. Have you ever heard of the Graham Caldwell aeroplane?"

"No," said Kalinsky. "I have not."

"Nor had I until that day. And very few people have heard of it at all. Working in an almost inaccessible part of the Highlands is a young Scotch engineer. He is apparently a genius on aeronautical construction, and he has been experimenting on a machine of his own which is as much in advance of any existing aeroplane as the present-day car is in advance of the previous type. His staff consists of two or three fitters and one trusted mechanic. It is a private enterprise without Government support, so there are no troops or anything of that sort guarding the place. And it was on this spot in Scotland that the doctor really had his eye fixed.

"The information came from one of the fitters, who was a humble member of the Key Club. And if one-half of what this man reported was true, the performance of the machine was simply incredible. I am no expert in flying, but even I was impressed by what I heard. A few final details still remained to be perfected; then the plans of the machine would be complete. And the doctor was waiting till that was done before striking.

" 'Does Hoskins know of this?' I asked him.

"He did not.

" 'What, then,' I said to Belfage, 'is your plan?'

"It was a simple one. When Waldron had been abducted one small cylinder of his gas, and only one, had been found in his laboratory. And this had been removed, and was in the house at the moment. The doctor's idea was to wait till the plans of the aeroplane were finished, and then go to Scotland with the cylinder. The fitter would introduce it into Graham Caldwell's office, and while the inventor and his mechanic were powerless, Belfage would steal the plans. He would then offer them to the highest bidder. If in addition to that he could get away with the secret of the gas as well, so much the better. But it was clear that he attached far greater value to the former."

"One moment," said Kalinsky. "Did this man Hoskins not realise that this cylinder was in existence? Because if he did, since publicity was all he desired, all he had to do was to have the gas analysed by an expert, and publish the result."

"Exactly, m'sieur. That point occurred to me. And that is why Doctor Belfage had not mentioned the cylinder at all. He had realised how valuable it would be to him with Graham Caldwell, and so, fearing Hoskins would do just what you said, he had lain low about it."

"So, Herr Veight," said Morgenstein, "if I understand you aright, the situation when you first came into the matter some – "

"Four weeks ago."

"Some four weeks ago, was as follows. Waldron was a prisoner in Hoskins' house at Horsebridge, where efforts were being made to compel him to reveal the secret of this gas. Unknown to Hoskins this doctor had the secret in his possession."

"He had the cylinder, Herr Morgenstein, but he did not know what the contents were."

"Quite; quite. He had the cylinder, but he could not find out what the contents were without wasting them. And once they were wasted they could no longer be used against Graham Caldwell."

"Exactly," said Veight.

"Since, however, the final plans of the aeroplane were not yet finished, Doctor Belfage in conjunction presumably with that other man you mentioned – "

"Meredith."

"Meredith was playing a waiting game, until the time was ripe to strike. They would then get the plans of the aeroplane which Hoskins knew nothing about; and, if they could – though that was a secondary matter – get the secret of the gas to themselves."

"Exactly," repeated Veight. "You have given the situation in a nutshell."

"And what, might I ask, Herr Veight, was your reaction to this little scheme?"

"In the words of the homely English idiom, Herr Morgenstein, it struck me that it was money for jam. In fact, beyond playing a waiting game there was nothing for Gregoroff and me to do. That the worthy doctor's ideas on who lived and died might have to be changed a little, was neither here nor there. Also it was advisable for him not to know that he was going to get very little out of it himself: it might have damped his ardour. He could not, of course, give either Gregoroff or me away to the police, without giving himself away at the same time. And so I suggested that he should introduce us to the imbecile Hoskins as two fanatical members of the Key Club from abroad, and that we should take up our residence either at Horsebridge or his house near Cambridge.

"It was to Horsebridge that we finally went. And a few words about the house itself would not be out of place. Originally it must have been the fortified keep of some medieval baron. Made of thick stone, it was completely surrounded by water, and the only means of communication with the shore was by way of a drawbridge. The old dungeons still existed, dank and mildewed, though they were shut off from the rest of the house, which was warm and modernised. And in these dungeons Mr Hoskins, the idealist, had confined Waldron.

"Well, gentlemen, it takes a good deal to surprise me, but I must confess that that man Hoskins had me guessing. We all know that a fanatic in any shape or form is capable of refinements of cruelty which would make a savage blush. One has only got to remember the crimes that have been committed in the name of religion. But Mr Hoskins won in a canter.

"In appearance he looks a most saintly creature. His hair is white; his features are ascetic. He walks with a slight stoop, and wears pince-nez. In short, he looks like the conventional ideal of a country clergyman.

"He welcomed us effusively; his gullibility was almost incredible. Everything that Belfage told him about us he swallowed; we were brothers with him in the great faith.

" 'Stay as long as you like,' he said. 'This creature Waldron is stubborn; he refuses to speak. In fact I sometimes think that it may be necessary to kill him. Better, far better, that one man should die, rather than thousands be murdered by his infamous discovery. I have tried to make him see reason; I have explained to him our ideals. But he is stiff-necked; he persists in harping on the fact that he is an Englishman, and that his vile gas is for England's use and hers only. He even has the audacity to call me a traitor. But I do not fear the ultimate result; there is no man yet who has ever survived the ordeal. The drug is infallible.'

" 'What are you doing, Mr Hoskins?' I asked, and even as I spoke a swarthy black-haired man entered the room.

" 'Tell them, Cortez,' said Hoskins. 'They are of our order. Tell them of the drug that breaks the strongest nerve.'

"The newcomer stared at us suspiciously; there was nothing gullible about him. Then he whispered something in the old man's ear, who shook his head vehemently.

" 'No; no,' he cried. 'They are of our order. Tell them.'

"The man called Cortez shrugged his shoulders.

" 'Marijuana,' he said in a surly tone. 'A Mexican drug.'

"And Gregoroff whistled under his breath."

Veight paused and lit a cigarette.

"Gentlemen," be continued, "it was a new one on me, but not on Gregoroff. Known to drug addicts as Mary Jane, its effects are literally terrible. As a general rule it is made into cigarettes, but it can also be administered subcutaneously. And after a while it reduces a man to such a pitiful condition of nerves that he ceases to be a man. He becomes a gibbering wreck, scared out of his life by the slightest trifle. His brain refuses to act; terror of he knows not what holds him in its grip, until in the end he puts a bullet through his brain or else ends up in a lunatic asylum. And this was the drug that the saintly Mr Hoskins was administering daily to Waldron.

"It was in every way an ideal prison. Hoskins was respected and liked in the neighbourhood; save for this one strange streak he was a charming old gentleman. And so he was the last man who would incur suspicion should a hue and cry be raised for Waldron. At the same time every precaution was taken to prevent discovery. The drawbridge was raised every night at sunset, and not lowered till the following morning; the tradesmen left their goods in the courtyard in front of the house. And so far as we could tell, nobody had an inkling of what was occurring. Waldron's relatives, if he had any, were evidently not worrying; the faked telegram had kept the servants quiet. Which left Gregoroff and I plenty of time to arrange our plans.

"One thing we soon found out: the Mexican, Cortez, had to be reckoned with. He was under no delusions concerning us, and he told us so quite candidly. A nuisance, but one that could not be helped, and he is one person who will have to be squared when the time comes. But he did not affect our scheme, which, in brief, was the same as the doctor's. With one or two small additions – additions we did not pass on to Belfage.

"We proposed to allow him to get the Graham Caldwell plans when the time was ripe, by using his cylinder of gas. We intended to accompany him, and if by any unfortunate chance a fire should take place while the men were powerless in the office, and after the plans had been removed, it would doubtless be attributed to natural causes. In fact we proposed that two fires should take place, the other being the hangar containing the machine itself."

"Good," said Kalinsky softly. "Very good. And the worthy doctor?"

Veight smiled faintly.

"Would not, I think, be missed. They are dangerous roads, m'sieur, and lonely roads in that part of Scotland. No, I think the doctor would not be missed. Then having got the plans, we proposed to return to Horsebridge – you remember, do you not, that Hoskins knows nothing about the aeroplane – and obtain the secret of the gas if we had not done so already. Such, briefly, was our intention."

"You speak in the past, Veight," said Kalinsky. "Is it not your intention now?"

For a moment or two Veight hesitated. Up till now he knew he had held his listeners; it was vital that he should continue to do so.

"M'sieur – I am going to be perfectly frank with you," he remarked. "Four days ago a most annoying thing happened. You have, of course, appreciated the essential importance of keeping Waldron's presence in Horsebridge a secret. Judge then of our dismay when Gregoroff while walking in the courtyard one evening suddenly recognised a man who was fiddling about with the mechanism of the drawbridge as a British Secret Service man, whom he had last seen in Warsaw. He acted at once. He is a man of immense physical strength, and the road outside was deserted. So he hit the so-called workman over the back of the head with a stick he was carrying; stunned him and dragged him into the house. Then we held a council of war.

"What had happened was unfortunately only too obvious. This man, whose name is Lovelace and who is an officer in the English Army, must have spotted Gregoroff in Warsaw at the time when he was finding out about the gas. Suspecting something, he had followed Gregoroff to England, and by some means or other had got on his track again. It seemed to us that Lovelace must have lost him to start with, otherwise we should have had the police on our heels before. In fact we hoped, and as things have since turned out hoped rightly, that we had got him in time. Nothing had so far been passed on. But we were confronted with the situation of having a British Secret Service man a prisoner in the house. Waldron was on the verge of cracking; and we had received information from Scotland that another three days would see the plans completed. And then this had come out of the blue.

"The first thing to decide was what to do with Lovelace. To kill him was far too dangerous; besides, Hoskins wouldn't hear of it. Moreover, there was no place to keep him prisoner, except the dungeon where Waldron was, which again did not suit us. And so we decided to take him to the doctor's other house, and put him in the central room there.

"We waited till it was dark; then, having given him something to keep him quiet, I started off by car with a fellow-countryman of mine and another man as guards. And on the way we ran into dense fog.

"Well, gentlemen, I will not weary you with a long story. Suffice it to say that Lovelace, having partially recovered from the drug, managed to give us the slip while we were creeping along through the mist. I had one shot and wounded him, but before we finally caught him again he had succeeded in throwing a stone with a message wrapped round it through the lighted window of a cottage. And that is what has caused the bother. For the message was found by the owner of the cottage, a man of the name of Drummond, who proceeded to make an unmitigated nuisance of himself."

"What was the message?" demanded Kalinsky.

"Gibberish; complete gibberish," said Veight. "In fact I would not have bored you with all this, seeing that everything is quite satisfactorily settled now, but for one thing. Drummond, as I say, became most troublesome, and collected three other men round him. They knew nothing, but they were becoming very inquisitive. And so it was necessary to take steps to stop them. They were all armed; they were all tough customers. However, by means of a simple ruse they were all four inveigled into the central room in the doctor's house. And there we had to waste Waldron's gas on them."

"Why?" said Morgenstein.

Veight smiled grimly.

"Because, gentlemen, from my knowledge of human nature, Drummond is a man I would prefer not to talk to if he has the full use of his limbs and a gun in his pocket. To a lesser degree the same applies to the other three."

"Did the gas work?" asked Kalinsky.

"Marvellously; marvellously. It is all Waldron claims for it. But – there is no more. That is the point."

"My dear Veight," remarked Kalinsky curtly, "that is not our affair. Why do you worry us with these details?"

"Because, m'sieur," said Veight quietly, "I take it that the plans of the Graham Caldwell aeroplane will be more valuable to you if England is not in a position to have them redrawn."

"Well?" snapped Kalinsky.

"While we still had the gas it would have been possible to ensure that result, and make it appear an accident. Now that is out of the question. It can only be murder plain and unadorned."

Kalinsky shrugged his shoulders.

"I am not increasing my offer," he said.

"And I am not asking you to, m'sieur," answered Veight. "But I am asking for a certain amount on account. I have a very wholesome regard for the English police, and I have no wish whatever to give their hangman a job. I must have money to make my plans, and ensure a safe getaway."

"You say this message was gibberish," said Kalinsky. "What do you mean by that? Why should anyone take the trouble to send a meaningless message?"

"It may have been a code, m'sieur. At any rate we could make nothing of it."

"Perhaps not. But what about this man Drummond? He may have solved the code."

Veight smiled grimly.

"It doesn't matter much if he has. He and his friends have been prisoners for three days in the room I told you of. The house is shut up and empty; the room is soundproof. I fear they may be getting a little hungry, but that can't be helped."

"And where is this secret-service man you wounded?"

"At Horsebridge. He is unconscious, and so can be safely left in one of the ordinary bedrooms. I can assure you, gentlemen," continued Veight, "that everything is exactly as it was before this regrettable *contretemps* occurred, save that we no longer have the

166

gas to help us. It is therefore for you to decide. Do you wish there to be no chance of the plans being duplicated?"

At a sign from Kalinsky, Morgenstein rose, and the two financiers withdrew to the window, where they conferred in low tones. And Veight watched them anxiously, though his face was expressionless. What were they going to say?

He had told them the exact position of affairs quite truthfully. But he knew – none better – that men of their type did not advance money on mere promises. And yet it was essential that he should have some, if he and Gregoroff were going to escape from the country.

He lit a cigarette to soothe himself: the last three days had been trying ones. Present always had been the fear that Drummond and his friends had found out about Horsebridge, and had handed the information on before they were made prisoners. Then as the time passed and the police still left them alone, that fear had gradually died. But the atmosphere remained.

Doctor Belfage had completely lost his nerve: the Drummond episode had finished him. Only a ceaseless application to the bottle had kept him going, and even then it had been unsafe to leave him alone for fear that he might give everything away in a sudden access of terror. And Cortez had been a trouble. And Meredith. In fact the whole gang gathered together at Horsebridge had been suffering from suspicionitis. Nobody trusted anybody else; the only point on which they all combined was in continuing to fool Hoskins. After that the trouble started.

Meredith, in particular, had been showing his teeth. From the first he had resented the appearance of two foreigners, though until the *affaire* Drummond he had not shown it openly. But since then he had taken no pains to conceal his belief that Gregoroff and Veight himself were playing a double game. Which, in view of the fact that it was perfectly true, had not helped matters.

The girl, too, Doris Venables, had proved a complication. Even now he did not know where she came in; it had been necessary to keep her permanently under the influence of drugs in her room in Horsebridge to prevent any chance of her screaming. And it had all increased the nervous tension. Only Hoskins himself seemed impervious to it: he was too occupied torturing Waldron to bother about anything else.

He came out of his reverie; Kalinsky was speaking.

"I will tell you what we have decided, Veight. You will appreciate that we have no means whatever of testing what you have told us. We have to rely entirely on your word. At the same time, neither Herr Morgenstein nor I think it likely that you would be so very foolish as to waste our time with a tissue of falsehoods. So we will assume that everything is as you have said."

Veight bowed; this sounded a promising beginning.

"That being the case," continued Kalinsky, "the whole problem boils down to whether or not you can deliver the goods, and further if the goods, when delivered, are what you claim for them. Will five thousand pounds be enough for your immediate needs?"

"Ample, m'sieur," said Veight.

"Good; you shall have it. And that we will regard as over and above the rest of the money, and not as a payment on account."

"You are generous, gentlemen. I thank you."

"On receipt by us of the tracings of the aeroplane and the formula of the gas you will receive ten thousand pounds out of the fifty we have agreed on. When we have satisfied ourselves that they are of real value you will receive a further fifteen, making twenty-five thousand in all. Do I make myself clear?"

"Perfectly, m'sieur," said Veight slowly.

"The remaining twenty-five thousand, Veight," continued Kalinsky, "will not be handed over until we have indisputable proof that we and we alone hold those two secrets. There may be duplicate plans of the aeroplane already in existence; the formula of the gas may be known to someone else. If so, the removal of the people concerned will not avail much – but that is your affair. If, on the contrary, no duplicates already exist, then the removal of the people concerned will solve the question. That again is your affair. So my offer can be summed up in short. Five thousand for current expenses; ten for the delivery of the goods; fifteen when the goods are proved satisfactory, and a final twenty-five when it is proved we have a monopoly. Do you agree?"

"There is one point that occurs to me, m'sieur. Supposing we have a partial success. Supposing, for instance, the plans of the aeroplane become your monopoly, but the formula of the gas is known elsewhere. What then?"

"You would receive half. In the case you have mentioned, instead of receiving the final twenty-five thousand you would receive twelve and a half."

Veight rose to his feet.

"Gentlemen, I accept. In a case of this sort we have to trust one another. You are trusting me to the extent of fifteen thousand pounds; I am trusting you for the remaining forty, or whatever may be due. You will be here, m'sieur, for some days?"

"In all probability. If not, you know the permanent address in Paris that always finds me."

"Then I will bid you goodnight, gentlemen. You will hear from me in the course of four days at the outside."

With a bow he left the room and walked along the corridor towards the lift. Taking everything into account, he felt well satisfied with his evening's work, and his brain was already busy as to the best means of still further lining his own pocket. He shrewdly guessed that the two men he had just left were planning war at an early date, and inside information of that sort could be profitably used.

For a few moments he stood outside the swing doors watching young London arrive to revel. Mere girls and boys – happy and carefree, with healthy appetites and tireless legs. What would they be thinking in a few months' time?

"*Ein wunderschöner Abend, Herr Veight,*" came a voice from behind him.

He swung round as if he had been shot. Who had spoken to him about the evening? But all he saw was a superb being in a gorgeous uniform, surrounded by bevies of lovely girls and their attendant swains.

"A taxi, sir?" said the superb being politely.

"No," snarled Veight. And then, obeying a sudden impulse, he added: "Did you hear anyone speak to me in German?"

The superb being raised his eyebrows.

"German, sir? Really. Most peculiar, sir."

With another snarl Emil Veight turned on his heel and strode into the Strand. For though the words were German, the accent had been English.

CHAPTER 11

He hailed a taxi and gave the name of his hotel. But, try as he would, he could not get the incident out of his head. Emil Veight was the last person in the world to court publicity, and at the moment he was particularly anxious to blush unseen. But the fact remained that someone had recognised him as he left the Ritz-Carlton. Whom could it have been?

The police he dismissed as unlikely: no one in the group had looked in the slightest degree like a plain-clothes man. A secret service agent was a more probable solution: he was pretty well known amongst that fraternity. And, if so, it would require no great astuteness on the speaker's part to connect his visit with Kalinsky.

He frowned; the whole thing was annoying, coming as it had on top of his very successful interview with the two financiers. He felt justifiably aggrieved about it. And then an idea struck him, and he peered cautiously through the little window at the back of the taxi.

His hotel was a quiet one north of the Park, and the street behind him was deserted. It was an ideal spot from which to see if he was being followed, and he signalled to his driver to stop. But though he waited a full minute no one came in sight, and at length he told the man to drive on. Whoever it was who had spoken to him was evidently no longer interested. And he began to wonder if he had not unduly exaggerated the significance of the incident.

A fast open car was drawn up outside the hotel, and Veight glanced at it in some surprise. From what he had seen of his fellow-guests a hearse would have seemed a more suitable vehicle, but the mystery was solved as he entered the lounge. Seated in an armchair was the gigantic figure of Paul Gregoroff. And it was obvious at once that the Russian had something important to say.

"Have you got a sitting-room," he asked, "where we shan't be disturbed?"

"It's perfectly safe here," answered Veight. "No one sits up in this place after ten. What's brought you up to London?"

"Have you seen the evening papers?" cried Gregoroff.

"I have not."

"Then read that."

The Russian pointed to a paragraph and Veight ran his eyes down it. Then with a whistle of surprise he read it more closely.

COUNTRY HOUSE GUTTED BY FIRE
SCARCITY OF WATER HINDERS FIREMEN

From our Special Correspondent. Cambridge.

Yet another country house must be added to the list of those that have recently been destroyed by fire. Hartley Court, a largish residence standing in its own grounds, about three miles from Cambridge, was completely gutted in the early hours of this morning. Two fire brigades which were soon on the spot found their efforts hindered by the lack of water due to the recent drought.

The reason of the outbreak is obscure, as the house had been empty for some days. And this fact also permitted the flames to get such a hold before they were seen from a cottage on the other side of the road that, even had the water supply been adequate, but little could have been done. There seems no doubt that defective electric wiring, resulting in a short circuit, must have been the cause of the trouble.

Some excitement was occasioned by the discovery of human bones in the ruins. But it transpired that the owner, Doctor Belfage, had some complete skeletons in his laboratory which he used for lecturing purposes.

Veight put the paper down on the table and lit a cigarette.

"How does this affect us?" he remarked thoughtfully.

"Up to date it hasn't," said Gregoroff; "but that's not saying that it won't. Everything depends on how long the yarn about the skeletons holds good."

"Belfage put that up, did he?"

"On my instigation. The instant I heard about the fire I realised this complication would occur, and it is quite natural for a doctor to have some in his house."

"Why shouldn't it continue to hold good?"

"However fierce the fire, and I gather it was an absolute inferno, there are bound to be some traces left besides the actual skeletons. At least I should imagine so."

"Trapped as they were in that room, it seems possible to me that the process would be pretty thorough. However, that is beside the point. Let us assume that you are right. What then?"

"To start with, Meredith will undoubtedly split on us if he finds himself in any trouble. Up to date he has kept out of the way, and Belfage has done the talking. But once the insurance people come on the scene Meredith will have to appear."

"Even if he does, what is he going to say? Unless he is completely insane he must stick to our original story and profess entire ignorance of anybody having been left in the house. Burglars who inadvertently shut themselves into that room would be a plausible theory."

"Supposing something is found which identifies the bodies, such as a cigarette case?"

"Once again – entire ignorance. The house was shut up after the meeting of the Key Club – the tradesmen can confirm that – and he has absolutely no idea what has happened since. And there's one thing you can be sure of. Any story they may have written down on paper will have been destroyed."

"There's something in what you say," said Gregoroff slowly. "At the same time, I wish it had happened after we were clear away. If Meredith can queer our pitch he will."

"On that point I certainly agree with you," said Veight. "He and that damned little quitter of a doctor have got to be watched. To say nothing of Cortez. And it's on that very matter that you and I have got to come to a decision. I've seen Kalinsky; Morgenstein was with him."

"Satisfactory?"

"Very. Five thousand for current expenses; fifty when they handle the goods, provided – "

"Provided what?" said Gregoroff softly as the eyes of the two men met.

"There is no chance of anyone else handling them."

"Just as we thought," remarked Gregoroff. "Damn Drummond and his friends! That gas would have been invaluable."

"There's no good worrying about that now," said Veight. "What we have got to decide on is a plan of campaign, and it's not going to be too easy."

He pulled up a chair closer to Gregoroff and lowered his voice, though the lounge was quite deserted.

"Let us first of all eliminate the impossible. What I would have liked to have done would have been for you and me to have gone on our own to Scotland after the aeroplane plans. But there is no object in discussing that. If we attempted it Meredith would communicate anonymously with the police. And I know Scotland – particularly the Highlands. I did some work there in 1914. Those cursed Scotchmen can spot a foreigner a mile off, and they don't like us. It is equally impossible for us to let them go on their own. They would either bungle the whole thing and put the inventor on his guard, or else they would disappear with the plans. So we've got to go together. Do you agree?"

"I do," said Gregoroff.

"Let us go a bit farther. Meredith is only after the tracings; we, on the other hand, want rather more than that. And the point we have to decide is the best method of getting rid of Graham Caldwell and his assistants without being suspected ourselves."

"Meredith and the doctor may have to go too," put in Gregoroff.

"They may, and nothing would please me more than if they did. But we've got to think of ourselves, my friend. You can't get away with things in this country as easily as on the Continent. And what I am wondering is this: Would it be possible to dispose of Graham Caldwell and his man in such a way that Meredith and the rest of his precious brood get run for murder?"

The Russian stared at him.

"That's a grand idea if it can be worked," he said at length. "But can it?"

"I believe it can," answered Veight. "Always provided one thing – that we get the two of them to Horsebridge."

"I don't quite follow you," said Gregoroff.

"While we had the gas, as I explained to Kalinsky, their death up in Scotland could be attributed to accident. As you know, our plan was based on that. Now it can't be; at least it wouldn't be safe to rely on it. Now we are agreed that they have to be killed, and we are agreed that it is necessary for us to go there ourselves. Now you, my dear Gregoroff, are not exactly an inconspicuous member of the society, and I have already mentioned that I know something about the inhabitants of the district. And since it would be out of the question for us to avoid being seen, the result is obvious. With one accord they would connect you, and through you, me, with any murder, however skilfully it was done. The very loneliness of the place doubles the difficulties. Within five minutes of the thing being discovered every policeman in Scotland would be on the lookout for us. Which would prove singularly awkward when the plans of the machine were found in our possession."

"Very true," admitted Gregoroff.

"I have therefore come to the definite conclusion that by far our best chance of success – I go further, our only chance of success – lies in getting these two men to Horsebridge."

"And how the devil do you propose to do that, seeing that it is the one thing Belfage and Meredith don't want? Their whole idea is to keep that fool Hoskins from knowing anything about the aeroplane."

"They must be made to want it," said Veight calmly. "And it can be done by pointing out to them the vital importance of keeping the airman's mouth shut while negotiations for selling the plans are in progress. What does it matter if Hoskins does know? I admit that before we used the gas we were not going to tell him. But now that is all changed. And, as I say, what does it matter if he does know? The only plans will be in our possession. Let the old man think what he likes. We can pretend to have copies made for distribution to every government. That will keep him quiet. To Meredith we can pretend that we are only waiting for Waldron to speak, when both secrets can be sold to the highest bidder."

"And then? What then?"

Veight leaned even closer to the Russian.

"Have you ever heard of adrenalin?"

Gregoroff shook his head.

"Adrenalin," continued Veight, "is used for asthma. I know, because I suffer from it at times myself, and I always carry a supply with me. And it has one very strange property. Though quite harmless when taken in the proper way, it causes death if it is injected into a vein. Now it will be necessary to keep the two airmen under the influence of drugs to prevent them raising a disturbance, which will be Belfage's job as usual. And my suggestion is quite simple. When we have got what we want we will kill both of them and Waldron by giving them an injection of adrenalin. The fact that the doctor is more or less permanently drunk is all to the good. He will think he has killed them by giving them an overdose of morphia. And then, my dear Gregoroff, we will fade rapidly out of the picture, leaving the dear doctor and the rest of the crowd to explain away three dead men as best they may."

"But it is a marvellous scheme!" cried the Russian with genuine admiration. "It is sheer genius."

"I flatter myself," said Veight complacently, "that it has a certain merit. Small unforeseen details are, of course, bound to crop up, but we must deal with them as they arise. In the main, however, I think the scheme is workable."

"Eminently so," said Gregoroff. "I congratulate you most heartily. There is, however, one point that occurs to me. How do you propose to get Graham Caldwell and his mechanic to Horsebridge? They will have to be drugged, and the sight of two unconscious men in a motorcar travelling through the country will be apt to cause some comment."

Veight rubbed his hands together.

"Once again, my friend, I think I have solved your difficulty. The English, as you know, are a peculiar race, and at this time of year many of them are in the habit of attaching to the backs of their cars a strange-looking contraption on two wheels called a caravan. In this they tour the country, eating tinned foods and living in the height of discomfort. But what could be better suited to our purpose? In the first place it supplies a *raison d'être* for our going to the Highlands at all. We are tourists – sightseeing. In the second place, it supplies an admirable hiding-place for our prisoners. There are two bunks, and curtains which can be drawn, so that one can drive with absolute safety through the largest towns, with both of them inside."

"Upon my word, Veight, it is a pleasure to work with you," cried Gregoroff. "So far as I can see, the scheme is as nearly fool-proof as it is possible to make it."

"Two heads are better than one," said Veight. "If you can see any flaws, mention them."

"How do we do our final getaway?"

"Private machine and fly," answered Veight without hesitation. "There's an aerodrome not twenty miles from Horsebridge. We'll deliver the stuff to Kalinsky in Paris."

"I suppose there is no chance of him double-crossing us?"

Veight shrugged his shoulders.

"All I can say is that I don't think so. He's too big a man to make it worth his while. I certainly have never heard of him letting an agent down."

He got up, rubbing his hands together.

"Don't fear: he will pay up if we give him the goods. And unless something entirely unforeseen occurs we can't fail. Drummond and his damned friends are dead; Lovelace is helpless, and the Venables girl..." He paused. "That young woman is a bit of an enigma. I can't make out where she fits in."

Gregoroff laughed coarsely.

"Not for want of trying, from what I've seen of you," he remarked. "And as for that fool Meredith, he eats out of her hand."

Veight looked at him through narrowed eyes.

"Don't fall into that error, Gregoroff. I have never been in the habit of letting a woman interfere with business. And I repeat, I can't make out where she comes in. Ostensibly she is an enthusiastic member of the Key Club. But what is she really? Was it, as Meredith maintains, just feminine curiosity that sent her back to that cottage? Or is she in their secret service?"

"In either event it doesn't seem to me to matter much," said the Russian. "She's safely under the influence of dope and will remain in that condition until we are clear of the country. And after that it doesn't matter a kopeck who or what she is. What is far more to the point is what happened at your interview this evening. I must be going soon, and so far you've only given me the barest details."

For a few moments Veight was silent; then, sinking his voice, he uttered one word – "War."

"Did they say so definitely?" cried the other eagerly.

"My dear Gregoroff," said Veight, "the Kalinskys and Morgensteins of this world very rarely say things definitely. But I waited a little before actually entering their room, and I heard one or two of their remarks. And even had I not done so the thing is obvious. We both know quite enough to realise how matters stand in Europe today. And the only doubtful point was what Kalinsky was going to do about it. Tonight's interview has answered that question. He means war, and I believe he means it soon. And that is where you and I can considerably increase that fifty thousand pounds. We may only be small men financially, but when a small man has *certain* inside information he can soon become big."

The Russian nodded.

"That is true," he said.

"Kalinsky is not buying our stuff to frame it. Kalinsky isn't insisting on having the monopoly of it for nothing. Kalinsky is playing deep, and it is up to us to play his tune. And there's one place I shall not be visiting when the music starts – London. There won't be any preliminary orchestra this time. No question of ultimatums expiring in twenty-four hours."

"Which is what these fool English can't believe," remarked Gregoroff.

"My friend, they are incredible. With London a mass of smoking ruins, they would send an indignant note, saying, 'Play the game, you cads: we weren't ready.' "

Gregoroff laughed.

"At the same time," continued Veight, "since we are playing for big stakes ourselves, I would like to be sure that the counters are full value. I don't think there can be a possibility of error, but all the same, I would like to see that aeroplane in action. Even if it is not *all* that has been claimed for it, and all that I told Kalinsky it was, we can still sell the plans to him. But in the jargon of the people who race over here, we shall know the true form of the horse. And that will help us in making our bet."

"I gather they try it out every day," said the Russian.

"Exactly. And I suggest we see it on its trial flights, before we finally destroy it. With my caravan idea it should be easy. We can take our hotel with us to within a couple of miles of the place."

"It's a beautiful idea – that caravan. But you realise Meredith, and probably Cortez as well, will insist on coming with us."

"Of course. Let 'em. I allowed for that. They can do the dirty work," he added with an evil laugh. "If you and I, Gregoroff, are not capable of dealing with those two miserable specimens we'll give up the game for good."

He glanced at his watch.

"I think I'll come back with you tonight to Horsebridge. Not expecting you, I had intended to sleep here and go up tomorrow, but there's nothing to keep me."

"Where are you going to get this caravan?" asked Gregoroff, as Veight rang the bell.

"You can get them all over the place. I'll hire one locally. Let me have my bill," he continued, as a bleary-eyed youth appeared round the corner.

"Bill! You can't 'ave no bill. H'everybody 'as gone to bed."

"Then somebody has to get up, or I shall go without paying it."

"Ho! you would, would yer? Can't go without paying yer bill. Send for the perlice, I will, if yer tries them gaimes wiv me."

Veight turned to the Russian.

"In some ways I would like to be in London on the date we have been discussing," he remarked softly. "You'll send for the police, will you?" he continued to the night porter. "Now I've been here one night. I am still alive because I have eaten no food here. I will therefore pay you for two nights, as it is so late. How much will that be, *schweinhund*?"

" 'Oo are yer calling naimes? Mine's 'Orace."

He hiccoughed loudly.

"Pardon! 'Ad tripe for me supper. Comes back on one like, don't it? Two quid, yer said. Right oh! Suppose it'll be orl right."

He pocketed the notes and shuffled off into a noisome recess under the stairs, from which there emerged a series of devastating explosions, showing that the tripe was still active.

" 'Ere's yer receipt," he said, appearing once more. "Shall I get yer bag?"

"No," said Veight. "All you can do is to get out of sight and hearing. I won't be a moment, Gregoroff: I've a few things to put in. I'll join you in the car."

He went upstairs, and the Russian, lighting a cigarette, went down the steps into the street. It was past two o'clock, and not a soul was in sight. An occasional car flashed past the end of the street along the Bayswater Road, and in a neighbouring basement an amatory cat made music. There was no moon, but in a couple of hours it would be dawn, and it would take him just about that time to reach Horsebridge.

He got into the car and started the engine. It was a fast machine, though a good deal slower than the one stolen by Drummond, and as he thought of that episode he cursed under his breath. Even the fact that he had struck the damned Englishman in the face, and that the swine had since died in agony, was not enough. He would have liked to have murdered him personally.

Unlike Emil Veight, who only killed as an absolutely last resource, Paul Gregoroff gloried in it. Beneath a very thin veneer the man was a merciless savage. Human life meant less than nothing to him. Willingly would he have done in the four men in Hartley Court with his own hands, had he not been dissuaded by the others. In fact his readiness to kill was a constant source of anxiety to those with whom he worked. He never seemed to realise that what might be done with impunity in Russia was a very different matter in Western Europe.

With an effort he dismissed Drummond from his mind, and concentrated on the work ahead. He felt a genuine admiration for Veight's scheme, which he readily acknowledged as a masterpiece. Try as he would he could see no flaw in it. There were difficulties which he could see, and unforeseen ones which would almost certainly arise. But in the main the conception was magnificent. Particularly the idea of the caravan. It tickled his sense of humour to think that they would be able to stop and ask a policeman which way to take the two men they were going to murder. And the adrenalin. Very, very good.

"My dear Veight," he said as the German flung his bag in the car and sat down beside him, "once again I congratulate you. I have been thinking it over while I waited for you, and I cannot see any possibility of failure."

"Nor can I," said Veight. "But I'm glad you confirm my opinion. Yes, Gregoroff, my friend, I think we shall be able to retire in the near future. How long will it take us to get there?"

"Two hours. One must admit one point in favour of this country: its roads are wonderful."

Save for an occasional lorry there was no traffic at all. Villages loomed up in the glare of the headlights and fell away behind them as the car ate up the miles. And gradually over the flat country towards the east the dawn began to break.

There was a coolness in the air. Here and there little patches of ground mist lay in the fields, and the smell of damp earth came faintly to their nostrils. And suddenly Veight spoke.

"I remember it like this away back behind the line during the last war."

Gregoroff glanced at him quickly, but did not speak.

"Strange, isn't it," he continued, "that we two are helping to start another. Don't think I'm becoming sentimental," he added with a laugh, "but at moments like this one cannot help marvelling at the congenital idiocy of mankind."

"All the better for us," said Gregoroff cynically.

"Agreed. But one can wonder at a state of affairs even while one profits by it."

"You'll be talking about the happy hours you spent at your mother's knee soon," sneered Gregoroff, and Veight frowned. Unscrupulous blackguard though he was, there was a streak of the genuine artist in him, which at times recoiled with disgust from the crude inhumanity of the Russian. But he said no more and they drove on in silence.

At length, just as they reached the last village before their destination, the sun rose. The actual house was about a mile farther on, and soon it came in sight, standing in its sheet of reed-fringed water. And with it Veight's mood vanished – he was once more the man of action.

"Let's get it clear now, Gregoroff," he said. "We want a few hours' sleep; then we must get down to things. The sooner we get up north the better, so we'll have a conference with Meredith as early as possible. He or Belfage will have to make arrangements for the caravan, and it will be best not to bring it to the house. We don't want old Hoskins to know a minute before it is necessary. In fact he needn't know until we actually come back with the two men. I will fix up the aeroplane for us; if I can't do it in any other way I'll buy one and hire a pilot. I shall say that it is wanted for an important business deal, and that it must be ready to start at a moment's notice."

"We, of course, say nothing about Kalinsky," said Gregoroff, as he backed the car into the garage.

"Good God! no. Are you mad? We hint at a possible buyer, to whom we will go accompanied by Meredith. And it is vital they should know nothing about the aeroplane."

Gregoroff produced a latch-key as they walked over the drawbridge.

"I follow," he said. "I wonder if that damned man Waldron has cracked yet."

He opened the door, and they stepped into the hall. In front of them the staircase led up to a mullioned window through which the sunlight was streaming. In the room to their right the remains of a meal littered the table, and Gregoroff entering poured himself out a whisky and soda.

The house was in complete silence as Veight went up the stairs and he paused by the window to look out. The whole expanse of the mere lay in front of him, and for a while he stood there staring idly across the water. The morning was still : in the undergrowth that stretched down to the edge not a leaf stirred. And he was on the point of going on up to his bedroom when he stiffened. The top of one of the bushes fringing the water had shaken.

"Gregoroff," he called softly. "Gregoroff – come here."

The Russian joined him.

"What's the matter?" he demanded.

"Watch the bank just beyond the waterlogged boat," said Veight, and even as he spoke the bush shook again.

"There's somebody hiding there," he continued softly.

"It might be an animal," said Gregoroff, but Veight shook his head.

"The undergrowth is far too dense for a sheep or a cow," he said. "And only a big animal would make that bush shake. It is a human being. We must go and investigate."

Silently they let themselves out of the front door and crossed the drawbridge. Then they followed the narrow path that skirted the pool. They were screened from view, but progress was slow. In places the path petered out completely and they had to force their way through brambles, but at length Veight, who was leading, held up his hand. They were just abreast of the boat.

They paused, listening intently, but save for the bird chorus they could hear nothing. Then very cautiously, a step at a time, they pushed forward. Suddenly, with an agitated squawk, a moorhen scuttered across the water, and Veight cursed under his breath. Then all its friends followed suit, and the possibility of surprise was gone.

"Come on," said Veight. "Damn those birds."

He pushed forward rapidly, regardless now of noise, with the Russian just behind him.

"Here's the spot," he cried. "It was just beside that coloured shrub. This is the actual bush that was shaking. And," he muttered, gripping Gregoroff's arm, "animals don't eat sandwiches."

On the ground at their feet were the remains of a meal, and they both bent down to examine them. Some ham and bread; the core of an apple; a piece of paper and some string.

"The devil take it," said Veight softly. "That apple core hasn't turned brown yet, so whoever it is he's only just gone."

Once again they stood and listened, and this time in the far distance they heard the noise of someone crashing through the undergrowth; then silence.

"Who the devil can it have been?" said Veight. "Tramps don't eat that sort of sandwich, and a tramp wouldn't have bolted. What's the matter?"

"Look at the house, man; look at the house," Gregoroff was breathing in his ear.

Through an opening in the bushes Veight looked. Leaning out of a top window, staring over the water in their direction, was Doris Venables.

"The girl, by God!" Veight muttered. "This must be dealt with at once."

CHAPTER 12

To all appearances she was fast asleep when they entered the room. The door had been locked as usual with the key on the outside; the window was wide open.

"There's no good shamming, young woman," said Gregoroff harshly. "We know you're not asleep."

There was no answer; only the deep-measured breathing of someone under the influence of drugs.

"If you go on pretending," said Veight, bending over her, "I'll rip the bedclothes off. I thought that would do the trick," he added with a short laugh, as she made an involuntary movement.

"Now, Miss Doris Venables, are you going to be sensible or shall we have to take drastic measures?"

"How dare you come into my room!" she cried furiously. "Go at once."

"Shall we cut out the innocent-virgin stuff?" said Veight calmly. "We are in your room and we intend to stay here until you've answered a few questions, and answered them to our satisfaction."

He bent over and stared into her eyes.

"There's no dope in her at all," he remarked to Gregoroff. "Go and get that miserable bungler Belfage, and bring him here."

"It might be as well, Veight, to question her first. We can get hold of him afterwards."

"All right," agreed the German. "Now, my girl, are you going to stop in bed, or would you prefer to put on a dressing-gown and get up?"

"I'll get up if you'll leave the room."

"We will avert our gaze, Miss Venables," said Veight ironically. "Is this what you want?"

He picked up a wrap lying on a chair, and tossed it on to the bed.

"Now hurry, please; we have no time to waste."

He turned his back, and a moment or two later she spoke.

"What are these questions you want to ask me?"

"Good," said Veight. "I am glad you are going to see reason. And really – I must compliment you on your appearance. A most enchanting picture."

"Will you kindly ask your questions and go?" she remarked icily. "I find your presence in my room quite insufferable."

"Then the sooner you answer, and the more truthful those answers are, the quicker you will be rid of us. What were you doing at the window a few minutes ago?"

"Looking out. I woke up, and seeing it was a lovely morning I got out of bed."

"Who was the man you were looking for?"

"I don't know what you are talking about," she said. "I didn't expect to see any man. Why should I? I don't even know where I am."

"I'm afraid, Miss Venables, our visit is going to be a long one. If you remember, I laid stress on your answers being truthful. You are not being truthful. Who was the man who was hiding in the undergrowth on the other side of the lake?"

"I tell you I didn't even know there was a man there, much less who he was."

"I fear, Gregoroff, that we shall have to adopt other measures with this young lady; measures, my dear, that you will not appreciate. For the moment, however, we will let that question drop, and turn to another. Ever since I have had the pleasure of knowing you, you have posed as an ardent member of the Key Club. Why?"

"Because I am one."

Veight raised protesting hands.

"You really must not go on in this stupid way. You are no more a member of that fatuous institution than I am. What I want to know is why you pretend to be."

"I tell you I am one," she cried. "You can believe it or not as you like."

"I suppose you'll ask me next to believe that you are a friend of Meredith's – a man with a criminal record, who has served a sentence for forgery."

She gave a slight start.

"I didn't know that," she said.

"You do now. Why did you go back to Captain Drummond's cottage that afternoon?"

"To make sure the message telegraphed by Mrs Eskdale was correct."

"And why did you want to make sure of that? I am waiting for an answer, Miss Venables," he added after a pause.

"I thought she might have made a mistake."

"Really! And if she had – what then? You, with a quickness for which I congratulate you, got rid of that man Drummond on the pretext that the message was a cipher giving the name of the place where your mythical cousin Harold had been taken to. You also, and on one of the few times in our acquaintance, quite truthfully told me that you thought it was the address of our headquarters in code. Why did you want that address? Whom did you wish to trace there?"

"I tell you, I – "

"Finding things a little difficult to answer, are we? Should I be very wide of the mark, Miss Venables, if I suggested to you that in the hurry of the moment you had not taken a copy of that wire, and that when I tore it up you couldn't remember the contents? And that that was why you went back to the cottage? Thank you, you needn't answer. I see I am right."

For a while he stared at her thoughtfully.

"I must confess you arouse my curiosity, young woman," he said at length. "Are you in the service of the British Government?"

"I am not," she answered promptly.

"Then if that is the truth you are playing a lone hand. Once again I ask you, why?"

She shrugged her shoulders indifferently.

"I have already told you, Herr Veight, that you are quite wrong. I really cannot go on repeating myself; it's too boring."

"So," said Veight softly, and at that moment Doctor Belfage entered the room, bringing with him a strong odour of spirits. He had pulled on a dirty dressing-gown over his pyjamas, and a two days' growth of stubble adorned his chin.

"Thought I heard voices," he muttered foolishly.

"You drunken swine," snarled Veight. "You were told to keep this girl under the influence of morphia, weren't you? Well, look at her."

"Gave her a shot last night," stammered the doctor.

"Shot be damned!" cried Veight furiously. "You were too full of whisky to know what you were doing. And what's the result? We found her trying to signal to somebody outside. And that's your doing, you miserable fool."

"Signalling? My God! Whom to?"

"That's what I'm trying to find out. And that's what I'm going to find out. Now look here, my girl, I've had enough of this fooling. You were anxious to find out where our headquarters were. Well, you have. They are here. And now you are going to sample what goes on in them. Up to date we haven't worried about you; you have been kept quiet. Now, entirely owing to that wretched bungler, we have got to worry about you."

The girl rose to her feet, and faced him fearlessly.

"How long have I been here, you brute?"

"Three or four days," answered Veight. "A nice rest cure."

"And what are you going to do with me?"

"Apply a little suasion. Show you some of the sights of the house. Unless you tell us who that was outside."

"I tell you I don't know," she cried. "And if I did I wouldn't tell you. Don't touch me." Her voice rose. "Don't dare to put your beastly hands on me." She backed to the window. "I swear I'll jump out if you do."

And even as she spoke a sudden change came over her face, and she gave a little choking cry.

"Tommy. Tommy darling. What have they done to you?"

Standing in the doorway was a man with a chalk-white face. A dirty bandage was round his head, and he was swaying dangerously on his feet.

"Doris," he whispered. "I thought I heard your voice, dearest."

Heedless of the other three she went to him and flung her arms round his neck.

"You devils!" she cried fiercely, as she led him towards the bed. "Sit down, darling. You oughtn't to have got up."

"Things become a little clearer," said Veight with interest. "I see you know Captain Lovelace, shall we say – fairly intimately."

"I'm engaged to him," cried the girl defiantly.

"Most romantic." The German lit a cigarette. "At last we are beginning to understand things a little better. So it was to help him that you pretended to belong to the Key Club."

"It was," said the soldier weakly. "And if you've got a spark of decency or manhood left in you, you'll let her go."

"Much more clearly," continued Veight. "That's why you wanted the message: you guessed he'd be here. It proves one thing, however, Gregoroff. You got Lovelace in time; he has passed on nothing. Tell me," he turned to the soldier, "as a mere matter of interest, what you meant by that strange message you threw through the window of the cottage. 'Rosemary BJCDOR.' It doesn't make sense to me, though of course it's a code."

Ginger Lovelace stared at him.

"Rosemary," he muttered. "I don't understand… I…" And suddenly he grew silent, and passed his hand over his forehead. "I can't remember… It's all a sort of dream…"

"Poor darling," said the girl, putting her arm round his shoulders.

"It doesn't matter," said Veight. "I only asked out of curiosity."

"Let him go back to bed," she cried.

"All in good time, Miss Venables," remarked Veight. "It wasn't I who asked him to get up, you must remember. And there are one or two things to be decided first."

"Have you still got that poor devil downstairs?" said Lovelace.

"We have. He is proving a little stubborn. But it won't be much longer now. And the quicker it is the better for you."

"What do you mean?"

"My dear Lovelace, I have no personal animosity to you. I can honestly say that I am delighted to see you are well enough to get up, and I hope that you and this charming lady will enjoy many years of happiness together. But when you insisted on butting into our plans you left us no alternative but to keep you quiet. And had you not tried to get away in the fog your head would not be so painful now."

"Cut out all that bunk," said the soldier. "What are you going to do with us?"

"Again render you harmless until we have done what we came to do, and then you will both be free to do whatever you like."

"More dope?"

"More dope."

192

"Can't you let Miss Venables go?"

"Really, Lovelace, you pain me. Let the girl who is engaged to you go! No, no, my dear fellow. You will both remain here as the guests of the estimable Mr Hoskins for a few more days, and then let the marriage bells ring out."

"What the devil is all this about?"

Meredith had entered the room unperceived.

"Ask that damned doctor," said Gregoroff savagely. "Let's get on with it, Veight. I'm sick of this. Fetch a syringe, Belfage."

"I don't understand," cried Meredith as the doctor shuffled out of the room.

"That swine is so sodden with drink that he doesn't know if he's coming or going," said Veight. "He forgot to give the girl an injection last night, and we found her looking out of the window. Now then, Belfage, stick it into his arm."

With shaking fingers the doctor inserted the needle, and a few moments later Lovelace fell back on the bed unconscious, while the girl watched them with eyes like those of a tigress.

"You brutes!" she kept on muttering. "You brutes!"

"Quite so, my dear," said Veight calmly. "It may interest you to know, Meredith, that these two are engaged to be married, which accounts for much that was obscure. However, we needn't go into that now. As I told you, we found her looking out of the window, and there was a man hiding in the undergrowth on the other side of the lake."

"What's that?" Meredith gave a violent start.

"Miss Venables' explanation up to date has not, I regret to say, entirely satisfied me. And so I propose to see if we can't get another. I think that the spectacle of our friend downstairs might open her mouth."

"You say there was a man watching the house?" said Meredith uneasily.

"There was a man hidden in the bushes," answered Veight, "who bolted when he heard us coming, and presumably he wasn't bird's-nesting."

"My God!" muttered Meredith. "Whom can it have been?"

"That is what I should like to find out. Come along, young woman, and you shall see the effects of another drug we keep in the medicine cupboard – one that is specially suitable for people who won't talk."

"Where are you taking me to?" she cried, shrinking back.

"Down below. You were so very anxious to find out where this house was that you must really see all over it now you are here. Hurry up," he added curtly, "you've wasted too much of my time already."

He took her roughly by the arm and forced her towards the door.

"You'll find it rather damp and a little gloomy; but don't be afraid – we shall be with you."

He half dragged, half carried her across the hall to a heavy door studded with nails which was fastened with two bolts.

"The old dungeons, my dear. Perhaps you have heard of Bonivard in Chillon Castle. We have a modern edition for you here."

He drew back the bolts, and the girl gave a little cry as he opened the door. Stone stairs led down into the darkness, and a wave of dank, mildewed air came up from below and hit her in the face.

"After you," said Veight with elaborate politeness, and slowly, a step at a time, she went down. Water dripped on her head from the ceiling; the walls were wringing wet when her hands touched them. At first she could see nothing; but at length the place began to take outline in the dim light that filtered through a tiny window high up. A big buttress stuck out from the wall on one side, and from behind it came a rustling of straw as if an animal was moving about.

Suddenly she screamed; something had run over her bare foot.

"Only a rat, Miss Venables," said Veight. "There are several, and they are big ones. Who was it who was hiding in the bushes?"

"I tell you I don't know," she cried wildly. "O God, what's that?"

A strange moaning noise was coming from the other side of the buttress, and Veight led her forward.

"Our Bonivard," he murmured.

Lying on the ground was a man who gave a cry of fear when he saw them. She could just see his face, his twitching lips, his terrified eyes, and his hands plucking aimlessly at the air. And then a chain rattled; he was tied up to a ring in the wall.

"The gentleman after whom you used to ask so glibly," said Veight. "When would he give way? Do you remember?"

"What have you done to him?" she asked through dry lips.

"They're murdering me," came a choking voice. "I'm going mad."

"No, no, my dear Waldron. Not murder. The very instant you decide to speak, all this will stop."

"You inhuman devil," cried the girl, and Veight laughed.

"The funny thing, Miss Venables, is that it isn't me at all. The saintly owner of the house is responsible for this. And he, I assure you, is an Englishman."

"That drug; what is that ghastly drug?" moaned the prisoner.

"Haven't they told you?" asked Veight. "It is not a nice one, Waldron, and its result in time will be to send you mad. It is, Miss Venables, a Mexican drug called Marijuana. You see before you the result. It instils such fear into the mind of the taker that he ceases to be a man. He is mad with terror over nothing at all; his brain refuses to function; his will power goes. And finally he finishes up in a suicide's grave or a lunatic asylum."

His eyes were boring into her.

"Mr Waldron would like a companion here: another soldier. Who was it who was hiding in the bushes?"

"I tell you I don't know," she cried. "I swear I don't."

"Still obstinate. I think I had better send for Captain Lovelace."

"No, no," she moaned. "I beg of you don't. I'm telling you the truth, Herr Veight."

"What is all this?" A deep voice came from behind her. "What are you doing here?"

"You have not yet been introduced to your host, have you, Miss Venables?" said Veight. "This is Mr Hoskins, who is responsible for this."

"You vile brute," said the girl. "Why are you torturing him?"

"You to say that!" Hoskins' voice shook with rage. "You who belong to our order! Are you not aware that this vile man you see before you has invented a new and deadly form of gas for use in war. Until he tells me his formula he remains where he is."

He turned on Waldron.

"Speak, you wretch, speak. What is your gas? Tell me, that all the world may know."

And somewhere, someone laughed. It came from above their heads, and Veight swung round tensely.

"Who was that?" he muttered. "Who was that who laughed?"

"Aye! Who was that who laughed?" cried Hoskins. "There are men, Herr Veight, in this very house who mock at our ideals; who would, if they could, use this man's foul secret for their own ends. I have heard them talking, but they do not know me. Now, you devil man, will you speak? Or shall I send for another injection?"

"Send and be damned," said Waldron weakly. "You wretched traitor to your country."

"Country! What is country? It is country that produces war. Go, Veight, and get the doctor. Tell him this man will still not speak."

"All right." Veight's voice came from the direction of the staircase. "Keep the girl there till I come back."

Sick and faint with horror of the thing, she was leaning against the buttress. In front of her the wild-eyed old owner of the house was muttering to himself fanatically; a few feet away Waldron stirred restlessly on his straw. And at that moment a hand touched her shoulder. A scream stillborn died on her lips, for a voice was whispering in her ear out of the darkness behind her.

"A friend, Doris. Tell Waldron to *pretend* to give the formula away, and gain time."

Then silence, and her brain working overtime. Who was it who had spoken, and how came he there? What she had said to Veight was the literal truth with regard to the man outside. She had awakened in a strange room with the light pouring in at the window, and had naturally gone to look out; no one could have been more genuinely surprised than she had been at his accusation. But now she knew there were men on the watch; knew that someone had actually got into the house – someone who knew her name.

She pulled herself together: she must act, and act quickly. At any moment Veight might return: somehow she must get the message through to Waldron before then. And suddenly she saw the way. With a little cry she tottered forward and collapsed on the straw as if half fainting. Would the old man suspect?

Close beside her Waldron tossed and turned, but her eyes were fixed on Hoskins. And to her unspeakable relief he seemed quite oblivious of her at all. He was still pacing up and down talking under his breath, and after a while he walked halfway across the room towards the stairs as if impatient at the delay. She seized the opportunity.

"Listen," she whispered urgently. "Can you understand me, Mr Waldron?"

His movements ceased; he lay very still.

"Who are you?" he muttered.

"A friend," she said in a low voice. "Help is coming. Pretend to give away your secret. Do you understand? *Pretend*. Say you will. Gain time."

He made no answer; all she could see was the faint outline of his white, twitching face close to her. And then came the sound of footsteps on the stairs, and she rose quickly to her feet again. Had she succeeded? Had she got the message through into that drug-bemused brain?

Fearfully she peered over her shoulder into the blackness. Of the man who had spoken to her she could see no sign, but she knew he must be there, hiding somewhere.

"I can't go on any more."

Came Waldron's voice, weak and quavering, and a thrill of triumph ran through her. He had understood: he was going to do as she had told him.

"That accursed drug is torture; it's sending me mad."

He babbled on incoherently for a little while, while Veight and Belfage stood beside Hoskins watching him. And then Gregoroff joined them.

"Are you going to tell us your secret?" said Veight quietly.

"Secret! The secret of my gas. God! I must have sleep. My brain is going."

Again he rambled on, and Veight said something in a low tone to Gregoroff, whilst the girl watched breathlessly.

"Listen, Waldron," said Veight, stepping forward on to the straw, "you shall have all the sleep you want once you have told us your formula."

"I can't think," muttered the other. "I tell you, I can't think. I must have sleep before I can remember it."

Once more Veight and Gregoroff whispered together, and it was Hoskins who spoke next.

"If we let you sleep will you tell us afterwards?"

"Yes. I will tell you afterwards. But now I must sleep. It is days since I have slept." His voice rose to a scream. "Keep the rats away. For God's sake – keep them away! And the horror in the corner. It is waking up."

Doris Venables felt her scalp beginning to tingle: something big was stirring on the far side of the dungeon.

"I am sorry you don't like the doctor's pets," said Veight. "That is only a baboon, but he can be very nasty if he slips his collar. Speak now. You can remember, Waldron."

But the only answer was a vague babbling, from which the one word sleep continually emerged.

"It is better perhaps to let him sleep," came the soft voice of Cortez who had joined the group. "Marijuana acts this way sometimes. But if when he wakes he does not then speak, he shall sleep for good. How say you, Señor Hoskins?"

"I will speak when I wake," said Waldron brokenly. "Only take me from this awful place."

"Give him a shot, Doctor," cried Veight. "We must chance it. And now, young woman, we must decide about you."

The girl shrank back. Subconsciously she watched Belfage bending over the man on the ground with a hypodermic syringe in his hand; hazily she wondered if the unknown man would again come to her out of the darkness. And then suddenly she realised that something had happened to distract their attention from her.

Meredith had appeared, and he was talking excitedly to Veight and Gregoroff. His voice was low, and she could not hear what he said, but it was evidently news of importance.

"Good." She heard Veight's curt voice. "We will see this man at once. There is no time to be lost. Belfage – attend to the girl. And if you mess things up again, I'll smash you into pulp, you drunken brute."

She saw the doctor lurching towards her, and gave a little cry of terror. Surely the unknown would help her; surely... A hand was clapped over her mouth; she felt the prick of a needle in her arm.

"Carry her upstairs, Gregoroff. We must get down to this at once."

She felt herself being picked up by the huge Russian; realised she was passing through the hall where a strange man was standing. Then wave after wave of sleep and oblivion.

"She'll do," said Veight, who had followed her upstairs. "Now mind you don't say the wrong thing, Gregoroff."

The two men went down into the hall, where Meredith was talking to the stranger, while Hoskins with a puzzled look on his face stood by listening.

"It is ferry important that you should come as soon as may be convenient," the stranger was saying in the soft voice of the Highlander. "The plans are finished, but for how long Mr Graham iss intending to remain I cannot tell you."

"What plans?" cried Hoskins. "I don't understand."

"The plans of the Graham Caldwell aeroplane," explained the stranger in some surprise. "Surely you haf heard of it."

"It's this way, Mr Hoskins," put in Veight. "We had been intending to keep this as a surprise for you, but this man – by the way, what's your name?"

"MacDonald. Angus MacDonald."

"But now that MacDonald has come – "

"You will pardon me – Mr MacDonald," said the Highlander. Veight bowed ironically.

"Now that *Mister* MacDonald has come we can keep it as a surprise no longer. Up in the heart of the Highlands, Mr Hoskins, a man named Graham Caldwell has been experimenting with an aeroplane of his own invention. It is now perfected, and as an instrument of war it constitutes the most deadly advance in flying the world has yet seen."

"That iss so," agreed the Highlander.

"It was our intention to give you the plans of this machine as an unexpected present." He winked surreptitiously at Meredith.

"Now, I fear, they will be like the birthday present of more mature years that one chooses for oneself."

"How are you going to get them?" asked Hoskins.

"That will be ferry simple," said MacDonald. "My cousin, who iss a member of the Key Club, will be there on the spot to help you."

"What is the name of your cousin?" asked Meredith.

"The ferry same as myself."

"But the man we have been corresponding with is called MacPherson."

"Mister MacPherson is there as well. He too iss a cousin."

"So there are two members of the Key Club there," said Veight.

"That iss so."

"And what are you going to do?"

"I am continuing my journey to London, where I am a student in the University. I haf been on my holiday in the Highlands."

"How did you know of this house?" cried Meredith suspiciously.

"My cousins told me. I do not know how they knew. And now if you will allow me I will be getting along. I am not a member of the Key Club myself, but I am in sympathy with its wonderful ideals. I wish you all success, gentlemen; it iss a ferry great honour to haf been even such a humble help in such a worthy cause."

He bowed, and a few moments later the roar of a motor bicycle outside announced his departure.

"How the devil did they know of this house?" repeated Meredith. "That sot Belfage, I suppose."

"Don't let's worry our heads over that," cried Veight. "Once those plans are in the hands of the British Government we're done. That is to say, Mr Hoskins," he corrected himself hastily, "it is going to be very much harder to get hold of them. So there's not a moment to be lost."

"You are right," cried Hoskins. "What is your idea?"

"I suggest that Meredith, Gregoroff and I – "

"Cortez is coming too," remarked Meredith quietly, his eyes fixed on Veight.

"As you please," said Veight. "I suggest then that the four of us should go at once by car to the north of Scotland and obtain the plans by force if necessary. You and Belfage, Mr Hoskins, will remain here and obtain from Waldron his secret when he wakes."

"Good," said Hoskins. "I agree. I will go and talk to the doctor now."

"And what do you *really* propose, Mr Veight?" sneered Meredith as the old man went upstairs.

"Just what I said – with one exception. Those plans are going to be of twice the value to us if we can keep Graham Caldwell's mouth shut while we sell them."

"How do you suggest doing that?" said Meredith softly.

"By bringing him and his mechanic here."

"Here!"

"Yes – here. Doped, in a caravan."

Meredith stared at him, and then whistled under his breath.

"By God! that's an idea," he said. "In a caravan."

"When we've got 'em here we can foist off any yarn on the old fool. He'll look after them, leaving us free to sell in the best market. We'll stop in York or some big place on the way through and hire the machine."

"I'm on," cried Meredith. "And I'll vouch for Cortez. When do we start?"

"At once," said Veight.

"I'll get him. But don't forget one thing, Veight: no funny stuff."

"How the hell can there be any funny stuff, you damned fool? We're all in it together, aren't we? I'm not asking you to walk, am I? You're yellow, Meredith: plain yellow. Go and get Cortez. If we drive in turn we should be there by dark tonight even with the caravan. We'll have to fix the aeroplane for ourselves when we come back," he said to Gregoroff, as Meredith disappeared scowling. "And if ever I get that scum where he ought to be," he added softly, "may the Lord have mercy on his soul."

CHAPTER 13

For mile after mile the road stretches like a white ribbon over the high ground that lies between Lairg and Altnaharra. It is a narrow road with passing places every few hundred yards, and save for the inn at Crask no house exists. Occasionally a fisherman going north to Tongue passes in his car and is gone; once a day the mail van performs its allotted task.

On each side of the road the ground is flat and green. Tiny streams intersect it, making big patches of bog. But parts of it are hard and even: suitable for the landing of an aeroplane. And it was on such a spot that there stood two buildings and a tent. The buildings were obviously improvised. One was a small tin shanty and it was erected close to the tent. The other was much larger and had been placed some two hundred yards away. Beside the tent a dilapidated motorcar was standing, and a rough track leading to the road a quarter of a mile away showed how it had got there. On the front seat an Aberdeen drowsed peacefully, save for a periodical search for an elusive flea. But except for the dog there was no sign of life in the little encampment.

In the short northern night though it was well after ten it was still light enough to read. But the man who lay motionless on the small hill that rose halfway between the tent and the road was otherwise occupied. His eye was glued to a telescope, and the telescope was focused on the place, five miles away, where the road going south to Lairg dipped over the horizon and disappeared.

After a while he shifted his position to ease his stiffness, and glancing round he frowned. Black clouds were gathering over Ben Kilbreck, and rain would not improve his vigil. Not only would it increase his discomfort, but it would decrease the visibility during the half-hour of light that still remained.

For two hours nothing had passed. Save for the harsh call of a grouse, and the faint murmur of the coffee-brown stream that gurgled softly over the stones by the bridge under the road, no sound had broken the stillness. But the man, being a Highlander born and bred, was used to such conditions. He was in his element, though it would have made a townsman fidget.

Suddenly he gave a little grunt of satisfaction: coming over the rise was a motorcar towing a caravan. His watch was over, and shutting the telescope with a snap he rose to his feet. Then, with a final glance at the tent and huts, he walked slowly down to the bridge on the road.

It would be at least ten minutes before the car could get there, and he lit a cigarette, his features showing clearly in the light of the match. And to a student of physiognomy his face was an interesting one. His eyes were very blue, with the network of tiny wrinkles round them which mark an open-air life. But their expression betokened the thinker, and the firm mouth and chin denoted the man of purpose as well. No dreamer, this, even if he was an idealist.

At last the lights of the car – for by now darkness had fallen – breasted the rise a few hundred yards away, and throwing away his cigarette the man stepped into the road. It was possible, though not likely, that this was not the car he was waiting for, but that risk had to be taken. It proved groundless. With a grinding of brakes the machine pulled up and a voice hailed him.

"Is that you, MacPherson?"

"Aye," he answered laconically. " 'Tis himself."

"Your proof?"

MacPherson fingered the lapel of his coat.

"The badge of the Key Club," he said. "Any further proof you may be needing you'll find in the camp. And who may you be?" he continued as the man who had accosted him came into the light. "Are you Doctor Belfage? I was told he was a little man."

"My name is Meredith," said the other, "and I and my friends are acting for Doctor Belfage, who is ill. We are all enthusiasts for the cause. By the way, MacPherson, how was it your cousin found us at Horsebridge?"

"Because I told him. Your doctor who is sick said you were there. Come, let's be getting on with it. And I'll thank you to give me a lift as far south as Inverness."

He led the way along the path, and a muttered colloquy took place behind him.

"That will be all right," said Meredith at length. "We will take you to Inverness. Have you the two men safe?"

"You'll be seeing for yourself in a minute," answered MacPherson.

"Because," continued Meredith softly, "you had better remember we are all armed. In case, you know, Mr MacPherson; just in case."

"Is that so?" said MacPherson quietly. "The grouse are good this year, but it is not yet the twelfth."

"What the devil is the man talking about?" came a harsh voice. "And why is he dressed like a damned woman?"

"Shut up, Gregoroff, you fool," snapped Veight. "Haven't you ever seen a kilt before?"

"Probably not," said MacPherson affably. "Being true to our principles, he naturally did not wait to see them during the last war."

From behind came a chuckle, and Gregoroff snarled angrily.

"If you laugh at me, you filthy little Dago, I'll bash your head in."

"I did not laugh," said Cortez venomously. "Keep your hands from me," he screamed, "or I knife you!"

"I didn't touch you, you rat."

"Then who did? Something – it brush my face."

"It would seem, Mr Meredith, that your friends do not like the spirits of the moor," remarked MacPherson gravely. "Perhaps they are right. Strange things happen in my country. Maybe you will hear the death dirge if you are lucky – or unlucky."

"For God's sake let's hurry," said Meredith uneasily. "This place gets on my nerves."

"It is because you are not used to it," answered MacPherson. "But reassure yourself. We shall not be long now. The hut is just in front of us. If you will wait a moment I will light the lamp."

He opened the door and struck a match, while the four men crowded in after him.

"There is the inventor, Mr Graham Caldwell, and that is his mechanic."

Seated on opposite sides of the table and breathing stertorously were the two men. Their heads were sunk on their arms; between them stood an empty whisky bottle.

"I put a little something in their whisky," explained MacPherson calmly.

"Good!" cried Meredith. "Where are the plans?"

"In yonder cupboard," said MacPherson.

"And they are complete?"

"They were finished yesterday."

"You are certain there are no others in existence?" cried Veight, putting the tracings on the table in front of him.

"Absolutely certain," answered MacPherson. "I myself have drawn the greater part."

The four men looked at him.

"Could you redraw them?" asked Gregoroff.

"From memory? No, I could not. But why should I be wanting to? You have them, and shortly the whole world will have them."

He spoke indifferently, leaning against the window.

"Excuse me, Veight," said Meredith suddenly. "Not all of them in your pocket, if you don't mind. I will take half."

"Don't be such a suspicious fool," cried Veight angrily. "Anyone would think I was trying to double-cross you."

"Exactly what I do think," answered Meredith calmly. "Hand 'em over."

"Just so," said Cortez. "We will have half."

For a few moments there was a tense silence which was broken at last by the Scotchman.

"Are you not then all together in this?" he asked mildly. "What does it matter who has the plans?"

"Of course, of course," said Meredith hurriedly. "Just a little personal matter, Mr MacPherson. Mr Veight is wanting all the credit himself at headquarters – aren't you, Veight?"

"Here are two sheets," remarked the German, pushing them over the table. "And what the devil is the matter with you?" he continued to MacPherson.

For the Highlander, his hand outstretched, was pointing through the window.

"Look!" he whispered. "Look! The dancing light. The light of death!"

Flickering up and down, moving first this way and then that, was a faint blue-white light.

"It's only a marsh flame," cried Gregoroff harshly, but he crossed himself.

"There is no marsh there," said MacPherson sombrely. "It is the light of death. Soon you will hear the dirge."

"Don't talk rot," shouted Veight. "Are we children, to be frightened with such tales?"

The Scotchman turned and stared at him: stared at him till the German shifted uneasily on his feet.

"You poor ignorant man," said MacPherson slowly. "Do not mock at the Powers on the other side, or maybe," his voice rose, "they will strike you down. Do ye not ken that this moor is peopled with the dead – the dead who are earthbound? Listen." He held up his hand for silence. "What did I tell you?"

From far away, clear through the still night air, came a faint wailing noise. It rose and fell, sometimes dying away to nothing, then increasing in volume, but always the same wailing dirge.

"Bagpipes," muttered Meredith through dry lips.

"Aye – the pipes. But played by no human piper. It's the dead playing their own lament. Never have I heard it so clearly."

"Dead men or no dead men," said Veight angrily, "we're not going till we've done what we came for. The machine must be burned. Where is it?"

"Over yonder," said MacPherson. "The petrol is ready."

"Then lead the way. That foul noise has stopped; let's be quick before it starts again."

"You will not hear it again tonight," said MacPherson. "They never play twice. Follow me."

They trooped out after him, leaving the two unconscious men still snoring at the table.

"What a hell spot of a place," muttered Gregoroff, stumbling over the uneven ground. "How far is it to the shed?"

"Two hundred yards," answered MacPherson from in front, and even as he spoke a bellow of fear came from the Russian.

"God Almighty!" he yelled. "What was that? Something cold and clammy hit my face."

He thrashed his arms round his head like a madman, uttering the foulest imprecations.

"Blaspheme not," came the quiet voice of the Scotchman, "or maybe they that hear will take you at your word. Here is the shed; the aeroplane is inside."

A door creaked in the darkness, and then by the light of a match they could see the vague outline of the machine inside.

"The tins of petrol are against the wall," said MacPherson. "Pour two or three over the wings and fuselage. Tip the remainder on the floor, and let this invention of the devil be destroyed by the fire that purifieth."

"I would have liked to have seen it in action," said Veight, "but unfortunately that is impossible. The inventor is satisfied, is he?"

"More than satisfied," answered MacPherson. "There is no existing aeroplane that comes within thirty per cent of it for all-round performance."

The reek of petrol filled the air as they emptied the spirit over the machine, and a few minutes later the shed was a raging furnace.

"So may all such abominations perish," said MacPherson gravely as they watched the flames roaring up in the darkness. Fantastic shadows danced over the moor, and a heavy cloud of smoke drifted sluggishly away. But at length it was over; the blaze died down, and only a few smouldering embers remained of the Graham Caldwell aeroplane.

"Excellent!" cried Veight. "You have deserved well of the cause, Mr MacPherson, and we will see that your name is brought before headquarters."

They were walking back to the hut, where they could see the inventor and his mechanic still sprawling over the table. But even with the light from the window the darkness seemed the more intense after the fierce bonfire they had witnessed. And so, when there came from behind them a thud, followed by a bellow of pain and a hideous gurgling noise, they peered backward, unable to see what was happening.

"Murder!" The word was a gurgle. "He murder me."

"You little devil, Cortez!" Gregoroff's voice was animal in its fury. "Ah-h-h! You'd knife me, would you?"

"Stop it, you two," shouted Veight furiously.

"I tell you he's smashed my face in," roared the Russian, "and now he's stabbed me."

"I did not touch your face," screamed Cortez. "I touch you not at all."

"For men of peace," murmured MacPherson, "you would seem a little excitable. And indeed it appears that Mr Gregoroff has not only a knife in his arm, but that he has lost much of his beauty."

He had produced an electric torch, which he flashed upon the Russian. And in all conscience Paul Gregoroff was a parlous object. His nose was smashed and blood was streaming down his face. A knife still quivered in the upper part of his arm, and his teeth were bared like those of a snarling dog. He had let go of the Mexican, who, crouching vindictively, was watching him.

"Who did hit me?" mouthed the Russian.

"Not me," snarled Cortez. "I knife you, yes, because you throttle me. I never touch your dam' face."

"Somebody has," said MacPherson profoundly. "That could not occur on its own. Maybe it was one of the more dangerous earthbound spirits that haunt the moor as I have told you. It would be safer to come to the hut, I think."

"To hell with you and your earthbound spirits," roared the Russian, who was beside himself with pain and rage. "If it wasn't Cortez, it must have been you, Meredith."

"I was nowhere near you," cried that gentleman hurriedly. "Let's get inside the hut, away from the damned moor."

"Sensibly spoken, Mr Meredith," said MacPherson. "For though Mr Gregoroff's face is doubtless very painful, it is fortunate for him that he is still alive. It is certain that there is present an influence that does not like him: next time it may be his neck and not his nose that is broken."

He entered the hut and the others followed.

"Do you really mean to say," stammered the Russian, "that...that it was a ghost?"

The deep-seated superstition of the Slav was asserting itself, and MacPherson shrugged his shoulders.

"You may call it a ghost if you wish," he said. "I would prefer to say that it was one of the elemental forces that are abroad upon the moor this night. You have seen the light; you have heard the pipes: and you have escaped with your life. As I said, you are lucky... What will you be doing with the two yonder?"

"Well, Mr MacPherson," said Veight, "our idea was to take them south with us. We feel it will be safer to have them under restraint while the actual plans are being prepared for the various governments. That is the reason for the caravan."

"A grand idea," remarked MacPherson. "They should travel comfortably inside it. So if you would care to lift them into the car outside, I will drive them to the road."

"How will you explain their absence?" said Meredith suddenly.

"There is no one to explain it to," answered MacPherson. "But should any questions be asked I shall say they have gone south to the English and more than that I do not know. Dear me! and what is that?"

A sharp yell of pain had come from outside the hut, and Veight entered, wringing his hand.

"Something has bitten me," he cried angrily. "Something in your car."

"There, now! I'd forgotten her. It's the wee Aberdeen bitch. She does not take kindly to strangers. Winkie! Come here, lassie."

The little dog came trotting in, to receive a vicious kick from the infuriated German. And the next moment Veight was lying in the corner nursing his jaw, with a blazing-eyed man in a kilt standing over him whom he almost failed to recognise as the mild-mannered MacPherson.

"How dared ye kick my dog?" The voice was soft and incredibly menacing. "How dared ye?"

Veight scrambled to his feet, but a second look at the Scotchman's face was enough.

"Sorry," he mumbled. "Lost my temper, I'm afraid."

"Then be careful you don't lose it again," continued the soft voice. "Or maybe I might lose mine."

For a space the two men stared at one another; then the German turned away, and MacPherson, picking up his dog, made much of her. But though he said no more there was tension in the air. Four to one, and armed at that, but no one suggested that the Scotchman should help to lift the two bodies into the car.

Gregoroff had roughly bandaged his arm – the wound was only a flesh one – but his face was still an appalling sight. And just before they started MacPherson turned to him.

"You'll find water in the basin," he said. "I'd use it if I were you. And then we'll be moving."

"What about your car?" asked Meredith.

"It can bide here," answered MacPherson shortly. "I'll be out by the mail from Lairg tomorrow."

He turned out the light, and they jolted over the track to the road. And once again MacPherson was a spectator as they turned the caravan and put the unconscious men inside, where they were joined by Meredith and the Russian, who heaved a sigh of relief as the door shut behind him.

"Will you sit in front with me, Mr MacPherson?" said Veight as he took the wheel.

"I will not," answered MacPherson promptly. "There are some people I prefer to be behind, and yon little Dago with the knife is one of them. Come, girl."

The Aberdeen jumped in beside him, and they started off. A few spots of rain began to fall, but it was only a passing shower and they did not stop to put up the hood. But as a drive it was not a chatty one, and it was not until the car stopped on the bridge at Inverness and MacPherson got out that Veight spoke again.

"What was it really that hit Gregoroff?" he said.

The Scotchman looked at him with an expressionless face.

"Something verra hard, mon," he remarked, relapsing into a pronounced accent. "If it were not impossible I would say a croquet mallet. But I have never heard that the elementals play the game. Well, I will say good night, Mr Veight. You have the plans; you have the inventor and his mechanic, and your friend's nose should have recovered in a year or so. Heel, Winkie."

He strode away along the deserted road by the river, and after watching him for a while Veight let in his clutch and once more headed south. Perfectly correct: they had the plans and the men, there was no doubt on that score. But for all that a vague feeling of disquietude possessed him.

True the Scotch are a peculiar race, and a Scotchman who was also a member of the Key Club could not be expected to be anything but most eccentric. But the episode which stood out most in his mind, apart from the pain he still felt in his jaw, was the kicking of the dog. In an instant a man who up till then had seemed an inoffensive lunatic had become a dominant personality.

That the aggravation had been great he admitted. Not that he cared the snap of a finger about dogs himself, but other people did. And if MacPherson had merely shown anger or resentment he would not have been in the least surprised. But MacPherson had done far more than that: he had cowed Veight, which was an extremely novel experience for the German. And the question he was asking himself as they drove up the long hill out of Inverness was, which was the real MacPherson?

Of only academic interest, perhaps, but Veight was a keen psychologist. Men and their minds were supremely important factors in his profession, and he disliked being unable to classify one. And what was it really that had hit Gregoroff?

He believed the little rat beside him, for the very good reason that he would never have been such a fool as to attack a man twice his size except with a knife. It certainly had not been MacPherson: he had been with him well in front. Equally certain it was not an elemental spirit, though – and this was the point – it was possible that MacPherson really believed it was. Highlanders, he knew, were fey: it was quite conceivable that he genuinely thought the whole thing was supernatural. Ridiculous, of course, to a man like Veight: the light was obviously a will-of-the-wisp, the wailing noise some bird.

It left, therefore, only Meredith. What would have been more easy than for him to arm himself with some heavy piece of wood when they were burning the aeroplane, and attempt to kill, or at any rate stun, the Russian in the darkness? It might have been done almost noiselessly, in which case he would have been up against Cortez and Meredith by himself, without realising the fact.

A glint came into his eyes: the more he thought of it the more probable did this solution seem. And after a while he glanced sideways at his companion, whose head was nodding. Both sides could play at that game, and with infinite care he put his left hand over the back of the seat and felt for the jack which he knew was lying on the floor. He found it, and put it between his legs. If the thing was going to be done it would have to be done at once.

Dawn was breaking, and again he glanced at Cortez, who was lolling against the side of the car fast asleep. Then he lifted the jack, and brought it down on the base of his skull. The Mexican lurched forward and was still.

Veight still drove on, but fear was clutching him. He had not intended to kill the man; had he hit him too hard? He felt for his heart: there was no sign of movement. And Veight's own began to go in sickening thumps. Cortez was dead: he had murdered him.

Behind him the caravan bumped along, and instinctively he looked at his petrol gauge. It was only a quarter full, and he could not fill up with a dead man beside him. Why had he hit him so hard? He had only meant to stun him, and then do the same to Meredith. After which he intended to leave them both hidden somewhere off the road. But he had killed him.

Veight thought furiously; the one essential thing was not to lose his head. And gradually he grew calmer. A plan was beginning to materialise in his mind.

It would require nerve, but he realised all too clearly that this was no time for half-measures. He had not the faintest wish to be hanged by the neck till he was dead, and that was the finish that stared him inexorably in the face unless he could dispose of the body in such a way as to divert suspicion from himself. And to do that it would not be sufficient merely to hide it : sooner or later someone would be bound to find it. After which identification, and with MacPherson in the neighbourhood the certainty of his being implicated.

The same consideration precluded any possibility of pretending to stage a motor accident. Apart from the fact that a car does not hit a man on the head, his connection with Cortez would be bound to come out. And why should someone who started as a passenger in a car be knocked down by it?

No: there was only one thing to be done. And having made up his mind Veight felt all his customary coolness returning. It was an unfortunate complication, but it was not the first time he had been in a tight corner and got away with it.

The first essential was a suitable place, and here fortune was with him. The road was running through a fair-sized wood, and as far as he could see there was no house within sight. So he stopped the car and putting on a glove he took the revolver out of the dead man's pocket. Then he picked up the jack and went to the door of the caravan.

"Puncture," he said briefly, keeping the revolver out of sight. "Give me a hand, Meredith; here's the jack."

Blinking his eyes sleepily, Meredith took it, and as he did so Veight shot him from point-blank range through the heart.

"What the devil are you doing?" stammered Gregoroff. "Are you mad?"

Veight looked up and down the road: no sign of anyone. Inside the caravan the two drugged men still slumbered peacefully.

"Listen, Gregoroff," he said quietly. "I've had an accident. I meant to knock Cortez on the head and stun him. Unfortunately I hit him too hard and killed him. You've got to help me stage this show, or we're for it."

"You mean you are, you damned fool," answered the Russian.

"You seem to forget the man you killed in Drummond's cottage, my friend. Be quick; there's no time to lose. Get hold of his shoulders, and we'll cart him into the wood. His hand has tightened on the jack, which is what I hoped for, and he's hardly bled at all."

Between them they lifted the dead man out of the caravan, and carried him into the undergrowth for a distance of about thirty yards. Then they laid him down where he was screened from anyone passing by.

"Now, Cortez," cried Veight, and they made the second journey. "We'll leave the two bodies together, and with luck they won't be found for days. But if by chance the are found sooner, and we are implicated, our story is this. We all stopped here and those two began quarrelling. We got bored and left them, and know nothing of the affair at all."

"Pretty thin," said Gregoroff, watching Veight lay the revolver in the Mexican's hand.

"We shan't be in England when they're found," cried Veight. "And with that jack clutched in Meredith's hand it isn't by any means so thin as you think."

"What induced you to hit Cortez?" cried the Russian curiously.

"Because the more I think of it the more do I become convinced that it was Meredith who hit you, and that if he'd laid you out he and Cortez would then have gone for me," said Veight, taking a final look at the bodies. "That seems all right to me," he continued. "The two things took place practically simultaneously. Meredith hit Cortez from behind; Cortez spun round and shot him as he died. No fingerprints on the gun except any that Cortez may have left there himself. In fact, my dear Paul – well staged. Now all we want are the plans from Meredith's pocket, and we will resume our journey."

He stooped over and extracted the papers, and the two walked back to the road.

"I think," he went on, "that you had better still continue in the caravan. Your face is definitely noticeable. Put another quarter grain of morphia under both our passengers' tongues. We don't want any chance of them coming to and shouting."

Suddenly he glanced up, listening: in the distance could be heard the drone of an aeroplane. It grew rapidly louder, and, flying low over the trees, a scarlet monoplane came into sight. It roared overhead, and as it passed above them they saw a man leaning out and looking down. Then it was gone and the noise of the engine died away in the south.

"An early flyer," said Gregoroff uneasily. "And he's seen us."

"What does that matter?" cried Veight irritably. "Your nerves seem pretty rocky this morning, Gregoroff. There's nothing unusual, is there, about a caravan on a road? And it is ten to one he'll never give it a second thought, even when the bodies are found. Get inside; the sooner we're back at Horsebridge the better."

CHAPTER 14

During the long drive south Veight reviewed the situation from every angle, for, though he had denied it to Gregoroff, he realised that the whole thing was pretty thin. True it was the best that could have been done under the circumstances, but he saw only too clearly the dangers of the position if the bodies were found before he was out of the country.

Meredith was known to the police, and through him the line would lead direct to Belfage. And with the ex-doctor in his present condition of nerves that might mean anything. He would certainly blurt out that Veight had been up to Scotland with the caravan, and that would mean a searching interrogation by the police.

Why had Meredith gone into the wood with a jack in his hand? Why, if he and Cortez had quarrelled, had they not done so by the roadside? What had they quarrelled about? And finally, what had been the object of the whole journey? Why go up to the Highlands and return the next day?

To the first three questions the answer was simple: since the tragedy had taken place after the car had gone, he could plead complete ignorance. Why had the car gone on, leaving two of its occupants stranded by the roadside? That was a bit of a poser. Because he, the driver, was the only one in the car. The others had all been in the caravan, and he had driven off believing they were inside again. When later he found they were not, he had gone too far to turn back, and assumed they would come on by train. That held water, and Gregoroff would come in there. He had thought they were in the car, and so he had said nothing.

So far, so good; it was to the last question that, try as he would, he could not evolve a satisfactory answer. To pretend that an ex-convict, a dope peddler and two men like Gregoroff and himself had gone to Scotland in a caravan for fun or to see the view was too farcical for words. In addition to that there was MacPherson to take into account. The fact that his own part in the performance was not at all creditable might not be enough to prevent him speaking if he found out who the dead men were – which he certainly would, since their names were bound to appear in the papers. That risk, however, being outside Veight's control, would have to be ignored. But what was he personally to say to account for the trip? And the more he thought it over, the more did he come to the conclusion that a half-truth was the only possible solution. They had heard of the Graham Caldwell aeroplane, and they had gone up to see it. Unfortunately they found the inventor had left for England; and even more unfortunately the machine had accidentally caught fire while they were there.

Yes, reflected Veight, that was the only solution, *if* he was interrogated. If! The whole crux lay in that word. With any luck, as he had said to Gregoroff, the bodies would not be found for at any rate two or three days. And by that time he would be well away, even if it entailed forfeiting the secret of the gas.

Like most men who live by their wits, Veight was an optimist, and as the day wore on his spirits rose. Possibly the Cortez episode was the best thing that could have happened. He had realised all along that fooling them at the last moment was going to prove difficult, and now all need for that had disappeared. Belfage and old Hoskins would be child's play, but Meredith had had a nasty suspicious mind. And so, by the time he turned the car in over the drawbridge, Emil Veight's equanimity was fully restored. His story was cut and dried; Gregoroff was word perfect, and he felt that the first instalment of Kalinsky's money was already as good as in his pocket.

There was no one in the hall when he and Gregoroff carried the airman and his mechanic in, and the house seemed very silent. But as they laid them down on the floor Hoskins appeared from his study brandishing a paper.

"It is you, is it?" he said. "I thought it might be Belfage. The formula, my friends: the formula of that devil Waldron's gas."

"Excellent," cried Veight. "And here are Graham Caldwell and his mechanic, to say nothing of the plans of the machine."

"A great day, gentlemen: a triumph for the club. But tell me – where are Meredith and Cortez?"

Veight laughed.

"A most absurd thing has happened, Mr Hoskins. We all got out this morning just after it was light, and when we drove off again we left them behind by mistake. I thought they were in the caravan with Gregoroff, and he thought they were in the car with me. They will doubtless come along by train."

"Dear me!" said Hoskins, "how very unfortunate. But what have you been doing to your face, Mr Gregoroff?"

"I fell down on the moor up there and hit it on a rock," answered the Russian.

"Quite a chapter of accidents," cried the old man. "I wish the doctor would return. I want him to see this formula, so as to be quite sure there is no mistake. Then by tonight's post, my dear friends, it shall go to every government."

"Just so," said Veight quietly, and his eyes met Gregoroff's. "Just so, Mr Hoskins. Where is the doctor?"

"He went over to his own house after lunch. Something to do with the insurance people and Hartley Court. But he should be back at any moment now."

"Might I see the formula?" asked Veight casually.

"Of course. Here it is. Waldron only recovered sufficiently a short time ago to write it. And even then I had to threaten him with more of the drug. Do you know anything of chemistry?"

"I fear not," said Veight, glancing at the formula he held in his hand. "Have you taken any copies of it yet, Mr Hoskins?"

"No; I was waiting for the doctor to make certain that devil has not deceived me."

"He is still below in the dungeon?"

"Yes. And he remains there till the letters are dispatched."

"And Captain Lovelace and Miss Venables?"

"Upstairs in their rooms."

Once again Veight glanced at Gregoroff, who gave the faintest of nods. And the next moment they closed in on the old man, who gave one frightened little squeal like a snared rabbit and then subsided limply, and his eyes roved from one to the other in terrified bewilderment as they forced him into a chair.

"What are you doing to me?" he wailed.

"Now listen, Mr Hoskins," said Veight quietly. "And pay very close attention to what I am going to say. We shall not do you any harm provided you do not give us any trouble. But knowing your strange outlook on life we shall have to take certain precautions. Gregoroff and I want this formula, which you have been kind enough to give us, and so we propose to keep it."

"But aren't you going to send it to all the governments?" cried Hoskins incredulously.

Veight roared with laughter.

"We are not, my dear sir. Ah! would you, you old devil?"

For with a furious shout of rage Hoskins had sprung out of the chair and had hurled himself at the German. His eyes blazed with fanatical fury; his hands clawed at Veight's pocket, and his frenzied shrieks of "Traitor!" rang through the house. And it was not until Gregoroff joined in, and hit the old man on the point of the jaw, that he finally sank back in the chair mouthing incoherently.

"You mustn't do that sort of thing, Mr Hoskins," said Veight quietly, "or you may get hurt."

"You devil! You devil!" muttered the other. "Are you going to sell that formula to one of the Powers?"

"Such, roughly, is our intention, my dear sir," said Veight with an amused smile. "You don't really imagine, do you, that we should have wasted our time in this depressing hole for nothing?"

"Never, while I live," cried the old man. "I will get the police... I will tell them..."

"I rather feared that you might try something of that description," said Veight calmly. "But I confess I did not imagine you would be quite so uncontrolled. So we shall have to take steps accordingly. You're a stupid old gentleman, you know; very stupid. Where shall we put him, Paul?"

"Down in the dungeon with Waldron," said the Russian. "And we'll have to gag him."

"What about the other two?"

"Put 'em down there too. I want to discuss that part of the show with you."

"All right," said Veight briefly. "I think I know what you're going to say, but we'll talk it over."

They deftly bound and gagged the old man in the chair where he sat, then they lifted him up and carried him down the stone steps to the dungeon below.

"Someone to keep you company, Waldron," said Veight amiably. "He tells me that you have at last seen reason."

The engineer officer glared at them in amazement.

"What have you got the old swine tied up for?" he asked at length. His voice was still weak, but the cessation of the diabolical drug was already beginning to have its effect.

"A little difference of opinion, my dear fellow," answered Veight. "We have slightly divergent views on what to do with your formula. By the way," he continued, taking the paper from his pocket, "I most earnestly hope for your own sake that you haven't been trying any funny stuff. This is the correct formula?"

"Go and try it for yourself," said Waldron indifferently. "Are you going to set me free?"

"All in good time," cried Veight. "You look so attractive where you are. But I think I can promise you that in the course of a few days, at any rate, your troubles will be over."

"But that devil Hoskins swore he'd let me go at once," shouted the soldier angrily.

"Quite, quite," said Veight. "But, as you can see for yourself, our friend and host is no longer in charge of the situation."

"Where are the rest of your foul brood?"

"Getting along nicely, thank you. And now, Waldron, I have something to say to you. I am going to have this formula of yours examined by a qualified chemist. If he tells me that it is what you say it is – well and good. You will be free to go, and you can have a grand time getting your own back on that damned old bore over there. But if I find you've been playing the fool, you'll pray for marijuana once again instead of what I'll give you."

Waldron yawned.

"I wish you'd go and play elsewhere," he said. "I'm infernally sleepy."

"So," continued Veight, "I would strongly advise you, if you have been so stupid as to write this down incorrectly, to rectify it *now*."

"Do go away," said Waldron irritably. "I've told you to try it for yourself. I can't say more than that."

Veight turned away, and beckoning to Gregoroff, they went back to the hall.

"We'll have to chance it," he remarked. "It might take days to have this thing properly tried out."

"Precisely," said the Russian. "And we aren't going to wait for days. Nor hours. We're going to clear at once. Leave those two where they are for the time and come in here. I want a drink. But we've got to get this straight."

"You mean you want to quit without..." The German paused significantly.

"I do," said Gregoroff doggedly. "I know what we arranged, and I was prepared to risk it if Waldron was still sticking out. But now that you've got the gas and the aeroplane plans, I tell you it's madness to stay one moment longer than is necessary."

"But it means dropping twenty-five thousand pounds," cried Veight. "You're a fool, Gregoroff."

"I'm a damned wise man. It's you who were the blasted fool – killing Cortez. Look here, Veight, there's no good our quarrelling. What's done is done, and you know that the only reason why I regret the death of those two rats is that it's made it dangerous for us."

"Dangerous," sneered Veight. "Since when has our trade been anything but dangerous? If you think I'm going to lose twenty-five thousand pounds you're damn well mistaken. The instant Belfage..."

"Belfage!" shouted Gregoroff. "The drunken little sweep! We'll probably never see him again."

"The instant Belfage," continued Veight imperturbably, "has given those three adrenalin we go, and not before. There's a machine waiting for us; we've got nothing to do except motor to the aerodrome and get in."

"And how long do you suggest we should wait for Belfage?" demanded Gregoroff.

"You heard what Hoskins said; he'll be back at any moment. Then we'll make him drunk, which won't be difficult, and *voilà tout*."

"It's risky," grumbled the Russian. "But I suppose we'll have to chance it."

"It's worth while chancing something for twenty-five thousand apiece," remarked Veight calmly.

"That's true," admitted Gregoroff grudgingly. "But I confess I'd feel a great deal easier in my mind if you hadn't hit Cortez quite so hard."

He was staring out of the window, and his eyes narrowed suddenly.

"Who the devil is this crossing the drawbridge?" he cried.

Veight joined him, and gave a prolonged whistle of astonishment.

"It's Kalinsky himself. Now, what in the name of all that is marvellous has brought him down? You stay here; I'll deal with him."

He hurried into the hall, and got to the front door just as the limousine pulled up outside.

"This is a most unexpected pleasure, m'sieur," he said.

"Unexpected!" snapped the financier, who was obviously not in the best of tempers. "What do you mean by unexpected? After the urgent message you sent me I had no alternative but to come, though it was exceedingly inconvenient."

He entered the house and Veight closed the door in a complete daze.

"Urgent message, m'sieur? I haven't sent you any urgent message."

"Then who was that stammering fool who forced himself on me this morning in my hotel? Belfage he called himself; the doctor you told me about. Said he came from you, and that it was of vital importance I should come here this afternoon."

Veight gave a sigh of relief. The thing was now comprehensible, though why Belfage should have done it was beyond him. And then came a sudden stabbing doubt. How did Belfage know anything about Kalinsky?

"Confound it, Veight, have you lost the use of your tongue?" Kalinsky's angry voice broke in on his thoughts. "Twice have I asked you who these two men are lying about in the hall."

"I beg your pardon, m'sieur." With an effort he pulled himself together. Whatever had caused Belfage's action, it could wait. At the moment the vital thing was not to let Kalinsky even have an inkling that anything could be amiss.

"To tell you the truth," he continued, "I have had so little sleep during the past forty-eight hours that I hardly know what I'm doing. Those two men are Graham Caldwell and his mechanic."

"What's the matter with them?"

"Doped with morphia. We brought them down from Scotland in that caravan you saw outside."

"And the plans of the machine?"

"Here in my pocket."

He handed them to the millionaire, who glanced at them and then threw them on the table.

"They convey nothing to me," he said. "You are sure those are the correct ones?"

"Absolutely certain, m'sieur. They were in the safe in Caldwell's office, and the man who had actually done some of the drawing himself gave them to me."

"Did you see the machine?"

"It was dark when we arrived, m'sieur," explained Veight, "and so it was impossible to inspect it closely. We burned it."

"Then you didn't see it in flight?"

"No, we did not. But the member of the Key Club whom you may remember I told you about, and who was responsible for our information in the first place, confirmed the fact that its performance is simply amazing."

The financier lit a cigarette.

"Well, Veight," he said more cordially, "so far you seem to have done well. I may say that I myself through a roundabout source heard only yesterday that this machine is a marvel. I also heard that, so far as my informant knew, no plans, save these, were in existence. And so I say again that I consider you one to be congratulated."

"Thank you, m'sieur." Veight bowed. "Things have gone very well. Because I have here the other thing I promised you – the formula of the gas."

With a triumphant flourish he produced the paper from his pocket.

"This again conveys nothing to me," said Kalinsky. "Have you any proof that it is correct?"

"Frankly, m'sieur – I have no *proof*. I am not a chemist myself. But the English officer Waldron is below in the dungeon, and he realises that if it is not correct it will be even more unpleasant for him in the future than it has been in the past. You would perhaps like to see for yourself?"

"Later – possibly. At present I am rather more interested in the future of the two gentlemen I see upon the floor."

"That, m'sieur, you may safely leave in my hands," said Veight. "And I think it would be better for you not to know any more about it. I have thought out a scheme, which I flatter myself is not lacking in ingenuity, and which is certain to result in Belfage being hanged for the murder of these two and Waldron below."

"And what are your immediate plans?"

"To leave England at the first possible opportunity," answered Veight. "After which I shall report to you in Paris for the balance due."

"You shall have it," said Kalinsky.

He took out a bulky pocket-book, and Veight's eyes glistened.

"You have done well, Herr Veight," he continued. "And though for the life of me I can't see quite what was the need for dragging me down here, I am glad I came and saw with my own eyes. Here are ten thousand in notes as we arranged, and the balance of forty will be handed to you in Paris when – er – the remaining conditions have been complied with."

Veight took the notes and bowed.

"Thank you, m'sieur. I can assure you they will be."

Now that the first instalment was actually in his pocket he was itching for Kalinsky to go. Unfortunately, however, the financier showed no signs of so doing; he was inspecting his surroundings with obvious interest.

"Extraordinary," he said at length. "Most interesting. By the way, where is the madman you told me about who owns this house?"

"Keeping Waldron company in the dungeon," answered Veight. "He became quite annoyed when he realised the formula for the gas was not going to be used as he intended."

"Of course; I remember. These strange people send things to everybody, don't they? I should very much like to see the dungeon, Veight."

Concealing his impatience with an effort, the German led the way.

"Be careful of the steps, m'sieur. They are rather dark."

"Good gracious me!" said Kalinsky, staring about him. "It is unbelievable. And is this the wicked old man who tortured the gallant young inventor?"

Veight swore under his breath; the great man had evidently quite recovered his temper and was pleased to be facetious. Pray Heaven he would be quick about it.

"That is the gentleman," he answered, forcing a laugh.

"Well, well," said Kalinsky genially, "it takes all sorts to make a world, doesn't it? But what a bloodthirsty old ruffian you must be!"

He lit another cigarette and turned away.

"Well – I think that is quite enough, Veight. I do not find the atmosphere of this apartment very much to my liking. I think I will now return to London."

Veight heaved a sigh of relief; then grew suddenly tense as he heard the sound of hurried footsteps in the hall above.

"Veight!" came a hoarse shout. "Veight – where are you?"

The German stood very still: it was Belfage's voice.

"I'm below in the dungeon," he answered. "What do you want?"

"Who is that?" cried Kalinsky quickly.

"Doctor Belfage, m'sieur," said Veight, as the doctor, white and sweating, clattered down the stairs, to pause for a moment as he saw Kalinsky.

"Belfage?" snapped the millionaire. "That is not the man I saw this morning. What the devil is the meaning of all this?"

Icy fear was clutching at Veight's heart. He knew now that something had gone wrong, but he forced himself to speak calmly.

"It is quite all right, m'sieur," he said. "Some small misunderstanding."

Already his quick brain was working: at any rate he had ten thousand in his pocket. And then he realised Belfage was pouring out some confused jumble of words.

"Skeletons!" roared Kalinsky, now beside himself with rage. "What in God's name is this madman talking about?"

"Pull yourself together, you drunken swine," snarled Veight, shaking Belfage like a rat. "What's the matter with you?"

"The skeletons, Veight. The skeletons at Hartley Court. Two of them were females."

The German's hands dropped to his sides.

"Females!" he muttered foolishly. "Females! What do you mean, females?"

And from behind him Waldron began to laugh. And the laughter grew till it swelled to a mighty chorus. From all round him, from above him were unseen people laughing – just laughing.

"*Ein wünderschoner Abend, Herr Veight.*"

"Pardon! 'Ad tripe for me supper. Comes back on one like, don't it."

God above! The bleary-eyed youth at his hotel in London. And still that laughter went on rising and falling, until, as if it was a drill, it stopped abruptly. And the silence was more terrifying than the noise.

He could hear the heavy thumping of his heart; dazedly, sickly, he realised that everything had miscarried. But how? How? Beside him Kalinsky, now thoroughly frightened, was clutching his arm convulsively; Belfage in a state of collapse had sunk down on the steps. And then came a well-remembered voice from above.

"So we meet again, Herr Veight. Kindly come up into the hall."

Like a man in a dream the German obeyed Drummond's order. All power of connected thought had temporarily left him: the sudden shattering of all his plans had numbed his brain. He realised subconsciously that the hall was full of men. He saw Standish, and Darrell, and Gregson and a dozen others he did not know; he saw Lovelace and Doris Venables standing at the foot of the stairs; he saw as a man sees the background of a picture in relation to the central figure. And that central figure was the man standing opposite him on whose face was no trace of mercy.

Suddenly Kalinsky gave a cry, and pointed to one of the group.

"There's the man who came to me this morning and said he was Belfage."

No one answered; no one spoke, and then Veight heard a voice. It was his own.

"How...did...you...escape?"

He was still staring, hypnotised, at Drummond.

"The court will now commence," was the only answer. "Bring forward the other prisoner."

He pointed to Gregoroff, whose nerve had completely gone.

"You fool!" he screamed at Veight. "I told you we should have got away at once."

"You've never had a chance, Gregoroff," said Drummond. "For the past three days you have never been out of our sight."

"How...did...you...escape?"

Once more Veight's parched lips mouthed the sentence.

"Sufficient for you, Veight, that we did."

"A truce to this play-acting," snarled Kalinsky, who had recovered himself. "Do you know who I am, sir?"

"I have that misfortune," said Drummond dispassionately. "And anything that you may care to say in mitigation of your conduct will be carefully considered."

"Mitigation! Conduct!" shouted the millionaire. "This, sir, is an outrage."

"It is," agreed Drummond pleasantly. "And a far worse one will shortly be perpetrated upon you. But before that takes place we will converse awhile, Kalinsky."

White with passion, the millionaire strode to the front door. It was locked and the key was not there.

"Open this door, sir." He was stammering with rage. "Open this door at once. I insist."

"Mr Kalinsky insists. What an epoch-making moment! Ten thousand pounds is the sum, I think, you have just paid Veight for the documents in your pocket."

Very slowly the millionaire came back: the seriousness of the situation had come home to him. This ring of silent men meant business, and Kalinsky's soul grew sick within him. But his voice was steady when he spoke.

"Who are you, may I ask?"

"That is quite immaterial," said Drummond. "Shall we say that, at the moment, I represent justice? Perhaps a little rough and ready; nevertheless justice. What are the documents for which you have just paid Veight ten thousand pounds?"

"That is my concern," answered Kalinsky.

"Assuredly. Give me those notes, Veight."

Completely cowed, the German handed them over.

"Ten thousand pounds!" Drummond balanced the packet in his hand. "A lot of money, Kalinsky: they must be very valuable."

"They are worth it to me," said the millionaire in an offhand tone.

And once again a chorus of laughter rose, fell and died away.

"I am delighted to hear it," said Drummond gravely. "True we all have different standards of value; but it is most impressive to realise yours. Have you by any chance made Mr Graham Caldwell's acquaintance?"

Instinctively Kalinsky looked at the two men who still sprawled unconscious on the floor.

"No, no; the *real* Graham Caldwell," continued Drummond. "Those two were wished on Veight in Scotland. They belong, I believe, to the local branch of the Key Club. Here he is."

A freckle-faced young man with a cheerful grin stepped forward.

"What are the plans Mr Kalinsky has got?" asked Drummond.

"Bits of a Puss Moth and an old Bristol fighter," said Caldwell. "But even then there's a lot missing. A wheelbarrow would fly better."

"I wonder," remarked Drummond pensively, "if any government really wants a flying wheelbarrow. You can but try, Kalinsky. And you've always got the gas, haven't you? I hope that's all right for him, Waldron."

"Grand," said the sapper. "I wrote it down in a hurry, but the final process should undoubtedly produce a form of cheese mould."

"Think of it, Kalinsky," cried Drummond enthusiastically. "A wheelbarrow with wings, and a spot of gorgonzola. They'll put up a statue to you."

Kalinsky turned on Veight in a cold fury.

"So you've double-crossed me, you rat. Hand me back that money."

"You forget he hasn't got it," said Drummond, still balancing the notes in his hand. "And it is really we who have done the crossing – not Veight. So we shall be pleased to keep these for our trouble."

"I see," said Kalinsky with a sneer. "Plain theft."

"Oh, no! A little present from Veight. And so that there shall be no misunderstanding, Kalinsky, an anonymous present of ten thousand pounds will be made tomorrow to the disabled soldiers and sailors fund."

His eyes bored into the millionaire.

"You may, if you like, make trouble. I don't somehow think you will. If your part in this affair comes out, your name will stink in the nostrils of the world. And there is a certain poetic justice, isn't there, in this money going to men who fought, in view of what it was really intended for? War: another war. More millions in your pocket; more millions mutilated or in their graves."

"I don't know what you're talking about," muttered Kalinsky.

"Tidying up, sare," quoted Drummond. "Having found out Veight was coming to see you, I came first. And as Henri is an old friend of mine, I had no difficulty in persuading him to let me act as floor waiter. He thought I was doing it for a bet."

"Confound your impertinence," snarled Kalinsky. "My part in the whole affair was perfectly legitimate. I promised this damned fool Veight money for certain things. What I proposed to do with them is entirely my own affair. He has failed to get them, and that is the end of the matter so far as I am concerned."

"That, I fear, is where we must agree to differ," said Drummond gravely. "I heard most of your conversation with Sir James Portrush; I heard your delightful bargain with Veight. And neither I nor my friends think you at all funny. In fact we think you a profound bore, Kalinsky, a very tedious person. Which must be rectified. If you can't make people laugh by fair means, you shall make them laugh by foul. Bring that rope, Peter."

"What are you going to do with me?" cried the now terrified millionaire.

"You'll see," said Drummond as Darrell and Standish passed the rope under Kalinsky's arms. "And I would advise you to keep your mouth shut for the next few minutes. In with him, boys."

Gibbering with fright, Kalinsky disappeared through the window, and a loud splash proclaimed his destination. Three times was he hauled up; three times was he dropped back. Then he reappeared, and again the chorus of laughter was heard.

Dripping wet, with duckweed in his hair, the millionaire stood there emitting a powerful odour of stagnant slime, and almost crying with rage and mortification.

"Very funny; very funny indeed," cried Drummond approvingly. "I told you you could make people laugh if you tried. But it would be selfish on our part to keep you all to ourselves. Goodbye, Kalinsky; they'll be tickled to death at the Ritz-Carlton. Run him out, Peter; the swine is an outrage and an offence against God and man. Here's the key."

The front door closed behind him, and silence settled on the room, which was broken at length by Drummond.

"And that brings us to the lesser fry," he said quietly. "Veight; Gregoroff; even the egregious Doctor Belfage I see. But where are Meredith and Cortez? The party does not seem to be complete. And you were all so matey in Scotland, weren't you?"

"I believe you're the devil himself," muttered the German sullenly. "Were you up there too?"

"Of course. As I told your Russian friend, you haven't been out of my sight. By the way, Gregoroff, have you met any more elementals with croquet mallets?"

"It was you, was it?"

"It was. A ripe and fruity blow, I flatter myself. But, I think, if anything, it has improved your appearance."

"How the devil did you get out of that room?" said Gregoroff with a scowl.

"I don't think you have actually met Mr Seymour, have you? You did your best to shoot him on his motor bicycle, but that hardly constitutes a formal introduction. A rising journalist, Gregoroff, and a lad of sunny disposition as you can see. Moreover, it is entirely due to him that you are in your present unsatisfactory position."

The Russian's scowl deepened as he looked at the young reporter.

"With becoming modesty he maintains that it was a sheer fluke. I, on the other hand, consider it was an extremely quick piece of work for which he deserves the greatest credit. I had arranged to meet him the day after you so kindly locked us up, and somewhat naturally I failed to keep my appointment. He waited and waited, and under the inspiration of a ginger ale he fell into conversation with that lovely girl who dispenses gin in the bar. They talked of this and that, and after a while she mentioned the jolly little party overnight when we had met Doctor Belfage. She also mentioned Hartley Court. So Seymour decided it could do no harm to call there. I trust I interest you."

"Go on," muttered Gregoroff.

"Naturally he found the house empty. But the sight of an unlatched window downstairs was too much for him and he entered. It was all very still and silent, but as he stood on the kitchen stairs wondering whether to explore there came from close by his head a little click. He looked up: it was the electric-light meter, and subconsciously he noted the reading. Then he went all over the house and found nothing. It took some time, and at last he decided to go. And then occurred, Gregoroff, one of those little things which sometimes alter the fate of nations. As he passed the meter he happened to glance at it again: *the reading was different.* Somewhere in the house current was being consumed. Where?"

"You cursed fool, Gregoroff!" cried Veight. "It was you who insisted on leaving the light on."

"Come, come," said Drummond. "Mutual, I think. But with unerring accuracy, Veight, you have spotted what gave you away. To make certain, Seymour continued to watch the meter until it changed again; then, being a determined young man, he once more went over the house. And this time, by taking a few rough measurements, he realised there was an inner room, the existence of which he had not suspected before. The rest was easy. He tapped: he heard a faint answer. And four hours later a nice gentleman with a blowpipe affair had cut through the door. That is how we got out, Gregoroff, and had you and Veight met us then we should assuredly have killed you both. We were not amused."

Drummond lit a cigarette.

"But saner counsels prevailed. Mr Standish had already solved the real message which was flung through my window by Captain Lovelace. But you haven't seen that one, have you? How stupid of me. There have been so many flying round, haven't there? It was in code too – 'Mary Jane. Urgent. G G Pont.' "

Sullenly the two foreigners stared at him.

"In code," Drummond continued quietly, "to minimise the chance, if you found it, of your moving poor Waldron elsewhere. Mary Jane, with Cortez introducing the Mexican atmosphere, gave us Marijuana: G G – Horse: Pont – bridge, in French. Not a very clever code, as I am sure Captain Lovelace would be the first to admit, but men who are half murdered, Veight, are not very clever."

"He shouldn't have tried to escape," muttered the German.

"Shouldn't have tried to escape, you rat!" roared Drummond. "A British officer from a damned foreign spy! Don't scowl at me, blast you, or I'll give you a taste of Gregoroff's medicine. To resume, however," he continued. "Fearing you might return to Hartley Court and find the birds had flown, we decided to burn the house down. It was a pity that two of the skeletons we obtained with great difficulty were those of the fair sex, but they served their purpose."

"What purpose?" said Veight angrily. "Why didn't you strike then instead of waiting?"

"For two good reasons," answered Drummond. "First and foremost in order to touch that blackguard Kalinsky for ten thousand pounds. Secondly – but I presume you have never read the immortal 'Stalky' – we wanted to jape with you. And you can't imagine the amount of fun you've given us."

"And what do you propose to do with us now?" asked the German. "Put us in the lake too?"

"No, Veight: you have a more important role to play which you will discover in due course. Doctor Belfage as well, and the incredible old gentleman downstairs. I would have liked Meredith and Cortez... By the way, have you any idea where they are?"

"I have not, and for a very good reason," said Veight quietly. With the realisation that the situation was desperate, his self-control had come back. "Since you appear to know everything, it is quite refreshing to find that you do not. Just after it was light this morning we all got out to stretch our legs, and when we started off again I thought they were in the caravan, and Gregoroff thought they were in the car. So between us we left them behind."

"What an annoying *contretemps*!" cried Drummond. "If only I'd known that, it would have quite allayed my childish fears. But when I saw you and Gregoroff emerging from that wood this morning – "

"You saw us!" Veight almost screamed.

"I was in the scarlet monoplane," explained Drummond patiently. "The Graham Caldwell machine. You didn't burn it, you know: when we gathered your intentions an ancient glider was put inside the shed. To resume, however. When I saw you coming out of the wood, and there was no sign of the other two, I was filled with unworthy suspicions. So we landed a little later, and I communicated those suspicions to the police."

Veight swallowed twice, and his knuckles gleamed white on the back of the chair he was gripping.

"What a waste of time!" He forced himself to speak calmly. "They should be here at any moment now."

"I fear not," said Drummond sadly. "Veight, you must prepare yourself for a shock. The dead bodies of your poor friends were found in the wood."

The German had again recovered his self-control. His start of amazement was admirable.

"*Gott in Himmel!*" he cried. "Dead! But how?"

"Clutched in Meredith's hand was a motor jack; in that of Cortez a revolver. Meredith was shot through the heart; Cortez had his skull broken."

"They were quarrelling when we all got out of the car, Gregoroff, if you remember," said Veight thoughtfully.

"That is so," assented the Russian.

"And did you leave them there quarrelling: one armed with a jack and the other with a gun?" asked Drummond politely.

"I have already told you," said Veight, "that it was quite by accident they were left behind at all."

"Of course! Of course! How stupid of me. What were they quarrelling about, I wonder? The plans of the wheelbarrow; or can it have been the flying cheese? Or perhaps," he added hopefully, "it was just naughty temper at being left to walk. Anyway, that is your next role – the two principal witnesses at the inquest on Meredith and Cortez."

The German's jaw tightened but he said nothing.

"Playtime is over," continued Drummond. "Serious business begins. And when through the medium of a nice double murder the public are put wise to your recent activities, even they may begin to realise that this country is living in a fool's paradise over armaments."

The telephone bell started to ring, and he picked up the receiver. And as he listened a look of amazement appeared on his face. At length the metallic voice ceased, and Drummond very slowly replaced the instrument.

"The police, Veight," he said gravely. "They want to know if you and Gregoroff are here. As you heard, I told them you were. They are coming to ask you some questions."

The German moistened his lips with the tip of his tongue.

"You will be interested to hear that they have found Cortez's fingerprints on his revolver," continued Drummond.

"Naturally," said Veight. "You told me he shot Meredith, and that the revolver was found in his hand."

"Yes: lying very loosely. And the police want to know how it got there."

"I don't understand," stammered Veight, after a pause. "If he shot Meredith…"

"Precisely," remarked Drummond. "If! You see, the revolver was in his right hand: the fingerprints are those of his left."

For a space in which a man may count five there was silence, while the German, his face ashen, swayed on his feet. Then with a roar like a beast Gregoroff hurled himself on him.

"Damn you!" he shouted. "What did you want to kill him for?"

"So," said Drummond when they were finally separated, "it would seem that my unworthy suspicions were justified after all. But I think your message to the British public will be even more valuable when it comes from the dock and not from the witness-box."

CHAPTER 15

"The Chief wants to see you, Hugh," said Gregson. "You, too, Ronald, and Seymour as well. Old Portrush is with him clucking like an agitated hen."

Drummond grinned faintly, and followed the speaker along the passage to a large airy room overlooking Whitehall. Behind a big desk sat a grey-haired man with a pair of keen, penetrating eyes, while beside him Sir James Portrush clutched the inevitable attaché case.

"So you are the sinners who have been corrupting my young gentlemen," said Colonel Talbot genially. "The tale I have listened to from Gregson is just about the most completely immoral recital of utter illegality I have ever heard. In fact at a rough guess I should think you have all laid yourselves open to at least ten years' penal servitude."

"At least," agreed Drummond happily. "But we've had a grand time, Colonel."

"What staggers me," cried Sir James, "are these disclosures about Kalinsky. I can scarcely credit them. Why, only a few nights ago, I was having a long conversation with him on the European situation at the Ritz-Carlton."

"I heard it all," said Drummond, lighting a cigarette.

"You heard it?" spluttered Sir James. "But we were alone."

"I heard it through the keyhole," said Drummond calmly, and Colonel Talbot hurriedly bent down to pick up a paper. "I was the waiter."

241

"Really, Captain Drummond," cried the minister angrily, "that is quite inexcusable."

"If I hadn't," said Drummond, "Kalinsky would now have the Graham Caldwell plans. And Morgenstein. He was in it too."

"Nevertheless unpardonable," continued Sir James. "To listen to a private conversation! It's…it's not done."

"It was that night," laughed Drummond. " 'Dictators, knaves, or fools' – do you remember?"

Sir James flushed scarlet.

"This is intolerable," he snapped.

"Come, come, Sir James, be reasonable. You must judge every case on its own merits. And in this instance I consider I was justified. I knew Veight was coming to see Kalinsky, which by itself was enough to prove he was a wrong 'un. But if I may be permitted to say so – wrong 'un or not, the advice he gave you was the goods."

"I am infinitely obliged to you for your opinion," remarked Sir James sarcastically.

"And," continued Drummond imperturbably, "it will not be through any fault of mine if that advice is not broadcast to the country when Veight and Gregoroff come up for trial. They'll hang 'em as high as Haman – both of 'em, and that always interests the public."

"Do you mean to tell me" – Sir James appeared to be on the verge of a seizure of sorts – "do you mean to tell me that you have the audacity – the damned audacity – to pass on a private conversation you heard through a keyhole?"

"Most certainly," answered Drummond. "I won't say it was you, but I'm undoubtedly going to tell the public Kalinsky's remarks that night. Wait, Sir James!"

He held up his hand, and after an abortive splutter the minister subsided.

"You did not go through the last war as – er – as a combatant. We did, and we don't want another, any more than some of the pacifist young gentlemen today, who have never heard a shot fired in anger. We know the horrors of it first-hand; we are all out to prevent it again if we can. But we maintain that the present policy of cutting down our fighting forces to the extent they have been reduced, is the most certain way of precipitating it. Do you realise that if this young feller here had not got us out of that house, war *would* have come? I ask you – do you realise that? But for the tick of an electric-light meter war would have come. As you know, they intended to kill Waldron and Graham Caldwell, so that those two secrets would have been Kalinsky's sole property. Do you suppose he was going to use 'em for shaving-paper?"

"Really, Captain Drummond, I am not accustomed to being hectored in this way." Sir James had at last found his voice. "The Government's policy on such matters is – er – a matter for the Government alone."

"Well, at any rate, you know Kalinsky's opinion of that policy. And," Drummond added pleasantly, "though he may be a knave, Sir James, he most certainly is not a fool."

With a snort like an angry bull, Sir James snatched up his hat and rose to his feet.

"You, it seems to me, Captain Drummond, combine both qualities. Good morning, Colonel Talbot; I am already late for a Cabinet meeting."

"Totes on greyhound tracks still worrying the old grey matter?" asked Drummond anxiously. "But they tell me Flying Fish for the third race at the White City tonight is a cinch. Shall I put on a quid for you?"

"I am not interested in dog-racing, thank you."

"Great fun, you know. And you could always earn a spot of honest dough as a tick-tack man. All you've got to do is to wave your arms and legs about and make faces. Just like a Cabinet meeting."

The door shut with a crash, and then Drummond threw up his hands in despair.

"How long, O Lord, how long?" he cried. "It isn't that his opinion differs from mine, but it is that ghastly air of smug self-complacency that gets my goat. What's your opinion, Colonel?"

But that worthy officer was beyond speech. Tears were pouring down his face; his shoulders heaved convulsively.

"Portrush as a tick-tack man!" he gasped at length. "You're a thoroughly reprehensible scoundrel, Drummond," he continued in a shaking voice, "and your proper fate is to be hanged between Veight and Gregoroff. But at any rate you've made me laugh. Now tell me, how many crimes have you committed in the course of the last few days?"

"How many, Ronald?" asked Drummond cheerfully.

"The only one, Chief, is burning down the house," said Standish. "And a few odd trifles against some lower excrescences of the Key Club, which they brought on themselves. But with regard to Hartley Court, I do not think there will be any trouble. Hugh and I will settle matters with Doctor Belfage."

"All right. But I don't want to hear anything about it," laughed the Colonel. "You're a bunch of miscreants, and the whole thing is hopelessly irregular. Get out. And I shall be delighted if you'll all dine with me tonight. Cabbageface knows the house, and the port is passing fair. Incidentally Ginger and that delightful girl are coming. We must drink their health."

"Bye-bye, Hugh, for the moment," said Standish, as they reached the street. "I'm going round to the insurance wallahs now. See you again this evening."

The traffic roared past in a ceaseless stream, and for a space Seymour stood staring at it beside a man grown suddenly silent.

"I can still hardly believe that it has all happened," he said at length.

Drummond turned to him slowly.

"Make England believe that it *will* happen, unless…"

The sentence uncompleted, he strode off, and Trafalgar Square swallowed him up.

SAPPER

THE BLACK GANG

Although the First World War is over, it seems that the hostilities are not, and when Captain Hugh 'Bulldog' Drummond discovers that a stint of bribery and blackmail is undermining England's democratic tradition, he forms the Black Gang, bent on tracking down the perpetrators of such plots. They set a trap to lure the criminal mastermind behind these subversive attacks to England, and all is going to plan until Bulldog Drummond accepts an invitation to tea at the Ritz with a charming American clergyman and his dowdy daughter.

BULLDOG DRUMMOND

'Demobilised officer, finding peace incredibly tedious, would welcome diversion. Legitimate, if possible; but crime, if of a comparatively humorous description, no objection. Excitement essential... Reply at once Box X10.'

Hungry for adventure following the First World War, Captain Hugh 'Bulldog' Drummond begins a career as the invincible protector of his country. His first reply comes from a beautiful young woman, who sends him racing off to investigate what at first looks like blackmail but turns out to be far more complicated and dangerous. The rescue of a kidnapped millionaire, found with his thumbs horribly mangled, leads Drummond to the discovery of a political conspiracy of awesome scope and villainy, masterminded by the ruthless Carl Peterson.

S A P P E R

The Female of the Species

Bulldog Drummond has slain his arch-enemy, Carl Peterson, but Peterson's mistress lives on and is intent on revenge. Drummond's wife vanishes, followed by a series of vicious traps set by a malicious adversary, which lead to a hair-raising chase across England, to a sinister house and a fantastic torture-chamber modelled on Stonehenge, with its legend of human sacrifice.

The Final Count

When Robin Gaunt, inventor of a terrifyingly powerful weapon of chemical warfare, goes missing, the police suspect that he has 'sold out' to the other side. But Bulldog Drummond is convinced of his innocence, and can think of only one man brutal enough to use the weapon to hold the world to ransom. Drummond receives an invitation to a sumptuous dinner-dance aboard an airship that is to mark the beginning of his final battle for triumph.

SAPPER

THE RETURN OF BULLDOG DRUMMOND

While staying as a guest at Merridale Hall, Captain Hugh 'Bulldog' Drummond's peaceful repose is disturbed by a frantic young man who comes dashing into the house, trembling and begging for help. When two warders arrive, asking for a man named Morris – a notorious murderer who has escaped from Dartmoor – Drummond assures them that they are chasing the wrong man. In which case, who on earth is this terrified youngster?

THE THIRD ROUND

The death of Professor Goodman is officially recorded as a tragic accident, but at the inquest, no mention is made of his latest discovery – a miraculous new formula for manufacturing flawless diamonds at negligible cost, which strikes Captain Hugh 'Bulldog' Drummond as rather strange. His suspicions are further aroused when he spots a member of the Metropolitan Diamond Syndicate at the inquest. Gradually, he untangles a sinister plot of greed and murder, which climaxes in a dramatic motorboat chase at Cowes and brings him face to face with his arch-enemy.

Printed in Great Britain
by Amazon